An End to a Silence

W.H. CLARK

Copyright © 2015 W.H. Clark
All rights reserved.
ISBN: 1512136433
ISBN-13: 978-1512136432

This is a work of fiction. Any resemblance to actual persons, living or dead, or actual events or locales is entirely coincidental.

No part of this book may be reproduced in any written, electronic, recording, or photocopying without written permission of the author.

Cover Design: W.H. Clark
Edited by Eliza Dee of Clio Editing Services

For Trisha

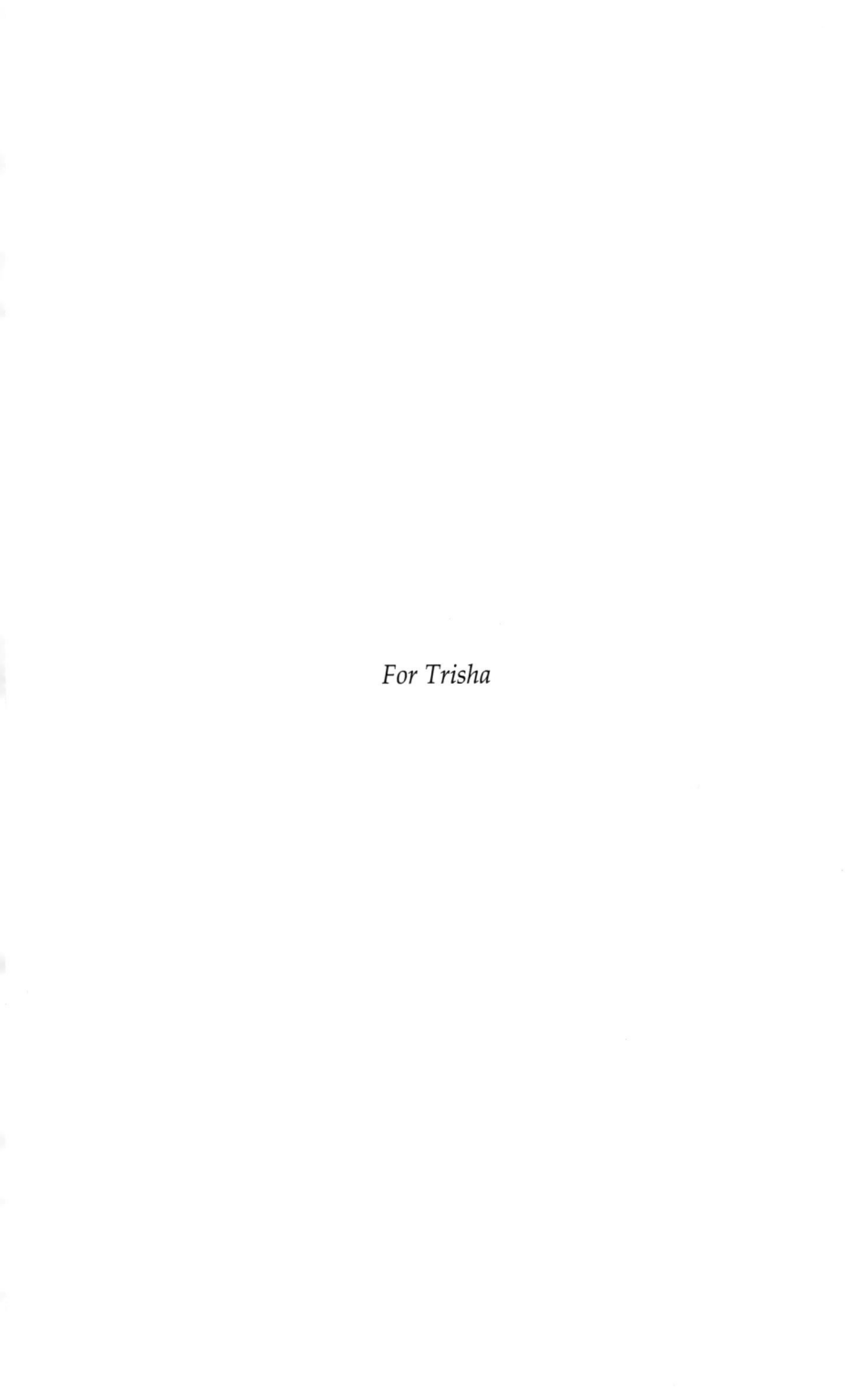

ACKNOWLEDGMENTS

Thanks to my early readers Doug, Trisha, Rob, Alison, Alison and Rachel for your time, feedback and suggestions.

Thanks to Eliza Dee at Clio Editing for making the American bits make sense and for making the English bits make sense too. Any errors and omissions are mine.

AN END TO A SILENCE

1

1985

The boy is still, already cold, even though a gentle summer evening breeze whispers of somewhere altogether warmer.

2

2010

Detective Newton sat at the counter of the Honey Pie Diner and finished his coffee. He took a last bitter sip and then stood creakily and walked the few feet down to the other end of the counter, where the attractive woman with the vivid red hair stood ringing up a check at the cash register. Her fingers tapped at the computer screen and made a click each time one of her long, painted fingernails caught it. And he watched her, not quite peripherally, through dimming vision. She placed a Styrofoam cup on the counter.

"And one to go."

"What do I owe you?" Detective Newton said. His head was cast down as he spoke, but the eyes looked up, like those of a chastised dog.

"Well, I ain't put my prices up since yesterday," she said, cocking a thumb over her shoulder at the menu board, and she smiled. Her name badge said she was called Cherry.

"Well, then," he said.

"Well, then," she said, and she stopped tapping at

the screen.

He put a hand in his pocket and pulled out a tattered bill. He handed it to her and as she took it, he held her hand gently. The smile slowly faded from her face and his found some color.

"Okay," she said, stretching out the word.

"I'm… sorry," he said, and he released her hand quickly, which released her smile again. "I don't… I just—"

"That's okay," she said.

"I was—"

"I said it's okay, detective," she said.

A fat man sitting behind Detective Newton shouted over his shoulder, "How we doing with that check?"

Newton jerked around and looked into the pudgy face of the man who had called out and Newton's eyes, angry dog, lingered there until the man looked away.

"Just another asshole," Cherry said, not quite loud enough for the man to hear. "I'd better get him off my premises."

Newton said, "Keep the change."

Cherry said, "Thanks." And she busied herself with the cash register again and Newton picked up his coffee and left, casting a glance at the asshole as he walked past.

She watched the detective walk out of the diner and then briefly stopped what she was doing and shook her head gently. The pudgy man turned around, but before he could say anything she said, "Check's on its way, sir," and under her breath, "fucker," and the check was produced with a few more fingernail clicks.

Outside, Newton patted his pockets vaguely with his free hand as a freezing wind blew straight through him. After a few moments he pulled out his keys, opened the door of his brown, boxy SUV, and hauled himself in, shivering. He placed the cup in the holder and then he leaned over and looked into the rearview mirror, turning it slightly for a better view of himself. He studied the old fool looking back and then he looked at the back of his hands and saw the spots of old age. He started the engine, buckled up and pulled away from the roadside, making an effort not to look back into the Honey Pie Diner at the woman with the vivid red hair who, for an excruciating moment, had been his beautiful wife of thirty years ago.

3

The phone rang in the station and McNeely answered it. She half stood up and looked over at Newton, who was sitting at his desk staring at the box in front of him. It stood alone on the otherwise empty surface save for a telephone, the coffee cup he had fetched back from the Honey Pie Diner, a tower of empty plastic trays, and a row of five pills of different sizes and colors set in a line. He picked up the first pill, popped it in his mouth and took a drink from the coffee cup.

"Got a call for you," McNeely, Westmoreland Police Department's Crime Scene Investigations Technician, said. She got no response. Newton picked up the second pill, put that in his mouth and knocked it back with another swig of the coffee.

"Detective Newton. You," she said louder and Newton looked over and pointed at himself. McNeely nodded and she prodded a couple of keys on the phone keypad. Newton's phone rang and he picked up. He swallowed.

"Yes?" Newton said.

"Adam. It's Jim. How are things?"

Newton didn't say anything.

"Hello?" The voice said.

"Jim."

"The medical examiner, Jim."

"I know it," Newton said. He changed the phone to the other ear.

"I have something for you."

Newton paused for a moment, staring at the unembellished partition screen in front of him.

"Shall I call back for a better line?" The medical examiner said.

"No, I hear you. Have you got a ticket?"

"A ticket?"

"You want help with a ticket?"

"A ticket? No, no. You misunderstand. I've got you a suspicious death. Just done a post mortem on an old man from Sunny Glade. He—in fact, Adam, you able to pop down and see me? This might be best in person."

Newton placed his hand over the mouthpiece.

"Where's the new guy?" he whispered loudly to McNeely. She shrugged without looking at Newton. He uncovered the mouthpiece and fiddled with his bottom lip.

"Okay," Newton said, and he hung up the phone. He sat there a while looking at his box. He took out a photograph and stood it up on the desk. It showed Newton and his wife, taken about thirty years ago going by the fashion. He stared at her vivid red hair done in the same style as Cherry from the diner. Then he picked it up again and put it back in the box. He scraped up the remaining three pills, tipped them into his mouth and took a big swallow of coffee, and then he stood and ambled over to the coat stand, where he took his coat and put it on. His heart missed a beat and he felt light-headed for a moment, which he put down to the two coffees he'd drunk, or maybe the pink pill.

He held there for a few moments before saying to McNeely, "I'm heading out."

"You bring me something back?" she said.

He looked at her.

"Ain't going there," he said. He turned towards the door and then he stopped, took a deep breath and held it there for a few seconds. He turned back and called to a compact man over the other side of the room.

"Sean. We got a possible crime scene needs preserving. Over at Sunny Glade." His voice had no color.

"I'll get on to patrol," Sean, the sergeant said.

"McNeely. Could you head on down there? You know where the new guy is?"

McNeely shrugged.

"Anybody have his number?" Newton said. Nobody said anything over the sound of clacking computer keys.

4

The new guy and Helen McNeely arrived at Sunny Glade at the same time, the new guy's gleaming red Alfa growling to a stop and the booming rock music cutting out with the engine. A uniform from Patrol standing outside quickly discarded his cigarette and stomped it into the ground with his boot.

McNeely made her way over to the new guy. Rock salt crunched under her feet and her breath chugged out in quick bursts.

The new guy took a glance around. The home glowed in the winter gloom and a cloud sank down on its roof, churned around the security lights and oozed down its walls. The gardens – roses and buddleia and copper birch hedges forming a barrier between the residents and the outside world – were only hinted at beneath the dimness of the day. Shadows of a mature mini woodland - a plantation of ponderosa pine, aspen, maple and ash - protected the northern aspect from the worst of the mauling winter winds.

"You got some serious horsepower there, detective," McNeely said, and she stroked the hood as the new guy straightened his Italian-cut suit.

"Just Ward," he said as he put on his hat over his short-cropped hair.

"And a serious hat," she said.

Ward smiled at her. He spoke briefly to the uniformed cop while McNeely fidgeted against the cold. Ward's suit didn't offer much protection from the arctic weather but he didn't seem discomforted.

Ward held open the door and waved McNeely in.

"Ladies first's what my ma taught me," he said.

"Obliged," McNeely said, and she rolled her eyes but smiled.

The receptionist, Jackie, greeted them with her usual cheery "hello," and then her face slouched into the serious face that she reserved for her children. "Has something happened? Well, I know something has happened but what might..." Her voice trailed off as Ward interrupted with a held up hand.

His firm Texan drawl fixed Jackie upright. "Sorry, ma'am, but could you point us to —"

"Oh, of course. Of course," she interrupted. "Down the corridor, past the dining room. I'll take you. Might be easiest."

"Thanks, but I think we'll be okay there, ma'am. Thank you for your help, though. The officer here will have a few words with you if that's agreeable." He winked at her.

Jackie's posture straightened. "Of course." She preened and gave Officer Stuart half her attention, the other half on Ward.

Ward and McNeely headed off, Ward tapping out a steady and loud clip-clopping rhythm with his black boots, which gleamed out of the bottom of his dark gray pants.

"Wow, real cowboy boots," McNeely said. "You really are a serious cowboy, ain't you?"

"Only a hundred percent, ma'am," Ward said.

The scene that greeted them was a serene resting place. A nice place to die, Ward thought. And then, before they could enter the room, a man appeared, blustering down the corridor.

"I'm Felix Grainger. The manager here." He wiped his hand on his pants before offering it to Ward, who didn't offer his back.

"I would like to speak to you later if that's okay. You going anywhere?"

"No, sir. I'm here as long as you need me. Yes, sir."

5

Newton was met at the mortuary by the medical examiner, Jim Packham. Newton tried to smile a greeting and patted him on his back as they turned to head to the autopsy room. Newton could smell it right away and instinctively sniffed a couple of times as if reacquainting himself with what death smelled like.

The old man's naked body lay uncovered on the cadaver dissection table, his trunk bearing a Y-shaped incision from shoulders to chest which had been stitched back up raggedly. Newton glanced at the body and then turned away, trying to think of somewhere else he'd rather be but failing to think of anywhere.

"I guess you got his clothes?" Newton asked, refocusing on the ME.

"Bagged, tagged and photographed," Packham said.

"We'll need those," Newton said.

"You got it, but the story isn't in the clothes. I did the usual checks for internal injury to organs and for cardiac anomalies but neither showed anything. It was the external examination that threw up something. Here on the ankle. You see?"

Newton squinted to see what the medical examiner

was pointing at.

"Might need your glasses," Packham said.

Newton reached into his inside pocket and took out his glasses, opening them slowly with his gnarled fingers.

"See it now?"

"A small red dot?"

"A small red dot indeed. Entry wound. From a hypodermic needle by the looks of it. That got me itchy. That raised my interest. I took a blood sample from the inferior vena cava and sent it for testing as an urgent. Got the results back and it seems the victim had a rather large amount of morphine in his system."

"That could be due to his medication, right?" Newton said.

"Well, no. Indeed no. Our deceased was not taking any morphine as pain relief. I checked. I have his medical records here if you'd like to take a look?"

Newton wearily shook his head once and waved a hand for the ME to continue.

"And anyway, that wouldn't explain the entry point on his ankle. He would take the morphine in pill form if he was taking any at all. Which he wasn't. So that's moot. No, our customer here had a very large dose of morphine administered by someone. I'm guessing he didn't do it himself. That kind of entry point might work for drug addicts but I wouldn't suppose our fellow here was an addict. And there aren't any other injection points or the telltale tracks that you find with addicts."

"Can we get a second blood analysis done?" Newton said.

"That's not for me. This guy is on his way to the

State Crime Lab. He's theirs now. But it is what I said."

"What makes you so sure?" Newton said.

"Because I've been doing this job as many years as you've been doing yours."

Newton shifted his weight onto his other foot and involuntarily rubbed the base of his back as an old pain flared. "Anything else?"

"He had newspaper ink on his fingers. That's all I've got. Apart from that he looks like a regular old man."

"Okay," Newton said, a dark pain shadowing his face.

"Do we have a time of death?"

"Approximately, yes we do. Between eight p.m. and twelve midnight on Sunday."

"Okay."

"So, this old guy has a story to tell. And I guess I turn that over to you to find the final pages of his tale. What are you thinking?"

Newton was staring at an area in the far corner of the room and then he said, "I don't know what I'm thinking, is the honest truth. I'll give it to the new guy to figure out."

"Of course. You go this week?"

Newton said, "Next week." He automatically flicked over the tag on the old man's toe. He stared at it for a few moments. Then he took a step back, his eyes wrenched open and the blood drained from his face. For a few seconds he forgot to breathe and then he took a big gulp of air. He mechanically clutched his back with one hand and reached into his pocket with his other, fingering around for a bottle of pills. William O'Donnell.

"Hey. I'm guessing you know the old guy," the medical examiner said. He touched Newton's arm. Newton shuddered under the medical examiner's hand. "You okay there, Adam?"

Newton turned abruptly to face Packham, his head snapping around. His eyes were empty for a second and then the pupils focused on the medical examiner. He strode to the end of the table and he stared down at the face he hadn't at first recognized.

Then he swayed back and turned to leave.

"I gotta go," was the only thing he said, and he called McNeely on his cell as he left.

Newton had left tire rubber in the parking lot of the morgue and was headed down North Dakota Avenue, a blur of buildings, trees and vehicles stretching out beside him. His foot felt heavy on the gas pedal. "Slow down there," Ward had said on the phone just now. But his thoughts were racing ahead of him and he had found it difficult to explain it to the new guy.

He took the turn onto Twelfth Avenue almost at a slide, his foot pumping more gas into the maneuver and his hands twitching momentarily in the opposite direction to the turn to prevent a full-blown skid. As he did so he saw, a moment too late, the woman and child crossing the road. The woman, however, had seemingly heard the revs of Newton's engine and her senses had sharpened enough for her to pause on the other side of the road and avoid being swept to her death under the SUV's wheels. Newton stamped down on the brakes and stopped a few yards away from the woman and child. He looked in his rearview mirror and then covered his face with his hands. He was trembling. He shook his head and tried to gather himself. *This shouldn't be happening to me,* he thought. *I should've retired three years ago when I could've. I don't want this. Not now. Not* this *dead man.*

6

One thing Ward had noticed right away was how tidy the room was. Two officers had sealed the room off to prevent contamination of the crime scene but first appearances suggested that the room had been cleaned. Whether that was a deliberate attempt to destroy evidence or just cleaning, Ward didn't know. Going by the spotless environment of Sunny Glade, wasting no time in tidying a dead man's room was consistent with the apparent obsession with cleanliness. A pity they couldn't get rid of the smell of piss.

Ward popped McNeely's cell phone closed and handed it back to her. McNeely stopped taking photographs and slid the phone back into her pocket. "Everything okay?"

"I guess so." Ward stroked his short-cropped beard, opened a drawer. Empty.

"Any idea what we're looking for?" McNeely placed her camera on the small table by the old man's bed.

"Nothing much to see."

McNeely's eyes narrowed as she studied Ward.

"I'm still trying to work you out, detective. You're different. No offense."

Ward removed his Stetson and placed it on his heart. "No offense taken, ma'am." His pale blue eyes settled on McNeely and he held her gaze.

"You're all right, though. Cowboy boots." She laughed. "You got cowboy boots."

Ward smiled briefly and reseated his hat.

McNeely studied the detective a few seconds longer. "You're okay. Different okay. And don't pay no heed to Newton. He's just playing out time. Running down the game clock. Has been for a while now." She reached into her bag for her fingerprint kit. "I'll dust around but it all looks pretty clean. Maybe too clean?"

"Whole building's too clean you ask me," Ward said. His eyes had settled on the picture of Bermuda that adorned the wall. He cast a glance around the otherwise austere room and then his eyes returned to the picture. "We need to find out where his belongings went."

The door opened and Newton lunged through. His speechless eyes fell on Ward. He pulled his body straight. He was panting and he placed his hand on his chest. He took a few sharp breaths before speaking.

"What have you got?"

"Newton, right?"

Newton said, "Wha'?" and then, "Yes, Newton."

"Okay, Newton. Ward." He pointed to himself. "And I got this," Ward said. "If you can tell me what you got and then you're okay to go." He studied Newton: the erosion on his dimpled face, the dark crescents below his eyes and the retreating gray hair. He thought sleep was a stranger to him. A kindred spirit.

"Okay," Newton said. "William O'Donnell." He waited a couple of seconds after speaking the name and then continued. "Seventy-eight years old. Cause of death: morphine poisoning administered through the foot. Approximate time of death: between eight and midnight on Sunday." He paused again and then said, "Guy's a murderer."

"Whoa," McNeely said, dusting the bedstead for prints as Newton bent to sit on the mattress. "Not the bed."

He straightened up again too quickly and pain showed in his eyes. "Bill O'Donnell. He murdered his grandson."

"He did?" Ward said.

"Sure he did."

"We're collecting evidence. For the homicide of an old man. You're saying this old guy murdered his grandson. He do time for it?"

Newton's shoulders slumped and he took a fat swallow.

"You're going to tell me what I'm missing here?" Ward said.

"Okay, some history," Newton said. "Back in 1985 a seven-year-old boy called Ryan Novak disappeared."

McNeely nodded recollection.

"The boy was never found. No body neither. The main suspect was this guy, his grandfather"—he pointed at the empty bed—"but there wasn't enough evidence on him." Newton left a pause. Ward and McNeely didn't fill it. Newton rubbed the base of his back and with his other hand reached in his pocket for his pills. He took them out and put them back. "The guy was never convicted."

"Okay," Ward nodded slowly. "And how does a twenty-five-year-old cold case help us with this here homicide? Do you think they're connected somehow, detective?"

Newton looked at McNeely and then back at Ward. "I think they might be."

"Might be? Okay. Even if we accept that he killed the boy, as you say he did even though he didn't do time for it, who does that put in the frame for this old guy's death? We need to be mindful not to go confusing the two cases, don't you think? So, I suggest that McNeely and myself go on with this crime scene and then we'll look at what we've got."

Newton clasped his hands together and bit his thumbs. "You're right, you're right. I'll be… I'll get out of your way," he said, and he stood up to leave. "Thing is, it was my case," he said. "It was my case."

Ward had stared at the picture of Bermuda for going on five minutes. And then he noticed the extra pushpin at the bottom, offset to the right-hand side. Then McNeely took his attention away.

"What have we got here?" She was staring at the windowsill with hands on hips. All the fingerprints that the dust had revealed. "Only a whole load of latents. The cleanest crime scene ever apart from this windowsill. Not just one set of prints but a whole load of them." She reached into her bag and took out a magnifying glass.

Ward went over to take a look. "All pointing inwards. Into the room."

"Mostly."

"What does that tell us?"

"Well, all the prints look like they're from the same person. So it tells us that somebody repeatedly entered the room through this window."

Ward took a closer look. "Are these palm prints facing the other way? In and out prints? Is this our guy?" He was thinking out loud, but McNeely replied.

"In the absence of any other prints in this room it's a good place to start. This is going to take a while."

"You need a hand?" Ward asked.

"We'll just get in each other's way."

Ward looked out of the window. The room, south-facing, looked over two thirds of the town, yesterday offering views of a crisp winter scene with remnants of snow clinging to rooftops and pavements hedged with dirty shoveled-up snow heaps from earlier clearing efforts. Today, the freezing mist blurred everything. An icy wind blew down from the hills which started ten miles north, the tail end of a small mountain range that snaked towards Canada, and brought a harder-than-average winter this year. Fifteen Fahrenheit was normal for a January day like today: it was five, and long icicles hung like silent wind chimes from the old man's window frame.

Ward returned to the picture. He considered the pushpin for a moment and then removed it. Expected something to drop from behind the Bermuda picture but nothing did.

"I think there was something here," Ward said. He got up close to the picture to see if there were any signs that something had been concealed behind it. He peeled back the corner of the picture and he could see a slight discoloring of the wall. Something had been pinned there. Something small. He did a rough measurement with his thumb and forefinger. About the size of a photograph.

"It's gone now," McNeely said.

"We need the old man's possessions. We also need to know who's been in this room since he died. We need to find out what this pin was holding."

7

The man holds the boy in his arms. The boy's eyes are open but don't see. The man's eyes are closed but tears spring from them. He rocks the boy, then pulls him in close. For minutes he stands there but he knows nothing of time. He holds him and he wants to for an eternity. He yearns to swap places with the boy, and a groan from the deepest depths of his soul escapes him. He sobs and looks towards heaven, an attempt at a prayer, a plea for forgiveness and mercy. He suddenly fears his final judgment. He stares into infinity and pities himself.

8

The conversation with the nursing home manager, Grainger, had been brief. Ward had asked him about any comings and goings on the day of the homicide, and Grainger had sweated his way through the questions, ending each answer with a "yes, sir." Said there was a girl with the victim shortly before he died. Paid regular visits. Ward had asked him about security and Grainger had pointed out surveillance cameras and had told Ward that all visitors were obliged to sign in on arrival and to sign out on departure. Yes, sir.

Ward had asked who had been in the room since the old man's death and Grainger had told him that the room had been cleaned and gave Ward the name of the cleaner. Said that he couldn't account for everybody who might have been in the room as it had not been locked. Ward had then asked him how drugs in the facility were secured and Grainger had told him that the pharmacy was secured by lock and key and that the on-call doctor and residential nurses had access to the key, which was locked up in the safe, for which he, Grainger, held the key. Yes, sir.

He had then asked Grainger to organize a full

inventory of the pharmacy, make sure nothing was missing. With particular attention to morphine. He would do that of course, yes, sir. Ward had dismissed Grainger with a thank you and had told him that there might be more questions later. Grainger had answered with a yes, sir.

9

It was a dark evening. Ward swung into the parking lot of the station, a modern building with plenty enough glass and a bit of steel girder and dark wood siding. He parked the car and turned off the engine and the rock music but didn't remove his seat belt. He stared straight ahead. He was still there when McNeely pulled in beside him a couple of minutes later. McNeely got out of her car and came over to him, tapped on his window. He wound it down.

"Welcome to Montana," she said.

Ward popped the belt. "Let's check this in. I'll update the lieutenant. See if you can find out what happened to the victim's possessions."

Newton was sitting at his desk. He faced his box of possessions, chewing at his thumb, occasionally examining it for intact skin to bite.

Ward dropped his hat on the desk next to Newton.

"I'll move my things," Newton said.

"No, stay. I'm fine over here."

Newton looked way past retirement, his gray pallor

underscoring the gloom of the day. He spoke without looking at Ward. "He did it." He glanced a hand across his thinning hair.

"I'm sorry?"

"Been twenty-five years sorry."

"We lose sometimes."

Newton's head cranked up to face Ward. "I worked the Ryan Novak disappearance for months. Still working it in my head. Something like that stays with you."

"We all have the ones that we don't solve."

"The nature of the job, son, I know, but this."

"You want to talk about it?"

"Aw shit, I don't know."

"Okay," Ward said, and gave Newton room to continue.

"It takes something away from you. It's not the failure. Stats don't count shit when it comes to the disappearance of a child. That's something that you're measured against differently and not by the department. By others. You front a failure like this in a small town like ours and you're the guy who didn't protect one of their children. You know how that goes down? You know what that does to you? I couldn't walk the streets without someone looking over at me and thinking, 'There goes the cop who let that bastard get away.' I still get that to this day. I sense it. The truth, son, that's all I need to know." He stopped. Ward saw the man of twenty-five years ago, scratching around for answers that disappeared around corners and into the darkness of dead ends.

"I hear you," Ward offered. He stood there looking at the old man who was shrinking before his eyes.

"Anyway, it's your case. I'll keep out of your way."

"Okay."

Ward took a step backwards and as he did he crashed into a uniformed officer, who fended Ward off like a defensive lineman.

"Watch where you're going," said the officer, a half smile, half grimace on his face. Teeth too big for his mouth and too white.

Ward's anger swelled but he didn't allow it to overflow from his puffed-out chest. "I'm sorry," he said as his fists clenched and he bit his bottom lip. "Ward." He unclenched his fist and offered his open hand. The officer didn't take it.

"No problem. Officer Mallory," said the officer, and he sat on the edge of Newton's desk, a smile running across his mouth.

Lieutenant Gammond was a short butternut squash of a man with slicked-back hair and a large mustache. Ward had knocked on the door and Gammond had said "come" but Ward was already in the office by then.

"Just come to update you on the homicide, sir."

"Ah yes," Gammond said, and he waved a pudgy hand at a chair for Ward to sit. "The old man. Hold it right there if you will." And he tapped at a few keys on his computer keyboard as slowly as he spoke. Ward sat.

"We've done our—" Ward started but Gammond held up a hand and continued to type with his other. Ward looked around the office, at the hunting photos, the photos of Gammond in uniform, the set of golf clubs, the homemade sign that read, "You don't have to be crazy to work here, you just got to do what I tell you." He saw the gun cabinet with three hunting rifles in it. He recognized the Mauser 98 and the Remington Model 700 but couldn't get the third.

"That one's a Krieghoff, son. Two rifle barrels and a twenty-gauge shotgun barrel. That'll bring down a dang country." He still tapped.

"You shoot that thing?"

"I done shot it once. Shoulder still smarts some."

Gammond stopped tapping, sucked through his bottom teeth as if he'd got a piece of meat stuck there, and said, "Okay, where're we at with the ol' feller?" He picked at his teeth with a manicured fingernail.

"As I was saying, sir, we've done our preliminary forensics gathering and taken statements. Should have results soon. I'll update you when we have something." He stood to leave.

"Sit down there, detective," Gammond said, and Ward hovered and then sat. "We ain't had a proper welcome sit-down-and-drink-a-whiskey chat." He reached into a drawer in his antique oak desk that looked like it was made from a single large tree and pulled out a bottle and two small glasses. "How we do things up here." He poured. "And don't tell me you'll pass because I won't hear a dang word of it." He handed the glass to Ward and sniffed his own before knocking it back. Ward did the same.

"See, we're civilized up in these parts." He stroked his mustache with thumb and forefinger. He stopped and seemed to lose his thoughts over somewhere else.

"I want Newton on the case with me."

"He's finished."

"He's got a few more days."

"What's he going to do in a few days?"

"Local knowledge. He knew the guy."

"Dang it, you're the homicide detective now, son. What'll you do with an old—" He stopped himself. "He'll be apt to get in your way. It's your job now. Why we got you up here."

Ward remained silent. Just regarded Gammond with eyes that didn't blink.

Gammond looked around like he'd lost something. "Dang it. You sure you want him on your case?"

"I am, sir."

"Well, he's still on the payroll, so I guess we got to put him to work. Okay, he's yours for the next two weeks." He poured himself another whiskey but didn't bother to offer Ward one.

"He mentioned the little boy who disappeared."

Gammond put his glass down heavily. "Well, detective, ain't no gain in that line of thinking. Totally unrelated."

"He doesn't think so."

"Like I said, ain't no gain in that line of thinking. What we don't want is for Detective Newton to go reopening ol' wounds. 'Stead of thinking down that track, see to it that he sticks to this here case. Use him by all means. He got nearly thirty years' experience. But that little boy case. That stays closed. And I got to be getting on now." He knocked back his second whiskey and Ward knew it wasn't his second of the day. "Good t'have you here, detective. And Ward, son, I want to be kept in the loop with ever' detail of this investigation. Ever' development, ever' line of inquiry, I need to know. Captain's orders."

"Why, who was this guy?"
"Jus' an ol' man."

10

The medical examiner's assistant was still there when Ward arrived. He buzzed Ward in. The mortuary was locked down after five. Presumably to stop any of the guests leaving.

"You must be Detective Ward," Dave Turner said, standing at the end of the corridor, mop in hand and wearing a blue plastic apron. "You've come to see our latest arrival?"

"If I could."

"No problemo. This way, hombre. Weather like this I don't know why we bother refrigerating them. Would be cheaper to just open the windows. If we had windows." He led Ward down a corridor and through a door which opened into the cold chamber. He walked, slumped shoulders, into the corner of the room and released the brake on a gurney with his foot, spinning it around and wheeling it over to one of the doors. He released a catch on the door handle, threw back the handle and opened the door. He placed the gurney in front of the drawer, locked the wheels, and slid out the tray which contained the old man's body. He unzipped the body bag and pulled down the sides so the old man's head, torso and arms were visible.

The old man's skin seemed to be slipping off his body and his underlying rigid muscle structure seemed tauter because of that. He was a scaled-down model of what he'd been thirty years ago. In good shape for a dead old man. Ward reached for the zipper and glanced over at Dave.

"Go ahead, my friend," Dave said.

Ward pulled the zipper all the way down to reveal the cadaver's feet and he examined the tiny entry wound, as deadly as a bullet but more subtle, he thought. He stepped back and pinched his chin, grabbing and stretching his beard as he pulled his fingers away. He was quiet for long enough to prompt Dave to speak again.

"You still in the room, amigo?"

Ward looked at Dave. "He look like a killer to you?"

"No, he don't, hombre. He looks killed to me."

Ward smiled and his eyes narrowed. "Exactly what I was thinking."

11

"It's half past eight, detective. Penny has her homework," said the man who had answered the door halfway through Ward's second knock.

"I promise this won't take long, sir," Ward said, chilling on the doorstep and removing his hat in an effort to show respect. "I just need to ask her a few questions. A man has died."

"Yes, you said."

"And Penny was one of the last people to see him alive."

A tall young girl, all legs and arms, appeared in the hall, half out of a doorway. "I'm okay, Dad. I heard about Mr. O'Donnell. Was he murdered?"

"I just have a few questions Penny," Ward said, ignoring Penny's question. "Then you can finish your homework. Sir?"

Penny's father stepped aside and let Ward into the house. As the heat hit him, his tensed muscles relaxed.

"The music room." She smiled at Ward. "This way."

Ward sat down on the piano stool while Penny settled herself onto a large cushion decorated in what looked to Ward like a Persian design. He'd seen lots of similar patterns before. She pulled her legs up and wrapped her arms around her knees.

"Don't worry about my dad. He's overprotective sometimes. Still thinks I'm twelve."

Ward smiled. "He's okay." He took out his notepad and pen. "I guess I have a few questions, but firstly I'd like you to tell me what happened the last time you met with Mr. O'Donnell."

Penny tossed her hair out of her eyes.

"I go in to read to him."

"Okay."

"It's community work. My dad encourages it. Wants me to be an upstanding citizen."

"You enjoy it?"

"I guess so," Penny said, her nose wrinkling a little. "Although it does smell of pee."

Ward smiled. "What sorts of things do you read?"

"Sometimes a book. A magazine. Whatever."

"Can you remember what you were reading on the day?"

"Yes, I can. It was the *Westmoreland Echo*."

"Okay," Ward said, writing in his notepad. "Did Mr. O'Donnell appear to you any different on that visit?"

"Only the fact that he scared the shit out of me."

Ward instinctively looked around to see if her father had heard her curse, but he wasn't in the room.

"How did he scare you? You say you were reading the newspaper to him."

"Yes, that's when he freaked out."

"You were reading and he freaked out suddenly? He'd been quiet until then?"

Penny nodded.

"What was the story, you remember?"

"No, I don't. Hang on. We might have a copy in the paper recycling." She left Ward alone in the room. He turned and lifted the piano lid and pressed a key down. Then another. Then he wished he could play like Jerry Lee Lewis. He lowered the lid as Penny returned.

"You're in luck." She opened the newspaper and jabbed a page. "This was it. This woman without any dignity selling herself on a billboard. Looking for a boyfriend." Her face showed disgust. "That story there." She handed the newspaper to Ward. He read the first few lines of the story about a Westmoreland woman and her quest to find a suitor by advertising herself on a billboard. He flicked through the paper and skimmed over various headlines.

"Just two seconds." He took out his cell and pressed a few digits. "Hey, it's Ward. We need to get somebody down to Sunny Glade tonight to go through the dumpsters. We're looking for a newspaper, the *Westmoreland Echo*. This is potential evidence." He paused for the reply, smiling at Penny, who was positively beaming back at him. "Thanks." He put the phone back in his pocket.

"Was he murdered? Am I a suspect?" she said, still smiling broadly.

Ward shook his head. "No, but you're very important to this investigation." Penny nearly burst at that.

"This is so fucking weird," she said, and this time it was she who looked around to make sure her father hadn't heard. She said the curse word as if testing a new mouth.

"Okay, you said he scared the... Mr. O'Donnell freaked out. What happened?"

"Only that he burst out shouting."

"Shouting?" He held his pen ready to write.

"Well, he never said a word normally. Never said a word ever. Most of them, they just gawk at the wall like zombies."

Ward sighed.

"But this day he said something all right. He asked for somebody called Doctor Brookline. He was kinda loud."

Ward's head snapped up. "Anything else?"

Penny made an effort to look like she was thinking hard. She hitched her dress up a little too far and started to scratch her knee. Ward saw her white panties and he glanced down at his notepad. Thought she was maybe enjoying the attention a little too much and becoming distracted. He carefully lifted the piano lid with his elbow and let it drop, the bang startling Penny back into the room. "Sorry, I must've caught it," Ward said.

The young girl pulled her dress back over her knees and wrapped her arms around them again. "I can't think of anything," she said, and this time he could see that she really was making an effort to recall something.

"You're sure of that?"

"Oh, hang on. He did say something else. Right after he'd asked for Doctor Brookline, he said something about..." She cast her head back. "Something about confessing. No, that wasn't it. Hang on. He just said 'confession.' That's what he said. That's all he said. And the Doctor Brookline thing."

"Can you think of anything else that happened that day? Anything, no matter how unimportant it may seem to you."

"I can't remember anything else. It was just the same as always. Apart from those two things I told you he said."

"Well, thank you, Penny. That's it." Penny looked downcast. "But I might need to ask you more questions at a later date. And if you think of anything else please contact me at this number."

He scribbled the number in his notepad, tore out the page and handed it to her, and at that she smiled again.

"Don't detectives usually have business cards?"

"They haven't come back from the printers yet," Ward said, and he offered her a smile. "Do you mind if I keep this newspaper?"

"No, of course not." She beamed.

12

The boy is wrapped in a bedsheet now, and is placed in the fetal position on the passenger seat of the truck. The man climbs into the driver's seat and starts the engine. He speaks to the boy. Words of comfort. Words of concern to a boy who might have grazed his knee playing in the yard. It seems right and it seems natural. The truck pulls away and the man makes a small circular movement over where the boy's head is, but his hand doesn't touch the sheet. "It's going to be okay," he whispers.

13

Ward remembered Jesús. *The poor little guy will be crossing his legs*, he thought as he turned left at the end of Penny's street, a few flecks of snow grazing against the windshield. He felt a heavy throb developing in his skull as he went over things in his head. An old man who Newton suspects of the murder of his grandson is a homicide victim himself. Are the two cases linked in any way apart from the biological connection? Did the old man know something about the person responsible for Ryan Novak's death, if indeed O'Donnell wasn't the murderer himself? Did the real killer come to finish off O'Donnell? But why now? Why wait twenty-five years to finally silence him? He'd said something about a confession to Penny, the girl who visited him.

But again, why now? What was his confession? Was it about the little boy, Ryan? But why wait all these years before confessing? Who else was threatened by the confession, if that's what it was, enough to kill the man? And what was it about the newspaper story that the girl had read to him that had made him suddenly panic and start calling for a doctor called Brookline? Had William O'Donnell simply gone senile? Who was

Doctor Brookline? And those fingerprints on the windowsill—who did they belong to? And why had someone repeatedly entered the old man's room through the window? Was that person the murderer?

As Ward pulled into his parking spot the questions bounced around his mind.

His motel room had a pink door like all the others. A row of national flags of countries from all four corners of the world danced energetically on the wind in a line on the roof, just visible above the motel.

Jesús, the little black mongrel with flecks of gray, more pronounced around the eyes, announced himself as soon as Ward stepped into the room at the Montana Sky Motel. His claws tapped an urgent dance on the hardwood floor over to Ward, and his eyes spoke of anguish. Time and arthritis had stiffened his limbs, which gave the impression that he was walking on chair legs.

"I am so sorry, Jesús." He pronounced it "Hayzoos." Jesús had come to be in Ward's permanent company following the death of a San Antonio gang member called Jesús Hernandez at the hands, or, more specifically, machetes of a rival gang. Jesús, the dog, not the guy — that would have been some resurrection for a man who had had all four limbs hacked off — had been found wandering Hernandez's apartment at the crime scene, seemingly in shock, and Ward had impulsively decided that he should go home with him rather than to the pound. Jesús still bore the tag with his real name, which Ward couldn't fluently pronounce.

Ward grabbed the mutt's leash which was hung up on a hook on the inside of the door and attached it to his collar.

14

At the Honey Pie Diner, Ward took the same seat as yesterday. The woman with the red hair, who hadn't been here yesterday, came over to Ward's table. The diner was empty save for a couple over by the far side, tucked into the corner furthest away from prying eyes and in light dimmer than the rest of the room.

"What can I get you?" Cherry asked. She wore a name badge.

Ward removed his hat, placed it on the table. "I'll have a coffee, please, ma'am. Black, I guess." He unbuttoned his suit jacket and straightened his narrow black tie.

"And something for your friend here?"

"Jesús will have the same," Ward said. Jesús looked up hopefully and then avoided eye contact when Cherry tried to make it.

"I think this little guy would love some water, don't you?" Her voice went gooey over the last two words.

"I'm sorry, he doesn't speak English. He's Latino."

"Ah," Cherry said, and she tipped Ward an exaggerated wink. She slipped her notepad back into the pocket on the front of her apron without writing anything in it and walked away. Ward checked her out as she ambled behind the counter, an extra emphasis on her hip sway, Ward thought. Jesús sighed.

"You need to pee again?" Ward asked.

"*No, mi padre,*" he answered himself. "*Puedo esperar.*"

"*Muy bien,*" Ward said, and his shoulders sagged as relaxation poured into him at last.

When Cherry returned with the coffee she spoke quietly. "You're a cop, right?"

"Right," Ward said. He looked down expecting to see his badge on his belt. It wasn't there. "The gun?" His holstered weapon was visible under his jacket.

"Jeez, this is Montana. Everybody carries a gun 'round here. You're sitting in the cop seat."

"I am?"

"Sure you are. By the window, good view of the room and of the entrance door. Good view of people coming in and out. You checked out that couple over there when you came in, suspecting an illicit liaison." She put an extra emphasis on the word liaison. "And you checked me out too after I'd taken your order. I saw your reflection in that mirror behind the counter there."

"Are you sure you're not the cop?" Ward asked, warming to Cherry, whose red hair negated the necessity of the name badge that Ward had fixed his eyes on. He gazed at it a few moments.

"There you go again, Texas Ranger, checking me out. My name badge this time." She winked again and Ward grinned.

"You got me there."

"Do we need introductions? You going to stay

around long enough to make that necessary?"

"Ward. And this here is Jesús." Hayzoos.

"Yes, we've met." Jesús tried out a glance at her and then looked down at the floor again.

"He's got social phobia. A little."

"Ward, is that a first name or a last one?"

"Well, now. Just call me Ward. It's the only name anybody ever uses anyhow."

"Very pleased to meet you both," Cherry said, and she turned and walked away. She glanced over her shoulder at Ward, who was still checking her out, then threw back her head and laughed raucously, drawing the nervous attention of the furtive couple in the corner.

"You need freshening up? Just to let you know I'm going to be closing in fifteen minutes." Cherry tipped her head in the direction of the couple. "Should I leave them the keys, you think?"

Ward smiled.

"Hey, you haven't even touched your coffee."

"I don't drink coffee, ma'am."

"Then why in heaven's name did you go and order one? I mean, I heard of folks quit smoking who carry around an emergency cigarette which they don't smoke, but I never heard of a person orders a coffee and doesn't drink it."

"I only came in for some water for the dog. Sorry about the wastage."

Cherry eyed him suspiciously. "Well, I guess I'll see you both tomorrow." She hung around. "You never said why a Texan cowboy ends up in the back of beyond. Don't get many southerners up here in Montana. They tend to feel the cold."

"Cold is a nice change." He grabbed his Stetson and sat it on his head. "Catch you around."

"Sure as shit will. It's a small town."

"Well, ma'am, goodnight," Ward said, and he let a gaze trace Cherry's well-made figure before he left.

15

He wondered why he could hear the sea whooshing in his ears. He stood in the kitchen and there was his wife Maggie and his daughter Jen and son-in-law Percy Mallory. Mallory was still in uniform. The three of them seemed to be having a conversation but Newton didn't hear them. And then he realized it was the blood whooshing in his ears and not the sea. Maggie was standing close to him and her lips were moving but he didn't hear her at first. It was only when she came right up to him and crouched below, looking up into his downward stare, that he heard.

"Are you listening?"

Newton said, "Yes," but he hadn't heard and Maggie knew that.

"I said that it's one of theirs. The chicken. The roast chicken." She was smiling when she said it but the smile changed to concern. "Are you sure you're listening? Are you okay?"

"Fine."

She studied him for a few moments. She touched his face gently and he tried a smile. "She necked it this morning."

"She did?" Newton said, late to the conversation and trying to show an interest to make up for it.

"That I did. Plucked it as well," Jen said.

"Doesn't Percy do the necking?" Maggie said, and Jen laughed loudly and rocked back as she did.

Newton thought he should get the joke but he mimed a silent laugh.

"He's too squeamish! He couldn't wring a wet pair of drawers."

Mallory glowed red. "Hey," he said, joining in with the teasing, but there was no humor in his voice.

"Well, I'm not sure I could wring a bird's neck. I'm sure your father couldn't neither." Maggie looked at Newton and he smiled robotically. "Well, let's set the table. Jen."

"Yes, Mom."

"I'll help," Mallory said.

Jen opened a drawer, took out cutlery and walked over to the table. Mallory followed her. He looked over his shoulder, where he could see Newton staring through the wall and Maggie busying herself with what she called "'companiments." Mallory grabbed Jen by her arm. She made like to yelp but Mallory's glare glued her mouth shut.

"Don't never make fun of me in front of your folks," he said through his teeth, and Jen looked around at her mom and dad, neither of whom appeared to be watching. "That's it. Just…" And he jabbed a finger toward her.

Jen dropped a knife, and Mallory let go of her before Newton or Maggie saw anything.

"That needs washing," Maggie said. "Get another."

Maggie said, "Has everybody got everything?"

"Sit down," Newton said. "Stop fussing and sit down."

"I agree," Mallory said. "Sit down, Mom. We've all got everything."

Maggie liked the fact that Mallory called her Mom. She smiled every time he did.

"Okay, I'm sitting." She sat and she glimpsed her husband with hands clasped together. "You look like you're about to say grace." And she shook her head. Newton untied his fingers and the blood ran back into them.

"I'll say grace, Mom," Mallory said, and Jen was about to say something but stopped herself.

"I was only kidding," Maggie said, and Mallory had a quick look at Jen.

"Say, what's this new detective like?" Maggie said. Mallory had started to eat and he kept his head down over his plate with one arm wrapped around it in a perimeter guard.

Newton said, "It's work. We have a rule about no work talk around the table."

Then Mallory did look up, but he still didn't say anything.

"Just look at this bird. It's like Thanksgiving all over again," Maggie said, but everybody else was already eating and none of them spoke.

16

Ward was stripped down to pajama pants, and he sat on the edge of his bed and prepared for the ritual of trying to get to sleep. Jesús sat and stared at him.

He could hear the wind getting up outside and he hoped that the sound would help him relax. He'd already had some beers but that hadn't worked.

There was a mirror on a dressing table opposite the foot of the bed. He studied the tattoos which decorated almost his entire torso and arms, and with his hand he covered the one of the little girl which sat on the left side of his chest, nestling amongst the tangled dragons. He tried to avoid his own gaze, but his reflection kept staring back at him, so he keeled back and lay there looking at the dreamcatcher hanging from the light fixture, fighting his thoughts. He stayed there a while and then shuffled onto the bed and pulled the duvet over himself. He waited for Jesús to jump up onto the bed and settle down by his feet, then reached and turned out the bedside lamp, but a little light still leaked into the room from outside.

He closed his eyes as tight as they would go and then relaxed them. He tried to relax every muscle in his body in turn, starting from his head and neck and working down. He concentrated on breathing slowly. When he reached his feet he took in a lungful of air and started counting back from ten like he'd been told. Each number was a step down to a special place where the memories were happy ones and the descent was slow and in time with his deep breaths. By the fifth step he could feel himself drifting off and then a panic took him and shook him back to ten.

On the sixth or seventh try he was gone. The wind whipped up outside and he twitched with each gust.

The field was a golden sea and waves rolled over it toward infinity. He looked all around and saw nobody and nothing else apart from the long barley stalks which appeared to flow one way and then the other on a churning high tide. He hugged his naked body against the cold but the wind was warm and yet he was wet. He looked up at the immaculate blue sky and wondered where the wetness had come from. He tasted the back of his forearm and he realized the wetness was sweat. The wind gusted around him and he thought he could hear the sea in his shell ears. He looked for a sign but there were just barley waves, and he didn't know what sign he was looking for or why he was there, but he knew he was meant to be there.

And then he looked down at his feet. They were covered in reddish mud, and he realized he was sinking. He lifted one foot out of the mud and the other went deeper, and then he lifted that foot and the first foot went even deeper. The next time he tried, neither foot would release and by now he had sunk almost knee-deep. He frantically looked around for something to get hold of to pull himself out but all that was there were barley waves, and he continued to sink, crying out for help.

He slumped to a sitting position and tried to pull his legs out of the mud, but he couldn't. His backside started to sink and he tried to lever himself back up. One hand plunged into the mud and stuck there. He waved the other hand in the air and shouted for help but still nobody came, and there were just barley waves and now the waves were over his head. And the wind swirled and the blue sky gleamed and an unseen sun beat down on him as he continued to sink. So he put his free hand on his head, closed his eyes and prepared to drown.

He heard a rustling nearby, and when he opened his eyes the scarecrow stood over him, its head tilted to one side in puzzlement. *Thank God, you've got to help me.* But the scarecrow just stood there with its quizzical look and its arms stretched out to its sides. *Won't you help me? Can you get me help? Please help me.* But the scarecrow just peered down at him and he had sunk more now until just his head and shoulders and one arm were not submerged. With his free hand he grabbed at the scarecrow, but he couldn't reach, and the scarecrow asked a question but he didn't know the answer. He closed his eyes and behind his eyelids there were just barley waves.

Jesús lay at the foot of the bed, his eyes on Ward gasping in his deep sleep. Outside, the cruel wind tugged at the flags on the roof and they flapped like tethered ghosts. Jesús hunkered down further into the duvet and whimpered gently.

17

Newton arrived to see Ward leaning over McNeely, who stared at her computer. Ward waved him over and Newton automatically looked around to see who Ward was waving at. Ward walked over to him and said, "You're on the case. We work it together."

"But I'm... I only got this week and next and—"

"I need your help."

"Oh, I don't know... it's just that..."

Ward took a step back. "I'm sorry, I shouldn't have—"

"No, no, I appreciate the... offer... and... but..."

"Okay, like I said, I'm sorry to have tried to drag you into this. I just thought that your knowledge of the old man and the Ryan case might be valuable. But I understand. Hey, only a few more days to go and then you're out of here. You don't have to fret over any of this anymore." And Ward turned his back on Newton and went back to McNeely.

Newton shuffled back to his desk and stood there a while staring at nothing. Then he walked out of the station.

Newton arrived just in time. The mortuary vehicle had its back doors open and someone was fussing around with something inside. Newton went straight into the building and spoke to an assistant, who waved him through without him having to show his badge.

There was a body strapped to a gurney and Newton knew it was O'Donnell inside the bag. There was nobody else in the room. He stood beside the body a few moments and then unzipped the bag to reveal O'Donnell's head. He looked familiar now. No longer just a shriveled body but the man who had taken Ryan. He felt an urge to peel open his eyelids and look into his eyes once more to see the lies that he was sure he could see twenty-five years ago. Would the opaque veil still be there, or did dead men's eyes reveal the truth? He knew it was a fancy of folly to think that, but the urge was there. He did peel back the eyelids but the eyes were cloudy and they refused to look back at Newton, so he got in close, but his own eyesight failed him and the eyes became blurs of watercolor splashes. He kicked the gurney.

"Son of a bitch," he said. "Son of a bitch. Fucking son of a bitch." And he grabbed the sides of the unzipped bag like they were the lapels of a jacket, dragged O'Donnell's face up to his own and said, "I know. I know. You can fool the rest of 'em, but I know. I know." Dropping the body back onto the gurney, he staggered back and collided with the dissection table, then steadied himself. Quick, short breaths came out of him and he placed a hand on his chest, and that's how Packham, the ME, found him.

"Adam," the medical examiner said, and then he saw the opened body bag. He calmly walked over and zipped up the bag, placing a hand on Newton's shoulder.

"I'm okay," Newton said. "I just needed to... I'm okay."

The ME nodded and squeezed Newton's shoulder.

When Newton arrived back at the station he went straight to his desk. Ward watched him sit down. He saw him pick up the papers that Ward had left there. Saw him read them. Saw a light flicker in Newton's eyes and some color come into his cheeks. The next moment Newton was on his feet and striding over to Ward.

"What's this?"

"Young girl used to visit O'Donnell. I went to see her last night. It's what she said he said."

"Confession? What'd he say about a confession?"

"He said the word 'confession'."

"You see what this is. He's confessing. The son of a bitch is confessing about Ryan."

"I have an open mind. Maybe he knew he was going to die and wanted a priest to confess to. All I can do is let the case play out and see where we are."

"Damn it, let the case play out. I told you he did it, didn't I?"

"For your peace of mind I'll let you know if I find anything. In the meantime I gotta be getting on with what I was getting on with."

Newton took Ward's arm firmly in his hand and said, "Okay, I'm in. Reporting for duty, detective. Or whatever it is I'm supposed to goddamn say."

Ward looked up at Newton. "Okay," he said.

Ward stood and led Newton over to McNeely. "We were just reviewing the evidence collected from the crime scene. McNeely ran some latents we found and we don't have a hit. We've sent hair fibers for analysis." Ward looked at Newton and wondered when the last time was he'd worked a homicide case. "We have Officers Jackson and Poynter interviewing everyone who was in the home at the time of death, an hour each side of the medical examiner's estimate. We have requested security camera footage and are waiting on that."

"Okay."

"We also await results on his clothes. There was a newspaper, the one that the young girl was reading to him on the night he died. We've had someone over there going through the trash but nothing."

Newton moved his weight to his left foot and appeared in pain. More than usual. "He had newspaper ink on his fingers."

"There are a lot of unanswered questions," Ward said. "We get the answers to some of those and we could be in the game." He drew up a chair for Newton to sit but he declined with a short quick shake of his head.

"Doctor Brookline? The girl said he called out his name."

"Our next port of call. You know him?"

"Retired doctor is all I know," Newton said. "Where are we on next of kin?"

"None surviving," Ward said, and he saw Newton grow an inch and then another. "His belongings were picked up by an Alice White. Before we got there. I was going to pay her a visit later."

"I know Alice," Newton said. "Used to be a nurse."

At that Ward said, "A person of interest, you think?"

"More an interesting person," Newton said.

"She would have access to morphine?"

"We can go see her later if that suits."

18

The truck pulls off the highway and the road becomes uneven. He slows down as if not to discomfort his passenger and makes steady progress up a short shallow incline, then begins a long descent through ancient plantation woodland. The road is still used by vacationers and it is kept clear from overhanging tree limbs, but he feels as if he's going through a tunnel, the headlamps of the truck carving out a hollow in front of him, a soft red glow from the taillights following.

A thin line of blue fire lights up the sky as it zigzags to earth and touches down close enough, and almost immediately a booming crack of thunder shakes the air and makes the man jump in his seat, jerking the steering wheel slightly to the left, enough to bump the truck out of the wheel ruts in the road and take off a bunch of tree branches with his side mirror. He straightens the truck then and the wheels find the well-worn ruts in the road again.

He continues for about a mile, occasionally humming an unrecognizable tune when the road becomes lumpy, and eventually draws up in a small clearing made for vehicles to turn. The road runs out and a wall of trees throws back light. A gentle breeze stirs the tops of the trees and the doleful squeal of branches kissing branches sounds to him like disagreeing violins. He cuts the lights and steps carefully down from the truck. A gibbous moon trickles enough light down for him to see his footing, but he takes a flashlight from beneath an oil-stained sheet in the bed of the truck. Out of habit he taps the flashlight against his hand before he turns it on. He walks around to the passenger side and opens the door. His cargo is still there and his heart falls to his boots. He gently scoops up the boy, sheet and all, and starts walking into woodland, his flashlight cutting through the undergrowth and highlighting jutting tree roots. A low branch snatches at the sheet and his forward motion draws away the veil from the boy's face. The scarce moonlight casts a cold blue wash over it. And Bill O'Donnell cries out.

19

The two of them were silent for the journey to Doctor Brookline's small bungalow off of the main eastward drag out of town. It was more blue collar than medical professional and every two hundred yards a different dog was to be heard barking.

Ward fiddled with the heating in the car but couldn't quite get the killer adjustment that made the temperature inside just right. It was either sauna or freezer. Stupid Italian engineering, he thought. In the end he pulled up his collar and settled on freezer. Newton did likewise.

The first thing to see at Doctor Brookline's home was that it looked abandoned. It looked like a repossession which was never resold. The front yard was overgrown with weeds and decorative plants and shrubs that now looked like weeds.

"We got the right address?" Ward said, his breath made visible in front of him by the subzero northerly. Newton shrugged. They opened the gate which creaked and jammed three-quarters of the way through its swing, the rust on the top of it flaking off in Ward's hand.

Four steps led up to a front porch. The deck had an ancient wooden chair whose upholstery had been eaten by weather and age. The chair was poked through with weeds which had emerged from the deck boards. Newton was first to the entrance porch, and he opened the screen door, which swung out unsteadily on crippled hinges. He knocked heavily three times on the inner door. Ward let the screen door prop against his back as he studied the yard, if it could be called that. It had the feeling of an ill-tended cemetery, the paving slab walkway suddenly seeming like end-to-end gravestones, and the house cast now as a derelict mausoleum.

Newton knocked again. Before an answer could come, he was trying to peer through the small side window, but drapes resisted his scrutiny. "Do you also have a bad feeling about this?"

"Probable cause?" Ward asked as he adopted a firm stance and looked for something to get a hold of to get extra leverage into his kick. Newton nodded at him and Ward drew back his leg.

"Hold on," Newton said, and he went to grab the handle.

"Gloves!" There was a shout in Ward's whisper as he dug into his pocket and then tossed a pair of latex gloves to Newton.

Newton's eyes apologized but he was clearly annoyed at himself. Said "damn it" under his breath. He pulled the gloves on and slowly turned the door handle. The door opened. "Doctor Brookline," he called. "Police officers." There was no answer. None was expected by either man but Newton called one more time as Ward drew his Glock 22.

"We're in," Ward said, and he entered slowly. Newton followed. They were in a corridor, four rooms off it, two on each side, and what appeared to be a kitchen at the end, though it was difficult to tell in the indoor twilight. Ward indicated the first room with a nod and Newton took up a position with his back to the opposite wall. He sniffed and Ward saw that and nodded to him. Both recognized the pungent smell of death. Newton drew his weapon and nodded okay.

Ward stepped across the threshold and pointed his gun into the dimly lit room, daylight shunned by dusty purple drapes that hung apologetically over the windows, secured by nails hammered into the walls and bent over with the last blow. Ward pulled out his flashlight and shone it into every corner. The room was empty save for an old couch covered with a crocheted blanket. Newton was already out of the room, and when Ward returned to the corridor he was startled by his call.

"Doctor Brookline. Police officers."

Ward followed him through the next door off the corridor on the other side of the house, and the smell grew stronger. Newton had sheathed his weapon and replaced it with his cell phone. "I'll call it in. Possible homicide."

Ward flicked the light switch with the knuckle of his middle finger, and light laid bare the extent of Doctor Brookline's decline.

This room mirrored the first one. The only differentiating features were one dead man slumped on the couch and a table next to him that held two discarded plastic medical syringes and a number of vials which had spilled over onto the floor. Another syringe hung from the man's arm, the hypodermic needle poking into a vein that had already dried up and collapsed.

Ward fished out another pair of latex gloves from his pocket and dragged them on. Newton saw him do it and said, "I guess I need to catch up, detective," as he picked up one of the vials carefully with forefinger and thumb and held it in front of his eyes, so close that he was almost cross-eyed. He took his glasses out of his pocket and slipped them on with one hand and looked again at the vial. "Morphine." He replaced it exactly where it had been.

"Shall we wait for McNeely to get down here?" Ward said. "We need to preserve this one."

"You think they're related?"

"You think they're not?" Ward didn't expect an answer. "I don't believe in coincidences."

"What does your instinct tell you?"

"I don't necessarily place a whole deal of faith in that neither. I've been married."

Newton didn't smile.

"Look at this." Ward's finger drew a line joining the dotted entry marks on the man's withered arm. "Guess he was an addict."

"He had access to morphine. Is this our killer? He kills and then kills himself with an OD?"

"I doubt that. By the look of him he hasn't been outside for a while."

"At least this scene hasn't been cleaned up."

Ward looked at Newton, took off his hat, rubbed the dark stubble on his head then replaced the hat. "I'm not so sure."

20

His arms and back ache terribly but he has carried on for an extra mile. The punishing journey has taken him through dense woodland and onto a smaller track now. He imagines horses dragging their freshly felled cumbrous freight from out of the forest and out of history and he feels like them. Like a ghost. He walks for another hundred yards up this track and then he slumps to the ground with the boy's increasingly heavy tiny frame pressing down on his trembling legs. He drops the dimming flashlight and casts a glance east, where the embers of a new sky smolder. A tepid breeze blown over this looming dawn fire gathers up whispered memories of his woodland past and swirls them all around him as trees shiver off the last of the night. He thinks of beyond the horizon, where day is already alight, and he knows he has to press on.

He heaves himself to his feet, shifting the weight of the boy to one arm so that he can lever with his other. He sees the flashlight on the ground but doesn't bend down to pick it up. He walks twenty more yards up the track and then he's off it again, blundering through thickening undergrowth and crowding trees, steering the boy's body between obstructions, threading and ducking in an ever more desperate but diminishing stride. He has to stop when a huge freshly fallen tree limb, ivory-colored sinews still showing, blocks his way. He goes deeper into the forest to skirt it and it becomes night again briefly. He hears the gentle footfall of two deer but doesn't see them as they catch his scent and tunnel into the remaining darkness.

He begins to talk to the boy, speaking of things they will do in the future, of hopes and dreams he holds for him. Of a future that only exists in the past. The dreams of a caring grandfather who knows now that he hasn't done enough. And how he wants to be punished. How he wants to pay for his silence. And he knows that one day he will. And he looks forward to that day.

And he curses his weakness.

21

"Time of death?" Ward said.

Packham said, "I'd say early hours of this morning. After midnight. Up to three a.m."

Ward said to nobody, "That means he died after O'Donnell. So Brookline's killer didn't take any morphine from here to kill O'Donnell. Could've been the other way around, though. We need that inventory from Sunny Glade."

McNeely stood up as Newton squatted down, trying to relieve the pain in his back and make it look like he was searching for evidence. Ward spotted it and was going to put a hand on Newton's shoulder but decided against it. He just said, "I think we're just about done here. If you want to wait in the car I'll help McNeely finish up."

Newton accepted the pity, and the look on his face told Ward he hated himself for it, but the pain was obviously too much. He waved away Ward's offer of help to stand and grimaced as he straightened.

"Hey, wait up, Adam," the medical examiner said, closing his bag. "I'll walk out with you."

"I'm feeling a sense of déjà vu here. This look too

clean to you?" Ward's eyes followed Newton and the medical examiner out of the room, and then he focused on McNeely.

"It looks like a shithole but I see what you mean. We ain't collected a whole lot that looks like a whole lot. Assuming this is a homicide and not a simple OD, we're looking at someone who knows not to leave anything behind. Someone who is clean in his work. A professional?"

"Let's not make that assumption yet. Let's just say he was very careful not to leave any trace."

"Same killer, you think?"

"Well, the first scene was clean, but then the old man's room had been cleaned by the staff at the nursing home. So any scrap of evidence he might have left was scrubbed up by the cleaning lady. Assuming he left any, and my feeling is that he didn't."

"Mine too. So we are working with one killer here," McNeely said.

"If the good doctor was murdered, I think so. The only obvious difference is the prints we found on the windowsill in the first victim's room. But why would a killer who is so meticulous leave so many prints at that scene?"

"You don't think the prints guy is our guy?"

"I would say it doesn't look likely," Ward said.

"So who is the guy who left the prints?"

"I don't know. But I would love to talk to him. And if that isn't our guy then the killer just walked into the nursing home unchallenged. I guess the security video will give us some clues."

"Could it be that the killer was already there? A member of the staff?"

Ward lifted his hat and rubbed a hand across his head. He didn't answer.

"No signs of a struggle here," McNeely said, trying to re-engage Ward, who had drifted off into his own thoughts. "Was the killer invited in? Was the victim too stoned to fight back? Did he just accept his fate? His life wasn't exactly worth a whole deal to himself by the look of things."

Ward stood there like a statue.

"Or maybe it was a self-inflicted OD after all," she added. "Don't need another homicide on the board."

Ward thawed and shrugged. "We'll follow the evidence. All we can do."

Newton was staring into the meager light of the overcast winter midday. He had listened to Packham talking about his new golf handicap but hadn't heard him. He only nodded occasionally and forced a laugh in the space where he intuitively thought it belonged. The medical examiner sensed distance and finally made it geographical, jumping into his sports car and zipping up the street like a youngster. His last words were "take care of yourself," and they were the only ones Newton really registered.

He was left to his thoughts as he froze in the car, which didn't have the engine running as Ward had the key. He knew that the murders of the two men and the disappearance of the boy had to be linked but he couldn't see why. The old man had mentioned a confession before he was killed himself. Newton was convinced that the confession related to the disappearance of the boy. The history that he carried around with him crowded out any other rational thought and created a tunnel which he struggled to look beyond. And that troubled him greatly. He knew what everybody down at the station thought of him. Knew what the new guy Ward thought. Thought he was old and past his best. But now and forever the ghost of Ryan Novak sat on his shoulder.

And then there he was across the road, no more than ten to fifteen yards away. A man wearing a checked, padded lumberjack jacket and a hat with earflaps, standing and looking toward the doctor's house. A few days' beard growth couldn't hide the familiar O'Donnell features, the large eyes of his late mother. And then there was the engineered jaw and tumbling brow of his late father. He knew that face. He knew that family so well. But he stared at this apparition and knew his eyes were playing tricks on him. It couldn't be him, of course not. A gasp escaped him as a small inexplicable panic gripped his heart and stabbed adrenaline into his bloodstream, and he feared he was losing it. Meanwhile, the man still stared at the house, his hands fidgeting in his pockets and a nervousness twitching under his clothes. And then he noticed Newton looking at him and immediately he turned away and started to walk quickly up the street. Newton tried to roll down the window but the electrics weren't engaged because Ward had the damn key and his shout of "hey, stop" only bounced around inside the car. By the time he opened the door and climbed out, his back only allowing slow movement, the man had begun to run. Newton tried his shout again but the man kept running, and Newton froze and couldn't give chase. He cursed himself and climbed back into the car, and in his confusion he simply pressed the horn and didn't let go.

It was Ward who was first out of the house and the screen door almost tore off its fractured hinges as he descended the few steps in one leap and made it to the car in seconds.

"What is it?" Ward asked as he tore open the driver's door and followed Newton's gape up the street.

Newton let go of the horn and looked up at Ward almost stupidly, his face drained of life. For a moment he was silent and then he said, "I'm sorry, I thought I saw someone. It was no one. He just ran, that's all, but I think he was just keeping warm."

Ward regarded him with a concerned and slightly annoyed look. "You saw someone? Maybe a witness? Someone more interesting? He ran, you say?"

"No, it was just... he's gone anyway. It was nothing really. I was just trying to get his attention is all." And Newton sensed Ward's irritation and he sensed his own sanity creaking. It was happening again. He was seeing ghosts. Damn it. He was seeing ghosts again.

Ward looked at Newton but Newton just stared straight ahead. "Give me two minutes," Ward said. "We're finished here." He tossed the car key into Newton's lap and slammed the door.

22

Alice White's time-wearied fingers knew only dainty movement here. House chores had become a struggle, but she still knew how to dress a baby with the most intricate care. They called her the Baby Dresser, the name as natural to her now as her baptized one, and she was revered in the small town where people regarded her with wonder for what she did. The tight-knit black community that centered on the gospel church considered her an angel.

The baby girl's right arm was caressed into the tiny pink cotton bodysuit that her parents had handed over. And then she threaded the left arm in. She snapped the five fasteners. And then Alice White's hands smoothed out unwanted wrinkles and folds and adjusted the garment, a hand sliding under the baby and nipping a deep pleat into the back of it to draw it into a more natural fit at the front, the side that people would see. The side with the embroidered smiling bear on it. The bodysuit was too large, as was usual for a baby this early, but she had the skill to always make them appear a perfect fit. Maria was the baby's name and she had lived three days. Her insides were all messed up and the doctors couldn't save her. But they had likely saved her from an almost certain future of pain and too many operations. She had been baptized on her second day of life while still in intensive care and had stopped crying briefly as the chaplain had spoken her name. And then she started up again and didn't stop until she fell asleep for the last time.

Alice hummed a gospel hymn, "Softly and Tenderly Jesus is Calling," her voice achieving a low timbre that could have been a note on a distant church organ. The viewing room that was adjacent to the hospital chapel was where she worked, and the sparse interior offered a fitting acoustic effect. There was one chair which was only used once the job was done and Alice sat there and said a prayer for the little soul and shed a tear. She always cried.

She had been a nurse for over thirty years and, although that career had ended, this career carried on and, really, it was her only true vocation. Her God-given gift. And with every baby she dressed, she knew in the deepest part of her heart that she was doing His work.

She dressed the very early premature ones in dolls' clothes as they were the only ones that would fit, and she worked extra hard to give some recognizable human form to these so that the parents could recognize them as a baby. They would bring their cameras and take photographs and weep and wail and Alice would be in the chapel next door muttering a prayer for them, asking God to deliver their baby to heaven and to mend the parents' broken hearts as quickly as possible.

She reached for her makeup box and searched for

something to put some life color into the baby Maria's lovely little cheeks.

23

Newton jumped as Ward opened the car door. The engine was running and Newton had whacked up the heat so that it was stiflingly hot. Ward immediately rolled down a window and finally found the perfect temperature. He didn't speak. Newton did as they pulled away and headed back to the station.

"Back there. It was nothing. Don't be getting the wrong idea about me. I don't spook easily or nothing."

"No problem."

When they arrived back at the station McNeely waved them straight over. She had gotten back just before Ward and Newton and she slurped a coffee and looked down at her computer and some papers on her desk. She picked some up and threw them back down onto the desk one by one.

"We ain't got shit from the first scene," she said.

Ward said, "How's that?"

"No DNA hits other than that of the victim. We have no fingerprint hits. We got the second blood analysis back and it confirms the first: morphine poisoning. But hear this. The security tapes." She said it as a question. "There aren't any."

"There aren't what?" Ward said.

Greg Poynter appeared by her side. "Went up there to collect it. Nothing doing. Been out of order for weeks. I checked it myself."

Newton looked at Ward and Ward said, "Goddamn it. So what do we have?"

"I brought back the guestbook." Poynter handed it to Ward, who didn't take it but nodded over at Newton, who did. "And all the statements we collected."

"It's a start. Okay, we check the book for previous visitors to the victim. We go over the statements to check for any irregularities, anything unusual or out of place. How's the evidence looking from the second scene?" He directed that question at McNeely.

"That will take some processing, detective. On the face of it we don't have a great deal. We'll run some prints, one or two clothing fibers. The ME will take a few hours or so on the body. Honestly, we don't have a whole lot."

"Statements from neighbors?"

"Still being collected," Poynter said.

"There is one thing," McNeely said. "The doctor had been served with a foreclosure notice. Looks like he didn't keep up the loan repayments. Maybe that's a reason for him taking his own life?"

Ward said, "Okay. Well, we have what we have. Keep working it." He gestured with his head at Newton. "I guess we go back to the first scene, see if there's anything we're missing. How about we go pay a visit to the owners of the nursing home? Anybody talked to them?"

"James Kenny," Newton said. "Owns most of the damn town. You see any construction works going on around here, you can bet a dollar to a dime it's Kenny Construction. He's an old-timer himself but money keeps you going like some elixir from the fountain of youth. Damn sure it does."

24

The massive dawn sun has already broken the horizon.
Bill O'Donnell cries dry tears now, from two sources of pain. He had considered dragging the boy's body but couldn't bear for any more damage to be done to him. Instead, he continues to carry him and the weight of his guilt seems to add another fifty pounds to the little boy.
He leaves another track that would have borne lumber-dragging horses and later trucks, those days merely a sepia memory, and now he's climbing to a small ridge where he knows that two miles beyond is his destination. He has to keep stopping to take in air and to straighten his cramping arms, but now he knows that the race against the sunrise is lost but the race against anybody else pursuing him is probably won. If there was anybody following they wouldn't know the woods like him.
He had lived here, had mapped the woods in his mind over forty-odd years, tracking whitetail and elk and fishing trout over in Blackfoot River. He knew hundreds of trees, peculiar by their bark patterns or branch formations, knew every turn in the rivers, and they acted like signposts to him.
He thinks of his daughter and dead wife and he feels like he's bringing the boy home for a burial in his spirit land.

And that gives him a small piece of comfort and he yearns for peace for the boy and for himself.

He reaches the top of the ridge and on the other side a steep drop appears to have sheared away the trees. In their place tumble sparse patches of mountain heathers and grouseberry. At the steepest part there are only rocks. He knows there is a long way down and a short way down, and instinct tells him to take the long route, which skirts the ridge as it falls away gently to the north, an ancient track that elk follow and probably created, carving an easygoing trail. That route would add an extra half hour to the journey but Bill O'Donnell doesn't feel he has that time, doesn't want this to take any longer than it needs to. He decides to take the short route.

He gently lowers the boy to the ground and lays him down. The body has stiffened. Then he reaches into his pocket and pulls out a length of thin nylon rope. He picks the boy up again and hitches him onto his back so that the boy's head rests on his own right shoulder. He bends forward so the boy doesn't slip, and then he takes one end of the rope and, with his right hand, he throws it over his left shoulder, the boy's too. He pulls the rope tight and fastens a knot at his chest, securing the boy to his back. He doesn't stand up, though, because he knows the boy will be dislodged. He throws the end of the rope over his right shoulder now and grabs it by his left hip, forming a crisscross over the boy's back. He pulls tight and, for the next few minutes, repeats this until he is able to stand without the boy working loose.

He takes the steepest part backwards as if climbing down a fire escape and he finds purchase in the rocks where he expects to. Only once does he nearly lose his footing on a thin seam of shale. Once the slope becomes shallower he can turn around and carefully pick his way down, his footing never quite sure under legs that want to go to sleep. And when rocks and sparse vegetation give way once more to lodgepole pines he falls to his knees. He can see the water through the trees, the lake created by loggers a hundred years earlier, and on seeing that he allows himself five minutes of rest. He unties the rope and gently lets the boy lie down, and then he sits and closes his eyes. And for a few moments he is asleep and he dreams and in his dream the boy is alive again.

25

Ward had called ahead to the office of James Kenny but he wasn't there. The customarily obstructive personal assistant eventually yielded and told Ward that Kenny was on-site at the planned development of the new science and technology wing at the Meriwether Elementary School.

When they pulled up at the school Ward knew straight away which one was Kenny. He had the calm demeanor of a man who was so in control he probably thought he could affect the weather. And despite his short stature, he towered over the men he was with and they were clearly intimidated by his presence.

Ward made no move to get out of the car. He stared at the man called James Kenny, property developer, multimillionaire. "Why do I get a prickly feeling about this guy?"

"Let's go say hello."

The man with the plans saw Newton and Ward, and this set him in a quandary of whether to acknowledge them or to keep telling Kenny what he wanted to hear, what he was paying this man to tell him. Kenny noticed his discomfort and glanced over to Newton and Ward and then back at the man and the two others he was with.

"We'll pick this up in five minutes," he said, approaching the oncoming detectives with handshake ready and outstretched. "Detective Newton and…" He grasped Newton's huge hand and squeezed it so that Newton wanted to say 'stop'.

"This is Detective Ward," Newton said.

Kenny grabbed at Ward's hand and Ward tried to make sure he got a good thrust into the handshake to avoid what he'd noticed Newton had suffered but he wasn't quick enough. He felt his metacarpals crunch.

"You're here to see me about the old guy." It wasn't a question but seemed like an order, as if he was driving a meeting to an early conclusion because he had to be at another one as soon as possible. He could've said, "Get on with it, you sons of bitches," for all the strength of his delivery.

So Ward slowed it down purposely and said, "The school getting some work done?"

Kenny momentarily seemed to be shaken down a rank or two by Ward's question but he quickly snapped back in charge, like a sergeant major snapping his heels together. He might as well have demanded a salute, Ward thought.

"So let's talk about the old guy," Kenny said. "Homicide? That's unfortunate." And Ward thought his choice of phrase was also unfortunate. But he didn't bite and he let Newton have a poke.

Newton said, "Would we be able to ask you a few questions, Mr. Kenny? You want to do it here or go somewhere warmer?"

"Here is fine. This won't take long, I'm sure. And

I'm used to the outdoors. All part of the job."

"Okay," Newton said. "I wondered if you could tell us about the security procedures you have in place at the nursing home."

"Ask a specific question, detective," said Kenny.

"Okay, well, let's start with the security cameras that aren't working," he said, and then he realized he hadn't asked a question. "Let me rephrase that. Were you aware that your cameras aren't working?"

"Being fixed today. Next question."

"What procedures do you have in place for controlling access into and out of the home?"

"You know the answer to that, detective. Next question."

Newton rubbed his back. "And the control of medication?"

"We have a small pharmacy which is secured at all times. All drugs are locked up."

"Who has access to the pharmacy?"

"The on-call doctor and the residential nurses."

"And who keeps the key?"

"The key is locked in the safe."

"And who has the key to the safe?"

"The manager of the facility has the key to the safe."

"Yeah, we've spoken to him," Ward said. "We've asked for a full inventory to be taken of all the drugs you got locked up there. Make sure none are missing."

"So that's what killed the old man? Drugs?"

"I'm afraid we can't discuss any details at this stage, sir," Newton said.

"Are you suggesting the drugs came from our pharmacy?"

"Again, with respect sir, we can't discuss any details

at this stage."

Kenny smiled. And then Ward spoke. "You ever take time to visit the home?"

Kenny paused and sized up Ward. "I often pop in to say hello to my guests. And to maybe pick out a room for when I might need one."

Ward tried a smile. "Were you there on Sunday night?" The question surprised Newton more than it did James Kenny, who briefly smiled.

"I would have to check back," he said. And then, "Yes, possibly. Am I a suspect, detective?"

"No, of course not," Newton said.

"As for suspect status, I don't think you are just yet," Ward said, and Newton looked at him as though wanting him to stop.

"Just yet. Ah. Mr. Poirot, you do play games," Kenny said.

"Did you know the man, sir?" Ward glanced over to the school then as he waited for the reply.

"I knew Bill O'Donnell, yes. He was a guest of the nursing home. I know all my guests."

"I'm sure you do," Ward said, "but did you know Mr. O'Donnell on a personal level?"

Kenny looked at Newton. "Your guy here is very thorough, detective. You got a good one there." And then he looked at Ward. "No. I didn't know him on a personal level."

"So you didn't visit with him on Sunday?"

"No, I did not. I was there only briefly to have a walk around. Run a finger over the surfaces so to speak. I do it most weekends as a matter of fact."

"Don't you find it a little strange that a man of his financial resources should be able to afford your prices, sir? I mean, it can't come cheap."

"I don't know what you are driving at, detective, so I'm not sure I can answer that question."

"Okay," Ward said. "I think we have everything we need for the time being. We appreciate your cooperation, sir." He looked at Newton to see if he had any questions, but a slight shake of the head said he didn't.

"Well, if you need anything else you know how to contact me." And with that comment Kenny turned his back on Newton and Ward and a wave to his three men brought them scuttling over to him.

Newton took a painkiller from the bottle and swallowed it with a grimace that might have been pain or the effort of a dry swallow.

Newton said, "Are you kidding me? You know who that is?"

Ward turned to Newton but his peripheral vision captured Kenny, a blur on the edge of his thoughts. "You know you said about instinct? Well, ignore what I said. It's now set to twitching."

"You think he's a suspect? Goddamn it, Ward, this is the richest man in town. In the county, probably. You don't think—"

"I don't like the guy. And I think he did know O'Donnell. In what capacity I don't know but he knew him all right. And he doesn't seem too concerned that there's a killer on the loose in his nursing home."

"Now hold on—"

"No. I'm running this case, remember? I asked for you to be put on the case."

"Why'd you do that?"

"Ask me that question a few days down the line."

"We don't go around upsetting the richest man in town is all I'm saying," Newton said.

"Why not? His wealth don't come into it."

"And his influence. He's connected. He knows everyone who's anyone at the golf club, damn it, and that includes your captain. So don't you go digging around too much with Kenny or you'll end up digging yourself into a hole you might not want to crawl out of. S'all I'm saying."

"Well," Ward said, "I got an advantage here in that I don't know or care about people's influence or reputation around here and I don't give a rat's ass who I might upset."

At that Newton just shrugged.

"And what's an old guy like O'Donnell doing, spending his last few years in a nursing home that costs around thirty thousand bucks a year?"

"Maybe he had a good insurance plan," Newton said.

"Well, correct me if I'm wrong but he don't seem like the kind of guy had a pension pot to piss in."

Ward waited for Newton, who sighed. "I think it's time you got a bit of background on the other case. Find you something out about O'Donnell."

"We're not working the other case. I got strict orders on that."

"Strict orders from who?"

"From Gammond. He don't want you reopening old wounds is what he said."

Newton was silent for a few seconds and then he said, "Let's go see Alice White."

"Next of kin?" Ward asked.

"Closest he'd got to any. It'll be a good place to start. Get you some context on the guy."

26

"I'll kick off the questions," Ward said. He and Newton had located Alice White at home on the quiet side of town. "Seems you know the lady and I'd kinda like to get to know her too, at my pace."

Newton nodded and clapped his hands to get some blood running through them. The cold seemed to age him, a pallid undercoat showing through his complexion, emphasizing the wrinkles and making visible the stress. He looked like old furniture too far gone to restore.

Alice White answered the door on one knock and her deep purring voice, like that of a content tigress, led them inside. The house was warm, old people warm, and Ward took off his coat. Alice White took it from him and set it on a coat stand by the door. He removed his hat and placed it on the hook next to his coat.

"Mr. Newton? Your coat, sir?"

But Newton shook his head. The warmth seemingly hadn't hit him like it had Ward. He bit his bottom lip as if to stifle something wanting to come out.

"We've met before, Mr...."

"Ward. Sorry, I'm Detective Ward. But I don't think we've met before."

Alice White coughed up a deep laugh.

"Not you, Mr. Ward. Mr. Newton and me have met. Long time ago."

Newton still didn't talk but nodded at her, took off his cap, and then looked down at his feet.

"I won't ask you to take off your shoes. Just wipe them on this here mat and come into the parlor. Fancy name I call my living room." The words seemed to wash over Ward and he felt relaxed by them as if enchanted.

She was dressed for a Sunday and Ward knew for sure that she always dressed for a Sunday whatever day it was.

In the parlor three cups were set out for tea. Cookies circled a doily-dressed plate, some in gold foil and some bare.

"The ones without the wrappings I baked myself for you this morning. Truth told the wrapped ones are for show and ain't nobody never touched those before when my best homemade cookies are on offer. Please sit."

Ward and Newton sat and then Ward noticed the single tear on Alice's right cheek, at odds with her broad smile which broadened further when she noticed Ward looking at her with concern written on his features.

"They leak from time to time in this cold. Sure it's an age thing."

Ward wondered how they leaked in this heat, though. He glanced around the room and the first thing that struck him were the photographs of children. Lots of photographs of lots of children.

"My babies."

Ward opened his face to ask a silent question.

"My foster children. Brought up no children of my own but many little ones have graced this house. Some troubled and some mellow but all wonderful in their own ways."

Ward smiled. "You got any now?"

"Oh no. Not no more. Getting too old to keep up with them. One thing always been true is that children draw energy. And at my age I ain't got enough of that most days to keep my own engine revving. Tea?"

"Oh, yes, ma'am," Ward said.

Newton said nothing but Alice poured three cups anyway. Ward eyed the cookies and Alice pushed them his way and he accepted the invitation readily.

"I'd like to ask you a few questions about William O'Donnell," Ward said. "Would you mind?"

"No, no, of course not." The smile still illuminated her face and Ward wondered if she knew what had happened to him, but he knew that of course she did. At least she knew he was dead.

"What can you tell me about him? Did you know him well?"

"I knew him very well," said Alice. "Very well. As well as anybody might know him I would say. But not as good as God knew him. I see the man but God sees the heart. What I can tell you, though, is the William I knew was a good man. A good man."

Again Ward allowed space for Alice to continue and she filled that space, the smile never leaving her face.

"I first met William at my church. One day he appeared. I can tell you which day because it was the

Sunday of his grandson going missing."

Newton looked up now and Alice brought him into the conversation with a slight, almost indiscernible nod of her head. Newton seemed to freeze in that gaze.

"Go on," Ward said, encouragement that wasn't necessary. He took out his notepad and began to write as she spoke.

"He hung around at the back and he kind of stood out. Took him for a hobo at first. And he was white. Not to say we don't have white folk at the church but not so many. When the service ended he stood aside to let people out but he stayed there. Never took his eyes off of Christ. I did the flowers back then and I was tending them when he walks up to the front and, as a good Christian, I ain't normally quick to judge but I confess on that occasion I thought he had an eye for the altar. We got a fair weight of gold and silver on there. But he just walked up and stood there staring up at Christ on the cross. I carried on with my business and kept a half eye on him, strange looking and sad as he was. Yes, he looked as sad as anybody I ever saw. I like to leave people be when they like that, communicating with the Lord. I'm not sure he knew it back then but he was doing that all right. God's always listening even when you not saying nothing. And William wasn't saying nothing. And then suddenly he spins around as if he's come out of a trance and he looked startled and he got me startled. I think he saw that and he just says to me, 'I wanted to get closer.'"

"Closer?"

"Closer to God. He told me later that he picked the Westmoreland Gospel Church because he thought we got closer to God with our 'dancing, singing and whooping hallelujahs' as he put it. Closer than the other denominations. And he was keen as corn dogs to get up close and personal with the Lord at that time."

"So would you say he was a deeply religious man?"

"No, Mr. Ward. I wouldn't say that. For sure he would be there every Sunday and some Saturdays too, and he started to help out with odd jobs around the place, but he wouldn't be described as deeply religious. Never saw him sing nor pray. Not outwards anyway. Some, they sing inwards and I think maybe William was one of those. He once told me he didn't pray because he was scared to hear silence coming back. He just wanted to know God was there. To trust he was there. He had faith because he needed faith. I think that's it. I think he needed it because of little Ryan. Not a day passed for that first year that he wasn't out looking for Ryan." Her voice was as sweet as her cookies and Ward helped himself to another, rapt in her story.

She stood then and walked over to the dresser and opened a drawer. She took out a photograph and handed it to Ward.

"Here's a picture from a couple years ago at one of our events. He always smiled for the camera, though his teeth weren't perfect." She laughed.

Newton lowered his head and Alice paused to look over at him.

"Mr. Newton. I feel what you thinking but I tell it as it is, as facts I know. William wanted to get closer to God. And you thinking that was because he took the life of his Ryan. I knew William as a kind man, not the sort of man that would do such a thing, but it don't matter what I think. You always suspected William, I know. But it don't matter much what you think neither. Fact is, only God can judge and if William done anything like you say he did, then I guess by now God has sat in judgment on him."

Newton didn't say anything but sat there with hands gripping knees and head bowed again.

"And you ain't touched your tea, Mr. Newton. No mind. I'll get us a fresh pot while you two talk amongst yourselves."

She stood up slowly and steadied herself before moving on out of the room. Ward looked over at Newton and for a minute he thought he was looking at a man on death row.

"It's bullshit," Newton said. "I've heard all this bullshit before. She knows something more and she ain't telling. O'Donnell just appeared from nowhere on the day the boy was reported missing and gave me this story of his truck going missing and him going off to look for it. Something didn't add up."

"Did he report the truck missing?"

"So what if he did? Yes, he did. But to me that don't add up to a convincing alibi. I'm telling you, Ward, there's something else here. And I think she knows. Why was he at the church anyways? He suddenly goes to church. A black church. Don't make sense. Never made sense."

"After losing his grandson I guess he might go to church. It's not that unusual for someone to go pray for something like that."

"It don't match the timeline."

"How's that?"

"Because he went to church before he knew the boy had gone."

Ward stared sleepily at Newton. "Okay, look—"

"I had him, Ward. I had him. He was at the church before Ryan was reported missing. His truck went missing. He took the boy and then after he'd killed him he went to pray for his own soul."

"Okay. We need to focus on the old man's homicide for now. I need to get background on the man. She's the one person knew him best. Got to be something in what she's telling us even if it's not the full story. God will strike her down if she's telling lies. That's how it works, right?"

Newton shook his head and was about to speak when Ward's cell phone vibrated in his pocket. He looked at the display and decided to take the call. The call lasted less than a minute and by the time Ward hung up Alice was back in the room with a fresh pot of tea and more cookies.

"Was that a phone I heard? That would be the station, I figure." She sat down slowly, smiling at Ward and holding his stare. He looked over to Newton, who sat upright now. The phone was on vibrate and hadn't rung out loud.

"Mrs. White. I have a few more questions. Did you receive any money from William?"

Alice White poured tea. A fresh cup for Ward, but Newton placed his hand over his cup to decline.

"Yes, I did, Mr. Ward. You don't need to ask me that because you got access to William's bank account. Regular payment each month of five hundred dollars."

Newton's jaw loosened.

"May I ask why? What was the money for?"

"Let me tell you about William O'Donnell. He was a kind man. As generous as they come. He gave of his time to the church and he gave to the glory of God. He knew of my work with children and he gave me money to help me support that. The money he gave was used to make a better life for those children. If there was any left over after taking care of the little ones I would donate that to the church and William was happy with that."

"Any idea where he was getting the money from?"

"Never asked. Money's a private thing for people and I ain't one to pry. He did work."

"Where did he work?"

"Mr. Newton will tell you. He worked at the elementary school as a janitor."

"Five hundred a month's a lot out of a janitor's salary. He can't have earned much."

"I never asked a man nor woman what they earn."

"But you understand it may appear a little odd that he would be able to give you all that money and he still managed to support himself too. You don't find that odd?"

"William lived frugally, Mr. Ward, like a good Christian man. I don't know any more than that. Can only tell you what I know. And I been open about that."

Ward tapped his bottom lip with his pencil. "Yes, you have, ma'am, and I appreciate that. I have just a few more questions if that's okay."

"That's fine with me. Fire away."

"When did the payments start?"

"A few years after we met. I tried to refuse at first but he was insistent and I figured if it could help the children it was a gift from God hisself and I never refuse that kind of gift."

"So that would be, what, twenty years ago, give or take?"

"Uh huh. Give or take, I suppose."

"So that would make it in the region of"—he did the math slowly—"a hundred and twenty thousand dollars total. That's a heck of a lot of money on a janitor's salary."

"Like I said, I don't know where he got the money from. That's the honest truth." She then reached behind her, twisting uncomfortably on her seat as she retrieved a shoebox from the sideboard. "You might want to see this. It's William's belongings from the nursing home."

Ward took it from her.

"In there's his worldly belongings. Don't amount to much. A wristwatch he never wore. A penknife. A Bible. Not a great deal else. Apart from his last will and testament."

Ward took a pair of gloves from his pocket, dragged them on and pulled out the will. He opened it and read it to himself. He glanced over at Newton and tilted the document so that they could both read.

"He left everything to you."

"Yes, he did. God rest his soul." And then the tear again rolling down her right cheek. She let this one fall and it wasn't followed by another.

"Okay." Ward let out a sigh. "I will tell you now that we are investigating a homicide here, Mrs. White."

"I know that."

"And this is potential evidence. Would you mind if we took these belongings for examination?"

"You take whatever you need. I want you to find the person who took William." Her smile was still there.

Ward picked up the Bible and flicked through the pages. As he did so a photograph fell out. It fell to the floor facedown and Ward saw the tiny hole where the pushpin had secured it to the wall behind the picture of Bermuda in O'Donnell's room at Sunny Glade. A picture the old man kept just for himself. There was writing on the back and Ward read it out aloud. "John 1 20." He turned the photo over and there, grinning up at the camera, was a small boy. About seven years old. It looked like any other normal happy domestic scene. A little guy standing in front of the TV, frozen for eternity. A single fading and creased memory of a lost life. The photo was old and faded, wrinkled from being handled regularly. Newton's eyes widened.

Ward said, "Is this William's grandson?"

"Yes, it is," Alice said after a slight pause, and Newton nodded.

"John 1:20," Ward said again, and he flicked through the Bible. He knew where to find John from his childhood. He could even recite John 1:29, the bit about beholding the Lamb of God, which taketh away the sin of the world. That had been drummed into him at an early age. But he didn't know what verse 20 said.

And when he'd read it silently, Ward simply showed it to Newton, who scanned it as though he'd got a terrible itch in his eyes. The first line did it: "'And he confessed, and denied not.'" Newton spoke the words and looked straight at Alice White, who placed one hand on top of the other on her lap.

"I know what it says," Alice said. "And I know what you thinking, Mr. Newton. But you taking that verse out of its true context. The full verse is 'And he confessed, and denied not; but confessed, I am not the Christ.' John's telling us he's not the Christ. That's all." She smiled.

"That's the second time O'Donnell's used that word," Newton simply said.

Ward was on the periphery of the moment between Newton and Alice, and he watched the pain in Newton's eyes and their refusal to accept the smile from Alice's mouth. He put the photo back into the shoebox and that broke the spell.

Ward said, "You say you knew William as good as anybody."

Alice turned slowly back to Ward, keeping her eyes on Newton as long as she could. She said, "Aside of God, yes."

"Do you know if he had any enemies? Do you know of anybody in his life who might want to do him harm?"

"Sir, no, I don't. William was a gentle man coming to the end of his days. Who would want to harm a man like that? Who?" She turned to Newton then.

Ward said, "I don't know. Maybe someone from his past who decided to even an old score. We don't know at this stage. But anything you can tell us could help us catch the person responsible. Is there anything you know that might explain why someone would want to harm him?"

"All's I know, Mr. Ward, is that there is evil in the world. Way the devil works"—her smile subsided when she said that—"is he confuses. Turns man against man. Ain't always no reason. Ain't always no motive. The devil is among us and he had his fingers in this business. That I know for sure."

Ward paused and thought for a minute. He looked at Newton and opened the way for him to ask his own questions, but Newton shook his head gently.

"Well, ma'am. We really appreciate you giving us your time. It's been a big help."

"My pleasure, Mr. Ward, Mr. Newton. If there's anything else I can do to help I'd be more than happy. Please catch the person who did this."

"We will, Mrs. White. I promise you."

Ward and Newton stood and Ward's eye was caught by all the photos around the room once more. He looked over them as he made his way to the door, and he flipped open an album which lay on a bookshelf. He gasped.

"Now they's my other babies, Mr. Ward."

On each page were two or three photos of babies, sleeping peacefully. He flipped the pages and noticed that some were wearing the same clothes. And some of the babies were so small they didn't look like babies at all but dolls. He turned to Alice but words didn't come.

"They is in heaven now, Mr. Ward. Ever' single one of them carried on the wings of angels to be with the Lord. They come to me to be dressed. Some call me the Baby Dresser for what I do. Gives an opportunity for their parents to spend some time with them before they go on."

Ward shook his head gently. "How… how many?"

"Some hundred or so."

Ward flipped pages and was finally stunned into silence. Alice looked at him and he felt a single tear on his cheek. Alice pointed at his face.

"That'll be the cold."

Ward wiped the tear away and walked to the door.

Alice touched his arm as he walked past and her smile dug into him now and pulled at something. He felt as if he knew some secret that she had just passed to him and he felt elation and sadness and wanted to get out of the house quickly. Newton was out already, and Ward took his hat from the coat stand while Alice passed him his coat.

"Come back when you ever want to know more," she said, and Ward knew that meant something else.

"I will," he said. "Thank you, Alice. Thank you."

Outside, Newton looked Ward up and down and then got in the car without a word passing between them. The gloom had turned to darkness, and the cold ripped away Ward's top two layers of clothing and cut into him. He had a feeling of not being there and he shook his head to clear the mist. He flipped open his notepad to try and remember what had just occurred. At the bottom of the last page he had written "Jesus is my savior. Christ is my redeemer" in large capital letters. He glanced at Newton, who sat in the car staring ahead. Ward said, "What the hell?" and climbed into the car, his hands shaking as he grabbed the steering wheel.

27

The Alfa pulled into the station parking lot and the headlights lit up two figures by the entrance. Newton recognized one of them right away and said, "What the hell are they doing here?" And Ward knew them to be local press. One photographer and one reporter. The camera flashed immediately as Newton hauled his body out of the car gingerly, his back going into spasm and wringing an anguished look onto his face. He held up his hand as the camera flashed again and again, at him, not Ward.

"Come on, guys," Ward said, and Newton lunged forward to knock the camera away as the photographer swerved his swipe.

The reporter whose name was Larsson said, "Can we have a comment on the Bill O'Donnell homicide case, detective?"

Newton squared up to him. "Go and nicely fuck yourself." Larsson shrunk back, apparently fearing one of Newton's clenched fists connecting with his face.

"I'm just doing my job. Same as you are. No need for the unpleasantries there."

Newton swung into the station and tested the door's

durability as it crashed against the stopper behind it. Ward was two paces back and Larsson made as if to grab his arm but thought better of it. It was enough to make Ward pause, and he looked Larsson in the eye. Larsson offered his hand and Ward waved him away like a shit fly. Then he noticed the card in Larsson's hand.

"You want to speak to me," said Larsson. "You need to speak to me. Take it."

Ward stood there and faced up to Larsson.

"This is not about you," said Larsson. "This thing goes way back. I guess you already got that. Take the card. Call me."

Ward took the card. Larsson smiled like a hyena. Ward tossed the card back at him and walked into the station.

"You know where to find me," Larsson shouted after him. "You will want to talk to me. Trust me."

"How the hell did they get this? How the hell did they get this?"

Ward could hear Newton's voice as he entered the building. McNeely was hunched over her computer and a couple of uniforms hovered around, clearly wishing they had been patrolling somewhere. Newton jabbed his finger at one of them, Poynter. "You?" Poynter shook his head. Newton turned to the other. "You?" The other cop held up his hands in a submissive denial. "Then who in hell leaked this? Anybody want to tell me?"

McNeely was the only one who spoke after a couple of beats. "They've been there a while. Hour or so.

Nobody has said a word."

And then Newton swayed, resembling a leggy sapling blowing in a strong wind. He grabbed the back of a chair and slumped down on another, just catching enough of his backside on it to stay seated. McNeely jumped up and grabbed his arm to steady him, as his unfocused eyes twitched in their sockets momentarily before they closed.

Gammond emerged from his office as fast as his pudgy legs could carry him. Ward noticed he wore stacked heels and wanted to laugh despite the current emergency.

"What the heck in the heavens is going—" He saw Newton. "Get a doctor. Get him some water."

"I'm okay. I'm okay," Newton said windlessly. "If I find that one of you sons of bitches has leaked this thing I will rip your heart out. I will rip your heart out of your chest. You hear me? You hear me?"

Nobody said a word and Newton closed his eyes again and drew a deep breath.

The next day's *Westmoreland Echo* would run with the headline "Cop in Boy's Disappearance Case Investigating Murder of Grandfather. Detective Out to Make Amends for Botched Case 25 Years Ago." Complete with a picture of Newton – no Ward in shot – grimacing at the camera, clearly hurting.

28

Cherry smiled a cat-just-fed smile at Ward as he entered the Honey Pie Diner, Jesús on a leash. Jesús kept focused on the ground as Cherry fussed over to him, cooing and gooing while stooping, showing cleavage and knowing that Ward was enjoying the view.

"My two new BFFs came back. Let me see if I remember this. A coffee for the little guy and a bowl of water for you, sir?"

"He likes his coffee black," Ward said, and he waited a while before seating himself. Cherry playfully snatched at his beard and said, "I like this."

Ward liked the touch and he settled himself by the window, same table as before, and removed his hat. He let Jesús's leash drop to the floor. "Might help myself to some pie of some sort if you got some," he said.

Bending down he rubbed Jesús's head and ears, and the little dog seemed to relax. He removed his coat, placing it on the seat next to him. He fished out his notebook and opened it to the last page to check if he had imagined what he had seen earlier. But it was there in his untidy handwriting. "Jesus is my savior.

Christ is my redeemer."

He wanted to shudder but the diner was too warm for that. He just sat there and shook his head. He tried to fit Alice White into the William O'Donnell case but didn't know where to put her. Was she a small piece of the jigsaw – a piece of sky in the top right corner? Or did she play a bigger part in this? She had been a nurse in her previous existence. She knew her way around a hypodermic needle. Was she the one to administer the fatal dose to end old William O'Donnell's life? Had she done the same to Doctor Brookline? Could she have done those things? Why would she?

Yes, she was the only beneficiary of William O'Donnell's will, but that didn't necessarily make someone a suspect. She couldn't be. Maybe she was helping the old man on his way because he had an incurable disease. But that would've shown up on the autopsy, surely. And anyway, she couldn't be a suspect. She couldn't be. That phrase kept repeating in his head. She couldn't be. And Ward also kept hearing "Jesus is my savior. Christ is my redeemer." At the back of his mind he couldn't help thinking she had something he needed to know. He just didn't know what the question was that he needed to ask to unlock that information.

And then his cell phone rang. It was Newton.

"Two things," Newton said. Ward thought he sounded different. More upbeat. "Firstly, I been doing some digging around O'Donnell's bank account."

"Okay."

"Statements going back twenty years. Five hundred a month as Alice White said. His salary would have easily covered those payments he made." Newton went quiet for a few seconds.

"Okay," Ward said. He stared at the neon beer sign that adorned the wall over the diner's counter. "What was the second thing?"

"What?"

"The second thing? You said two things."

"Oh, yeah. The autopsy on Brookline came back. Death by overdose of morphine. Only, no obvious evidence of foul play. No signs of a struggle. No forensics to speak of. Could be looking at a straightforward OD on that one. Or a suicide."

"Don't you think it's too similar? Gotta be connected?"

"I don't know."

"Okay."

"And I been thinking. Gammond doesn't want me digging around the Ryan case. He didn't say anything about you looking at it. How about you take a look? Fresh pair of eyes. I can have the original case materials ready for you in the morning."

Ward rubbed his forehead. "I don't know."

"There's a connection. I'm sure of it."

Ward said after a spell, "If I take a look, then I do it without Gammond knowing nothing about it. I'm interested. But listen here, Gammond don't find out. Nobody knows but me and you. I'll take a look but if it gets back to Gammond I could be looking at a move straight back to San Antonio."

"You got it." And then Newton ended the call and Ward stared at his cell for a moment.

Jesús let out a noisy yawn as Cherry arrived with his bowl of water and a large slice of apple pie for Ward. "Your pie."

Ward smiled at her and said, "Thank you, ma'am." Now he itched to get his hands on the case notes for the little boy's disappearance. His hand found a fork and he scooped a piece of pie into his mouth.

29

Cherry had her coat on and was turning lights out. Ward was the last customer and was getting ready to leave. He wasn't sure at first what the low rumble was but then he realized it was Jesús growling and, at the same time he realized that, he saw the man enter the diner. Cherry called, "We're closed, sorry," and then she saw the man and her face hardened.

"Everything okay?" Ward asked.

"It's fine," Cherry said, but Ward could see it wasn't fine. "You can go."

"I'd just as rather wait here if that's agreeable, ma'am," Ward said. Cherry didn't bother to argue but her confidence seemed to drain right away like a wrung sponge as she moved closer to him.

The man hunched himself up against the cold, his flimsy baseball jacket and cap not offering much insulation. Ward noticed he looked dirty. And thin. The man paused at the door and looked over the diner, and then he briskly walked up to the counter. His eyes were on Ward and Ward returned the stare. The man shrugged and looked at Cherry.

"This is a private matter," he said without loosening

his gaze on Cherry.

"S'okay," Cherry said. "What do you want?"

"I want some privacy." And then he turned to Ward. "So if you wouldn't mind, cowboy." He waved Ward away.

Ward stood his ground, said nothing, and the man sniffed loudly and wiped snot on his jacket sleeve.

"You either butt out or I knock you out," he said to Ward, but Ward remained unmoved by the threat.

"Troy, say what you gotta say to me and get the hell out of here," Cherry said, finding a crumb of confidence, drawn from Ward's presence.

"You ain't saying a lot, cowboy. Cat got your tongue?"

Ward felt his eyes drying as he hadn't blinked since the man had entered the diner. "I'm the strong, violent type," he said, and the man called Troy made an exaggerated gesture of surprise and then laughed nervously. His eyes seemed like they were doing a quick calculation and then he looked at Cherry again.

"Fuck it, then. Cherry, I need some money, so please"—he held out his right hand—"kindly oblige."

Ward kept quiet.

"Ain't got nothing to give. And ain't giving nothing. No more, Troy. No more."

Troy smiled. "I don't think you heard me. I need some money. Now please kindly oblige and give me some fucking money."

Ward remained completely still but his muscles tensed.

Cherry spoke again but this time louder. "I will tell you one last time, Troy. I am not giving you any more money. I'm finished with that. Finished. You listening to me? So please leave."

"Hmm. Well, I guess I will just have to take what I come for, won't I, bitch."

And Troy's hand shot out in Cherry's direction, but before it had half crossed the distance between them, Ward's hand flashed out and grabbed Troy's arm. In one fluid movement he squeezed and twisted the arm and with his other hand shoved Troy's upper body onto the counter. His hand slid up Troy's back and grabbed the back of his head, slamming his temple into the marble effect surface of the countertop. Troy let out a startled yelp. Jesús barked and pounced and Cherry snatched his airborne leash just in time to stop him sinking his teeth into Troy.

"Now, I don't know if your hearing is impaired there, but I heard the lady tell you loud and clear that she wanted you to leave, so we can do this the easy way or the hard way. From my experience of these situations, and I've been involved in one or two of them, the easy way is the most salubrious. So I'm the generous kind and I'll give you a couple of seconds to think that over. Give me a holler when you've made up your mind. Jesús. Quiet." And he squeezed Troy's neck, crunched his face into the countertop and twisted his arm up his back, and before two seconds had elapsed Troy was ready to choose.

"Okay, okay. Let me up. I'm going, I'm going. I don't want no trouble." And his voice was now more of a whimper. Ward squeezed hard on his neck and then released, shoving Troy away as he did so. Troy stumbled and nearly fell but managed to steady himself as his momentum carried him towards the door. He spun around.

"This is not over, bitch. And your new fucking boyfriend had better fucking watch out."

Ward made a movement as if to lunge at Troy and Troy was out the door quicker than a cockroach. He looked back through the window, but then turned and jogged down the street, his hands stuffed into his jacket pockets.

Cherry turned to Ward, tears pooling in reddened eyes. "I am so sorry about that." She fell into Ward's arms and he stroked her head.

"Now, there's no need to apologize there, missy. None whatsoever." She let the tears flow now. "I'm guessing that's your marital history right there."

Through a sob Cherry said, "I'm sorry. I'm trying to sort out a few issues."

"He into you for money?" Ward asked.

"He has a habit. I offered to feed him food but all he wants is to feed his habit."

"What's he into?"

"Oh, everything. Anything he can get his hands on. He'll do anything to get high."

"But he ain't getting high tonight."

"He'll probably end up knocking over a pharmacy tonight. Wouldn't surprise me none."

Ward's bright blue eyes widened and then shrunk into a squint. "He steal morphine?"

"Oh, he'll take anything looks like high. He'd kill for it if he wasn't such a coward."

Ward loosened his grip on Cherry and pinched at his chin.

"I told him no more but he comes back and I never had the strength to say no till now. Till now." She stared into Ward's eyes. "And now I'm scared he's gonna do something dumb."

"He ain't going to do a damned thing while I'm here. That I guarantee you, ma'am."

Cherry sniffled and laughed at the same time. "I love how you call me ma'am. Makes me feel like someone important somehow."

Jesús let out an audible sigh and they both laughed.

"You mind if I walked you home?"

"That's okay. I can find my own way home."

"You don't need to be being brave now. You have been threatened and it would make me feel a whole lot better if you let me escort you, make sure you get home in one piece."

"I got to stop at the bank deposit."

"There you go. You've got cash and—"

"Okay, all right. I'll take the escort. Sheesh." Cherry smiled when she said it.

30

The boy is in the boat. Bill O'Donnell had been relieved that the boat was still there but at the same time had known it would be. Nobody came to this part of the lake unless they had a good reason to and he couldn't see no reason, good or otherwise, to bother. No paths led to this point – the elk-carved track skirted off north and to backtrack south would mean picking your way through thick woodland where tangled scrub had also taken in the places trees had been felled and then later replanted and even the most determined explorer would most likely not want to pick their way through here. The boat had lasted over twenty years, thirteen of those since O'Donnell had left the woods in '72, but he had been back many times and had regularly patched it up and retouched it with Shellac. A tarpaulin cover, tied off at bow and stern and weighted down with rocks, had kept the weather out.

He carefully places the boy in the boat and then climbs into it himself and the early morning orange glow of the sun swathes the lake and jumps off in bright flashes, sparkling from the small waves that are pinched up by the gentle breeze that blows from the west, sweeping down off the mountains. He embraces the beauty of that and his *exhausted mind grabs at each twinkle, taken as a moment of solace, but, each time he grabs, his grief rips the moment from him and lets it drown again. This makes his heart leap up and down and in his shattered state he thinks for a minute that it will burst open and reveal a thick black goo of cold congealed blood. And then he vomits over the side of the boat but hardly anything comes out. The retching makes his body shudder and tense and he suddenly feels every single step he has taken in every muscle in his body.*

He wipes his mouth on the back of his hand and he places one oar in one of the oarlocks and, with the other, pushes himself off. He will stay close to the shore and that will take him longer but he feels like he wants to be near firm ground without knowing why he feels that.

He constantly fears he will fall overboard and drown and not be able to finish what he has started and that wearies him ever more and then he sleeps while still rowing and he knows that an unseen force is rowing for him and when he wakes he sees his wife and he sees his daughter and they are calling him from the shore and he turns to them and waves and they both wave back with both arms and he sees that they are distressed as they run along to keep up with his swift row strokes and he hurts so badly in muscle and spirit and he cries and cries out time and time again but then he wakes again and he is silent and the world is silent save for the slushing of the water against the bow. And he wonders where the morning birds are and he feels cold in his sweat.

He's nearly there.

31

They dropped the cash off at the bank deposit and stopped at a bar called Ned's Yard and Ward ordered two beers.

Cherry said, "You planning on staying in a motel forever or getting something more permanent?"

"I'm planning on staying in the motel for a spell. See how it goes."

"This town is better for having you. My experience of the police. Well…"

"I meant what I said back there," Ward said, "I won't let him hurt you."

"My hero," Cherry said as she removed her coat and scarf and hung them on the back of the bar stool where she sat. "So, tell me a little about yourself, cowboy. What's the story?"

"Not a deal to tell, ma'am."

"There must be something. Where did you grow up? What schooling did you get? What made you become a cop?"

He decided to answer the last question and left the others floating. "My great-grandfather was a Texas Ranger. My granddaddy too. My dad broke the chain and became a teacher but I decided I wanted to follow in my ancestors' footsteps. Sounded exciting, way my granddaddy used to tell it."

"And it isn't?" she asked.

"Well, you know. It's a job and not as glamorous as all that. It brought me here so I got to meet you and I'm glad for that." He took a long, slow drink of beer then so that he couldn't talk for a few moments. Give Cherry a chance to speak.

"You ever get scared? I mean of desperate people doing something foolish and shooting you?"

"No, ma'am."

She leaned back and took a good long stare at him. "You, sir, have a very nice way about you." She leaned over and kissed him on the cheek.

"Thank you," he said, and wiped the cheek.

"It's bad luck to wipe off a kiss you know."

"It is?"

"Sure it is," she said, and she kissed him again. "Don't you dare wipe that one off," she said.

"No, ma'am," Ward said, and she playfully punched him on the arm and he faked pain.

They talked for two more beers. When she had told him she had a daughter, she said she hadn't mentioned it before because she'd thought it might put him off.

"Now why would it do that?" Ward asked.

"You know. Not all guys like a ready-made family." And then she realized what she had said and quickly corrected herself. "Not that we're now a family or anything. Fuck, that ought to scare you off!"

"I don't scare easily," Ward said.

Cherry told Ward that five-year-old Laurie was with her grandparents over in Bozeman for a couple of days, feeling under the weather. Actually, they were Troy's parents but they had disowned him a while ago on account of his various issues. They were nice normal people, Cherry had said, and she wanted them to play a role in Laurie's upbringing. Troy, wisely, stayed away. His father Joe, an old-fashioned type who espoused hundred-and-fifty-year-old Montana values when it came to drug abuse, had said he would shoot Troy down dead if he ever stepped on his porch again. He took good care of his guns and Cherry didn't for a minute doubt that he would use them if Troy did show.

Cherry's own parents had leapfrogged Idaho and landed in Spokane following work and they weren't as accessible and, besides, she had her issues with her mother, and her father for that matter. They weren't 'live in your pocket' parents. They got on with their own lives and were biding their time before they retired down to Florida, at which point, Cherry assumed, she would probably only see them once a year on one of the major holidays. She was kind of philosophical about it and that surprised Ward, who was close to his family even though he didn't see them much either. But he talked to his mom and grandmother regularly by phone. His mother had tried to get him hooked up on Skype but that sort of thing just confused and exasperated Ward.

"Thank you, cowboy, for an unexpected evening" was the last thing Cherry said to Ward at her door. She kissed him briefly on the mouth and he didn't wipe it off. As he left he thought suddenly of Alice White and that made him feel uneasy and he wanted to go back to Cherry but didn't know why. He told himself he would call her when he got back to the motel but he realized he didn't have her number. When he did get back, he lay on the bed and stared at the dreamcatcher and knew that sleep was way beyond the horizon.

32

The *Westmoreland Echo* was the first thing Ward noticed on McNeely's desk. He was a little later this morning as he had driven straight to the Honey Pie but it was in darkness. Didn't open till eleven anyway but that didn't calm Ward's nerves, which had been on edge since last night. The story under Pete Larsson's byline carried a photo of Newton, and Ward knew that it would take another notch out of Newton's steadily faltering psyche.

So he was surprised when Newton emerged from his desk as sprightly as a keen young rookie. Newton strode over to McNeely's desk and plucked the newspaper from it and tossed it into the trash can.

"Ward," Newton said, and he walked back to his desk and picked up a box and gestured towards two more. Ward nodded and he picked up the other two boxes. He followed Newton towards the door and just as they had almost reached it, Gammond appeared.

"What you got there?" Gammond said.

Both detectives stopped and turned toward Gammond. Ward looked at Newton.

Newton said, "Just my things. Taking them home."

Gammond stared at the boxes for a long spell and nobody moved. Then Newton took the lid off his box and tilted it towards Gammond. Gammond saw the photographs that Newton had had on his desk. He waved a fat hand at them both and walked to his office.

In the parking lot Newton walked straight to Ward's Alfa Romeo, and Ward put his boxes down and popped the trunk. They put the boxes in the trunk and Newton opened the box with the photos inside. He lifted up the photos and Ward saw the papers relating to the Ryan Novak case concealed beneath them.

"Your wife?" Ward said, and Newton nodded. "We're going out on a limb here."

"I know it."

"Okay. I'll take a look at this later," Ward said, and he dropped the trunk lid.

Back inside the warm station McNeely said to Ward, "We are where we were. We have no meaningful forensics from the first scene. All we got is the latents from the windowsill. We've sent away for DNA tests on those but we won't get the results back for a day or two. Plus, if he's not in the fingerprint database, chances are he won't be in the DNA one. From the second scene we have even less."

Ward said, "Okay. We'll leave the second scene for now. Statements? How we doing with those?" He directed that at Poynter, who leaned on the dividing screen that backed against McNeely's desk. Ward wondered if that was his favorite position in the whole world.

"Everything we got is in the file on your desk, sir," said Poynter, standing up straight just long enough to say it before returning to his perch.

"Okay, I'll go through those. Let's keep looking. There has to be something we haven't found yet. I know it looks like we haven't got a whole lot but now might be time to throw all this in the air and see where it lands. Go back over the evidence. See if there's something we've missed. Look again at the crime scene photos. Try to think if there's anybody else we need to talk to. If we need to ask more questions we go ask them. Somebody out there knows something."

Ward's desk was like his motel room. Stuff still in boxes and arranged neatly, apart from the file containing statements that Poynter had put there. He had barely sat down at his desk since his arrival at the station. Never liked sitting at desks. He figured detective work was best done on foot and not in front of a computer screen. He was tucked into the corner of the open-plan office with a short screen offering minimal privacy. It was department policy. Suggesting openness and accountability. Ward was okay with that as he didn't intend to spend more time than he needed to there. He remained standing as he opened the file of statements.

A half hour later he looked at his watch. And he decided Cherry couldn't be put off. He grabbed his Stetson and coat and made for the door. As he did, Mallory was standing by the water cooler and he stepped in front of Ward and faced up to him.

"I hear you cowboys are all fags," Mallory said through teeth as big, white and gapped as a well-tended picket fence.

Ward wasn't expecting Mallory to be such an outwardly stupid dick as to insult a more senior colleague but he guessed that he had gotten away with being a dick for such a long time that it was accepted around these parts. Mallory was a big man. Tall and well built. But Ward confidently knew that he could drop him with one punch. But he just paused and sighed, looking at Mallory with doe eyes.

"You got nice lips," Ward said, and Mallory stepped back, his lips suddenly pursing and covering up his dazzling teeth until the lips seemed to disappear altogether. He let Ward pass and made a little sound of disgust from the back of his throat. "Catch you later," Ward said.

McNeely had seen the exchange from where she sat eating a salad from a plastic container, and she smiled. Mallory saw her and he stared at her for a couple of seconds then turned and walked.

"Asshole," McNeely said through a mouth full of leaves.

33

The Honey Pie was open for business and Ward felt relieved. But that relief was short-lived as Cherry wasn't there. The girl working was someone called Sally who had been called in to cover Cherry's shift.

"I need her phone numbers, cell and home," Ward said, and Sally eyed him with suspicion until he produced his badge.

"She's okay, right?" said Sally, as she wrote down the numbers on her pad and tore them off.

"Everything's fine, ma'am," Ward said. "I just need to talk to her." And he left the diner and called the cell number. Cherry answered after four rings.

"It's me. Ward," he said, trying not to show too much concern. "How you doing? I just went to the diner and you weren't there."

"I'm fine, detective," Cherry said, and Ward knew she wasn't. Something in her voice. She sounded like she had a mouthful of food but didn't sound like she was chewing. "Why'd you want to see me?"

"You sure you're okay?"

"I said I'm fine."

"Okay," Ward said. "I'm going to come and see

you. You at home?"

"No," Cherry said. "Yes. But I've got—I'm in the middle of something."

"I'm coming."

Cherry became quiet and then Ward thought he heard her choke back tears as she swallowed a couple of times. Maybe she was eating after all.

"Okay," she said.

When Ward got there he saw her glance quickly through the window and she opened the door and walked into the house, Ward following. She had her back to him as she fussed over some dishes in the kitchen sink. Ward approached her slowly and he placed his hand on her shoulder.

"It's okay," he said. "It's okay." And Cherry burst into tears and turned and hugged him. He hugged her back but she winced with pain and he eased off a little. He gently held her there for a minute, maybe two, taking the time to calm himself and to prepare himself for what he knew he was about to see. Cherry let go and stepped back, her eyes cast down to Ward's feet but he could see.

"Aw jeez," Ward said when he saw her face, bruised and bloodied. "Aw jeez." Her left eye was almost closed and was blue and she had a cut that crossed both lips and made it difficult for her to talk. The right-hand side of her face had a swollen blue grazed-up ridge where she had struck something hard, probably as she had fallen. He didn't see what damage there was under her clothes and she wasn't inclined to show him any more than he could already see.

"He came after you'd left," she said. "I told you he would do anything to get a fix. Look what he did. Nice work, huh?"

Ward fought back rage. She noticed it in his eyes and she held his hand.

"It wasn't your fault," she said. "This is what he does. He didn't take much. I didn't have much. Maybe that's why" – and she gestured to her face – "this."

Ward bit his bottom lip and when he finally spoke he spoke through gritted teeth, struggling to part his lips through the anger and the sorrow he felt inside. "I am so sorry," he said. "I'll call this in and get someone out here."

"No," Cherry cried, and again she winced against the pain in her middle. "I don't want that. The cops don't do anything."

And Ward felt even worse at that. He was quiet for a few moments but he knew she wouldn't back down. "Okay," he said. "Okay."

"I don't like the sound of your voice. Don't you do anything. Don't you dare get involved in this… in this shit. It's not your problem. I hardly even know you. Promise me."

He nodded and said, "You have my number now. If he comes back you call me." But he knew Troy wouldn't come back.

Cherry nodded and closed her eyes. When she opened them Ward was gone.

34

Ward entered Bill Bear's Mountain and River Outlet. He bought a pair of ski gloves. The sales assistant asked him, "Would you like a bag for that?"

Ward said, "No," and then, "Actually I will take a bag," and the assistant handed over the gloves in a large plastic bag.

"I'm sorry, it's the only size we have."

"That's fine," Ward said. He left and climbed into his car. He took the gloves out of the bag and stuffed them into his coat pocket. He scrunched up the bag and placed it behind his car seat.

It didn't take Ward long to find the house where Troy was staying. A rundown 1920s house in the west side of town, it was ready for demolition but had had a stay of execution due to City Hall red tape. It had been taken over by squatters of various bad character and degrees of drug addiction. Two women who turned tricks for drug money were the first people he saw when he entered the house without knocking. One sat on the stairs in the hallway smoking a cigarette and the other was standing and she approached Ward and tried to touch his crotch. He knocked her arm away and the whip of his hand almost broke her wrist.

"Motherfucker," said the whore. She was ready to take a swing at Ward but he shoved her away so that she sat on the stair next to her colleague. "Motherfucker," she said again but this time quieter. She took the cigarette from her friend and took a long draw on it.

Ward opened the first door. There were three rooms off this ground-floor corridor. The first room was dark but there were no curtains. The windows had been boarded up on the outside and the only light came from a candle burning in an old jelly jar and the occasional glow of the red tip of a joint that indicated where a body was. He could make out three in the room, spread out on the floor, on old duvets and cardboard boxes. Someone was curled up on two sofa cushions laid end to end to almost make a mattress. The smell offended Ward and he didn't want to stay in there longer than he needed to. He went around each body shape and knew quickly that none of them were Troy. So he left the room and took a deep breath outside. The two whores didn't pay him any attention at all this time.

He made his way into the next room, which appeared to be empty, and then he saw a lump in the corner. He strode over and tore the thin bedsheet away and got a "whatthefuck" for his trouble. It wasn't Troy but a man of about sixty who had no flesh on his bones and no clothes on his body save for an undershirt. Ward left the room and went into the next one, which had once been a kitchen. It was empty of people but full of other detritus which he could just make out as his eyes had adjusted to the gloom – empty beer cans, cigarette butts, empty food tins.

The whores parted, leaning away from each other at the shoulder to let Ward step past and on up the stairs. He reached the upper landing and stopped, reached into his pocket, pulled out the pair of ski gloves and put them on. There were four rooms off the landing, one being a bathroom. He ignored that and gently pushed at the door of the first room. There was somebody in this one. He could smell the rancid body odor and the marijuana smoke. Light entered through a small gap in the boarding on the window and he could make out two bodies, one sitting up but only half-awake and the other curled up in a fetal position.

The half-awake guy looked up at Ward and started to stand but Ward had seen something he recognized lying on the floor next to the other guy so he didn't notice the first guy come over to him. The first thing he knew was the wind displacement caused by a fist flying past his head, just catching enough of his face to register a bit of pain, which cut through Ward's adrenaline-fueled body. Ward waited till the punch had passed him and then he wrenched the arm out of the man's shoulder socket and spun him towards the open door, the arm flopping behind him at an unnatural angle. The bum tumbled out onto the landing, his head crashing against the banister, and he stayed down.

The commotion had brought the other body awake, and it sat up and made a grab for its jacket that lay next to its makeshift bed, the jacket that Ward recognized from the diner. Ward rushed over and stomped on

Troy's wrist, and something crunched and Troy cried out. Ward kicked away the jacket and then kicked out behind him to close the door, and as he did so Troy rolled on the floor, sniffling and cursing and clutching his arm.

Ward took off a glove and reached into his own jacket and drew out his pistol. Troy saw it and he stopped crying and shrunk back into his corner of the room, kicking up dust and narcotic remainders with his scuttling heels. Ward placed the gun on top of an upturned cardboard box that was being used as a makeshift coffee table and placed his hat next to the gun. He slipped the glove back on and in two steps he reached Troy, and Troy whimpered as Ward loomed over him. The first punch struck Troy high on the head and knocked it to one side. The second one struck him full in the face, straightening him up, and the world suddenly became even dimmer for Troy as his brain fought unconsciousness.

Ward wanted him to remain awake, though, so he turned his attention to Troy's body and he let go with two, three, four solid hits to his ribs, feeling more than one bone break under his fists. Troy yelped and cried like a trapped animal and then started gasping for breath. And then Ward hit him once more in the face, this time snapping his nose and he stepped back and Troy lay there, blood spilling from his nose and from a cut below his left eye.

"If you go near her again..." Ward said but he didn't finish the sentence. He took off his gloves, stuffed them into an evidence bag and then back in his pocket and straightened his jacket. He turned and picked up his hat from the cardboard box and put it on and then slowly made his way to the door, where he stopped. He heard Troy move behind him and when he turned around Troy had his gun. Ward could see blood coming from his mouth and right ear now and Troy held the gun shakily in his good hand, the other one hanging by his side. Ward just stared at Troy and then Troy pulled the trigger. An empty click broke the silence. Troy gaped at the gun for a second or two, struggling to draw breath, and then he pulled the trigger four more times, all giving him dull, ineffective clicks. Ward stepped toward him and Troy dropped the weapon and then sank to the floor, a piss stain spreading on the front of his jogging pants.

"If I had come with a loaded gun I couldn't be sure I wouldn't have killed you. Next time be assured that the gun will be loaded." He holstered the gun and left Troy with those words ringing in his already ringing ears.

35

A freezing wind blew into the station as Ward opened the door, and a few tiny ice crystals followed. He thought it wouldn't be long before there was a serious snowfall. Since he had arrived from Texas he hadn't really been much troubled by the cold but now he felt it seeping into his bones. He felt sick and his head throbbed in time with his heartbeat and he slumped into his chair and suddenly felt woozy. He closed his eyes for a few seconds and when he opened them he noticed that the middle knuckle on his right hand was showing signs of swelling and a dull ache spread up from it to his wrist. Shouldn't be broken, but he would put something frozen on it later. He tried to recall what he had done to Troy but couldn't. He remembered arriving at the house but everything after that was a blur. He vaguely remembered throwing the ski gloves in a dumpster.

He looked around the station and saw that Newton wasn't around. McNeely was eating an apple and Ward wondered if she ever stopped eating. Poynter called her Big Mac, which was an ironic moniker as she was skinny and small but she could eat her way through a ten-course meal and still stop somewhere on the way home for a late bite.

He caught her eye and she gave him a long searching look. She came over and said, "You look like shit."

"Thanks," Ward said.

"Things gone quiet around here," she said.

"So I see."

McNeely took a bite of her apple and her eyes lingered on Ward. "So, what's the story?"

"Too long to tell."

She nodded as if she understood. "Well, it's quiet around here." She took another bite of the apple and gave Ward space to come back. He didn't. He took off his hat and massaged his temples.

"Hand looks kinda swollen," she said. "You should get something cold on that."

"I know," Ward said, but he didn't offer any more and McNeely retreated back to her desk.

On her way back she shouted, "So goddamn quiet around here. We should party!" and Ward struggled a smile.

Then he saw the note on his desk – a telephone message to call the reporter Pete Larsson. He screwed it up and tossed it in the direction of the trash can but it fell short. He picked it up on his way out and he slam-dunked it this time.

36

He'd brought in the three boxes of material related to the little boy's disappearance and Jesús had watched him do it, following him around but never going out the door.

Ward sat on the bed and opened the first box of three – witness statements.

It was an hour later when he next looked up. Jesús was asleep with one eye that kept opening now and then to look at Ward.

Already he had two or three people he would like to talk to who had offered statements. Nothing really jumped out on a first read and he would take a second pass over it all but one thing that struck him was how the boy just happened to vanish into thin air. There were possible sightings here and there in the following days, all of which would have been followed up, but he knew from these kinds of cases that most sightings would prove to be fruitless. And numbers of sightings where a child was involved tended to be higher. People wanted to find him and they wanted to help. But every false sighting was a waste of resources and a distraction to the focus of the search. And it could result in the police being diverted away from the real location of the boy and sent on a wild goose chase across the county or even state. He'd seen it before.

But this case was different. Yes, there were sightings, and lots of them, but none of them convinced Ward on first reading. Apart from one. The boy had been seen talking to another boy the afternoon he'd disappeared. That boy turned out to be called Percy Mallory. Mallory had said he'd seen Ryan crying and had asked what was the matter but Ryan wasn't in no mood to talk and that was that. He was probably the last person to see Ryan alive apart from his abductor. It wasn't a lead. Just told Ward that this was a small town where everybody was connected with everybody. And he knew he couldn't go talk to Mallory. Knew Mallory would probably go running straight to Gammond to tell him Ward was digging in areas he shouldn't be.

Way he was feeling it, the boy had probably been abducted and murdered soon after. Probably picked up by a predator, a pedophile, and whisked away to his death. Probably buried somewhere in the woods and unlikely ever to be found save by worms. Best hope was that an animal would dig him up and uncover enough of him to be discovered by someone out hiking. But that hadn't happened yet and was now an unlikely scenario.

So where had he gone? Who had taken him? Was it the old man Bill O'Donnell, his own grandfather? He'd suddenly found God just before Ryan was reported missing. On the same day as he was out searching for his missing truck. Newton was right. It did seem odd, but it wasn't conclusive.

Was it someone else did it who then paid O'Donnell for his silence? The monthly payments to Alice White might be classed as suspicious. Was that where he was getting his money from? Maybe it was a guilty conscience made him hand money over to Alice for her work with children. Or the old man might just have been very generous. Nothing definite to say he'd received a payoff.

Ward decided he would investigate that angle anyway. It added up to a lot of money on a janitor's salary. Up to now he hadn't much else but he would carry on digging to see what was uncovered. He wrote a list out of people he would like to re-interview. A man who said he saw something weird on the night of his disappearance. The principal at the school where O'Donnell was janitor. Alice White again.

He wanted to interview O'Donnell himself but he would have to rely on the interview transcripts from Newton's interrogations. Was there anything in there that Newton had missed? Anything he had said that maybe should have been followed up? Newton's instinct had maybe been right after all and O'Donnell could possibly have had some involvement. But he remained unconvinced that O'Donnell had killed the boy. That still didn't seem to fit.

He opened the next of the three boxes. Newton's case notes and various reports in this one. Ward started to flick through them and one name was prominent throughout. William O'Donnell. He tracked Newton's growing obsession with the man and seeming desperation as he turned page after page and his headache got worse and he felt cold and lifeless.

37

Newton's SUV pulled into the parking lot of Sunny Glade. He cut his headlights and the world was an oppressive gloom. When he stepped out of the vehicle, he looked up at the sky and ice crystals fell onto his face and he shivered and hurried into the reception lobby. Jackie, the receptionist, greeted him with a smile. She knew him most recently from the photograph on the front of the *Westmoreland Echo*.

Newton picked up a brochure from the counter and flicked pages over and then put it back. He saw the yucca plant and the orchids but he didn't know if they were real, they were so perfect.

"Is there anything I can help you with today, sir?" she asked.

Newton said, "I'm just going to have a look around. Mr. O'Donnell's room." And then he saw the look in Jackie's eyes. The one that said you let one of our children be taken and you didn't catch the son of a bitch that took him. But she continued to smile and Newton shrugged off the feeling he had. Maybe he was imagining it.

"No problem. If I could just get you to sign the

guestbook," she said.

"Of course," Newton said, and then, "Say, would you mind if I took a look at that?" He signed the book and flicked back to the night the old man died. Was murdered. "Everybody who visits signs this, right?"

"That's right, sir."

"So this here is a record of everybody who visited on the night Mr. O'Donnell died?"

"Yes."

"You were working that night, right?"

"That's correct. I already spoke to that other police," Jackie said.

"No, that's fine. I just wanted to go over what we know just to be a hundred percent. Cross the t's and dot the i's."

"I understand that," she said.

"I don't see Mr. Kenny's signature on here. He said he was here that night. He always not sign in?"

"He's the owner. He doesn't need to sign in."

"Okay, that's fine," Newton said. "What time did he arrive?"

"I didn't see him arrive, but I saw him leave," Jackie said, and Newton's head snapped up.

"You didn't see him arrive? He come through a back entrance?"

"Only one entrance and this is it. Back door is locked off from the outside in. It's an emergency exit only."

"So how'd he get in?" Newton was trying not to sound too interrogatory and he smiled to reinforce that.

"I guess he walked in," Jackie's smile was a distant memory now.

"But you would've seen him, no?"

Jackie pulled herself upright and said quietly, "You know, I have to take restroom breaks."

"Of course you do. That's fine. Don't worry, you haven't done anything wrong. Like I said, I just need to double-check everything just to get this thing right in my own head," Newton said, and he turned the book back around and pushed it back to Jackie. "I'll just go take a look at the room now."

"Go ahead," Jackie said, and then Grainger, the manager, appeared.

"Detective," he said. "The other detective asked me to do a full inventory of the pharmacy. I got that in back if you can wait."

Newton nodded and Grainger went into a door behind the reception which led to an office. He emerged with a few sheets of paper with a computer printout showing names of drugs Newton had never heard of but suspected he would in a few years' time.

"This is the full list and I did a check against what we dispensed and everything tallies. Yes, sir. Nothing missing."

"That's great, thanks. Am I okay to take this?"

"That's your copy. Yes, sir," Grainger said. Newton took the report from Grainger and turned to go.

"Say, I don't suppose we can take down that tape on the door? You know something like that can get the other residents a little jittery. If that's okay. I don't want to—"

"Of course, I'll take care of that," Newton said, and this time he left Grainger and Jackie, who looked ready for a restroom break. He heard Grainger say "Yes, sir" behind him as he strode down the corridor and a ripple of music tumbled towards him from one of the recreation rooms and it sounded like something from the 1950s. Nostalgia was keeping these old people alive. Newton wondered if there was any part of his life that he'd feel nostalgic about.

He tore down the tape from outside the door and stepped in, pausing in the doorway. The room was untouched since he had last been there. The picture of Bermuda had been taken away as evidence, though what relevance it might have Newton couldn't figure out. McNeely was thorough. The bed was still ruffled from where someone had sat and Newton sat there now and as he did he stretched his back and he felt a twinge but not really pain, just a tightness. Progress, he thought, and at once he didn't feel so bad.

He looked around and took in everything and didn't see anything. He stood and went over to the window and looked down at the sill where McNeely had taken the latent prints. He looked beyond that into the grounds and wondered how tall someone would have to be to get in that window. He decided he couldn't see and so he left the room and tossed the police tape behind him.

Outside the building he picked his way around a narrow footpath, not designed for residents but for the gardener to tend his plants. His head reached just above the bottom of each window and he knew that whoever entered the old man's room was tall or very agile. That seemed to rule out James Kenny. He had no need to clamber through windows anyway as he had a free pass to the place. They hadn't gone as far as taking elimination prints yet. Newton thought Ward might insist on that soon though and piss Kenny off even more.

He turned around and was about to make his way back when he saw the man at the top of a small incline which was landscaped with grass and rose beds. The man wore something that had a hood and Newton started to walk towards him and the man started to walk away. Newton picked up his pace and so too did the hooded figure and by the time Newton started to run the man had already made his move.

Newton knew there was a wall in the direction the man was running and he lengthened his stride to try to catch him before he could make it over the wall. And then the man slipped on the moist grass, which had a fresh covering of ice crystals, and Newton again tried to lengthen his stride. As he did so he gulped in cold air which seemed to burn his chest and each lungful of air was harder to grab than the next and he felt the lactic acid building in his legs.

But he pushed on and he was now only a few yards short of the man as the man picked himself off the ground, leaving a large divot of grass behind where his boots had gained purchase. And then the man was off again, and he started to pull away from Newton as the wall got closer. A pain started to form in Newton's chest and seemed to spiral around inside his ribs before settling into a searing stab just beneath his breast bone. He momentarily pulled up and the air in his lungs seemed to catch there. He couldn't exhale and suddenly adrenaline took its own stab at his heart and the air rushed out of him and he took another few short gulps of air and the pain receded.

And then he set off again but by now the man was at the wall, where he paused and looked back at

Newton. He pulled down his hood and revealed the ghost of Ryan Novak. Newton stopped dead and just stared and blinked heavily twice to clear his eyes as the cold air swirled around him and scratched at his cheeks, which were turning redder. He wanted to say something but he couldn't find the breath to make the words. His chest heaved and ached and he thought he saw the man who looked like Ryan Novak take a step towards him. Newton rested his hands on his knees and wondered if he would fall over as his head felt like it was filled with helium.

When the man turned and climbed carefully over the wall Newton didn't move and didn't speak. He stared at the wall and wanted to cry out, but the cry was inside him and it rattled around his heart, and then he did slump down untidily and sat on the damp grass. The slope of the grass bank, coupled with gravity, forced him to lie down, and he looked up at the ice crystals, which continued to fall, millions of them, each catching the glow coming from the security lights that shone over the grounds of Sunny Glade. And then Newton realized that the man had held on to one of the light poles to help himself over the wall. He called McNeely. There must be prints on it.

Ward was driving but he still didn't feel good. He had the passenger window half-down and the freezing wind circled his head. His head had started to clear a little and the pain in his temples had subsided. But he felt very tired and his bones were lead-lined.

He had received a call from Cherry. She had asked if he would go pick up Laurie from Troy's parents' home in Bozeman. Didn't know who else to ask. He had immediately said yes. Cherry especially didn't want Troy's father to see her in the state she was in and Ward agreed that was probably wise. But the mention of Troy poured on the weariness and made him wince at the pain in his swollen knuckle, which he looked at now as he drove.

He rolled down the window on his side of the car and tried to stick his damaged right hand out of it but couldn't quite reach across himself to do it, and then the cold was too much for him and he rolled both windows back up. Speeding cars passed him every now and then and disappeared into the distance. A salt truck overtook him slowly and rock salt pattered damagingly against his car but he was too weary to curse.

His cell phone rang and he slowed a little and answered it. Newton still sounded short of breath and Ward was concerned about his shaky voice but said nothing.

"I have just seen someone who may be important to both cases," breathed Newton.

"Go on," Ward said.

"I saw him before back at the doctor's house but I didn't say anything then. I gotta tell you I thought I was seeing a ghost but I just seen him again."

"Who? Who did you see?" Ward asked and he realized he had pulled over.

"Ryan Novak."

Ward didn't answer at first because he thought he had misheard. Before he could ask Newton to repeat what he had said Newton had already repeated the name.

"I don't understand," Ward said.

"Neither do I, but I saw him just now and I saw him back there too."

"Did you talk to him?"

"He ran," Newton said. "He ran but then he stopped and he looked at me and it was him."

"Hold on. Let me think." Ward put the wounded knuckle to his lips and blew on it to cool it.

"Ain't nothing to think about, Ward. Ryan Novak was right there in front of me. Could tell he was an O'Donnell by his features."

"But you could be mistaken. It was twenty-five years ago. How could you be sure?"

"I know."

"So there is no Ryan Novak murder investigation no more, that what you're telling me? The kid's still alive and well?"

Newton was silent for a moment and then he said, "I don't know. I just don't know what the hell to think right now. My ass is soaking wet and I fell over and I feel old again, Ward. I feel old."

38

Alice White heard a noise and she stopped reading. She listened carefully and all was quiet. And then the noise again. A tapping on a window. She put down the newspaper and levered herself off her chair. She paused to let the strength come back into her gone-to-sleep legs. She hobbled over to the living room door and then the tapping came again from the kitchen. She turned on the hall light and shuffled to the back of the house. When she entered the kitchen she could see a figure beyond the door that led into the kitchen. She flicked on the light.

"Is that you?" Alice called. She fiddled with the key in the lock and then opened the door. The man stood there freezing.

"Yes, it's me, Ma," the man said, and he pulled down his hood and clapped his hands together to get some blood running through them. His face was a compendium of turmoil.

"Everything all right?" Alice asked.

"He saw me, Ma," he said.

"Who saw you?"

"The policeman. The old policeman. I was up at the

old people place and…"

Alice stared into the space at the side of the man and her eyes lingered there for a few seconds and then she looked back at him.

"Well, what's done is done. Did he recognize you?" Alice asked, and she held his hand and frowned at how cold it was and then she rubbed it.

"He maybe… I think so," the man said, and then, "Did I do something wrong, Ma? Do I need to go away?"

"No, no, of course not. The Lord showed you to him and this is all part of His plan." She took his other hand and started to rub that one. "You're cold as death. Come on, let's warm you up."

39

The Bozeman residence of Troy's parents was prairie Victorian style with an acre of impeccably landscaped garden which was tidy even though it was winter ravaged. A huge storage shed sat at the edge of the garden and a raised gazebo sat center stage, waiting to be used again come springtime.

The snowy mountain peaks loomed behind the house, their white tops obscured by sunken sky. Aged snow still lurked in corners of the garden, hardened to white icy crusts. When Ward stepped out of his car his breath seemed to freeze as it came out and he figured it was probably five degrees colder here. His hand throbbed. Troy's father Joe opened the door before Ward got there and he called out to Ward.

"What's your business before you come any further there?"

"I'm Ward. Come to pick up Laurie, sir. Cherry called?"

"You're a cop," Joe said, and Ward wasn't sure if it was a statement or a question but he automatically pulled out his badge and held it up for Troy's father to see.

"I don't need to see your badge. Cherry's say-so is good enough for me. Are you going to come in?"

Ward said, "Yes, sir, please," and he saw Laurie twitching a curtain and he smiled at her. She disappeared and when Ward entered the house she was there, standing behind Troy's mom, Dorothy.

"What did the son of a bitch do this time? That's why you're here."

Ward looked at little Laurie and wasn't sure how to proceed. He just said, "Aw, she had a fall and —"

"Bullshit," Joe said.

"Joseph," Dorothy said. "No need to curse."

"I'll curse. She's heard it before," Joe said.

"From you, mainly," Dorothy said.

"He beat her up?" Joe said to Ward.

Again, with Laurie standing there Ward wasn't sure what to say. So he didn't say anything.

"She already knows what a son of a bitch her father is."

"Joseph," Dorothy said again and Joe relented.

"Come in, Ward. You got a first name?"

"Ward will do, I reckon," Ward said. "It's what everybody calls me."

The house was spacious and extremely tidy and Ward liked that. The entrance hall was clad with wood from floor to ceiling. Ward was led into the large living room, which displayed various hunting artifacts and an elk's head on the wall. They all sat except Laurie, who stood behind her grandfather's chair.

"You like to hunt?" Joe asked.

"I used to like it some."

"What did you hunt?"

"Well, sir, I would hunt deer and hog mostly and

the occasional turkey," Ward said, and he detected a thawing in Troy's father's demeanor. "I fished too."

"You a good shot?"

"I would say so, sir. Better with a rifle than a fishing pole."

"You done military service?" Joe said.

"Yes, sir."

"Where did you serve?"

"I did tours of Iraq and Afghanistan," Ward said, and his face darkened at the mention of that.

"Army? Marine?"

"I was Infantry, sir. Sniper."

"Kills?" Joe asked, and Ward took a deep breath.

"Oh, I don't know."

"Bullshit," Joe said, and this time Dorothy just frowned an 'I give up' frown. "Sniper knows how many men he's killed. You guys keep a tally. Had one friend was a sniper and he kept a book. Described every single kill in detail."

"It's not something I usually discuss," Ward said, and Joe's eyes seemed to twinkle above a faint smile but he let it go.

"I was in the Marine Corps myself. Would have still been if I hadn't have been retired off. I could still do a job out in Afghanistan."

Ward nodded respectfully.

"You want to see my guns?" Joe asked, and Ward didn't feel he could refuse.

Ward said goodbye to Dorothy as she fastened up Laurie's coat and Laurie stood patiently and quietly without a hint of a fidget.

Dorothy said, "He's still my son, you know."

Ward fixed his hat in place. "I know."

All fastened up, Laurie grabbed the handle of her miniature pink suitcase and took hold of Ward's left hand. At the door Troy's father held out his right hand to shake Ward's and Ward offered it without thinking. He almost cried out in pain under Joe's grip and his knees buckled slightly. Joe let go quickly and he stepped back and his eyes lingered on Ward's. He slowly nodded his head at Ward and Ward turned and walked to his car, hand in hand with Laurie, his right hand throbbing and suddenly very hot, and tears freezing in the corners of his eyes.

40

Lieutenant Gammond wasn't observant for a cop. Newton had always felt he'd been lucky to rise up the ranks as he did and he found it hard to give him his respect. A feeling at the back of his mind scratched away from time to time and told Newton that Gammond had stolen his job. But he lived with it. The failure twenty-five years ago had thrown a spike strip under Newton's career, or that's how he saw it anyway.

But Gammond didn't see the anguish on Newton's face as he entered his office. He merely waved a hand and gestured towards the chair on the other side of his desk. Newton sat down instead on a chair on the other side of the room, by the door. Ordinarily Newton wouldn't have sat but he did this time. Something else that an observant cop would've picked up on. In fact, he didn't sit, he slumped. Gammond waved his hand again and Newton understood it to mean he wanted the door closed so he leaned to his left and shoved the door and it latched gently.

"Bring me up to speed on the O'Donnell case," Gammond said, and for a moment Newton was back in

1985 and heavy-lidded eyes cast up at Gammond and he was confused. He expected to see Lieutenant Carson sitting there, his bald head nodding too readily in that way it did as he listened intently to Newton's excuses for not finding the boy. Not getting close to a satisfactory resolution. Newton scratched his head briskly and looked around the office to get his bearings and suddenly he raced across twenty-five years and was back in the room.

"You want me to send Ward in when he gets back?"

"No, I want you to tell me."

"Progress is slow" is all Newton managed and Gammond nodded and Newton again thought of Lieutenant Carson.

"Any suspects?" Gammond said.

"Nobody of any great interest," Newton said, and he fished out his pain relief medication bottle but there was only one pill left. He threw it back and swallowed.

"You spoke to James Kenny."

"Right," Newton said as the pill went down slowly.

"He a suspect?"

"No."

"Said you had him cornered up there at the school and you did interrogate him some."

"Wasn't much of an interrogation if that's what he's told you."

"What's the angle there? Any?"

"Simply that he owns the nursing home. It was just procedural stuff, you know."

Carson nodded vigorously and Newton wanted to grab him and shake his stupid head off and then he realized it wasn't Carson at all but Gammond.

Gammond said, "Okay, good, right, well, let's try

and wrap this up quickly as possible."

And Newton thought he might get a pat on the head, "good dog", and tossed a biscuit.

"And the other case. The boy."

Newton was going to say Ward had that but he snatched his words back just in time. "We're not looking at that."

Gammond stared at Newton for a few beats and then nodded. "Good."

Newton didn't mention that he had just seen the boy, grown up.

Gammond seemed to have lost interest and he started to fuss papers around on his desk so Newton concluded that the meeting was over. He rose slowly from his chair, and as he did Gammond's phone rang. Before Newton could get his brittle body out of the room Gammond said, "Dang shit, we have a situation," and his face flushed as he stood. "I better go get the captain."

41

The shellac has dried up in the can. Bill O'Donnell pokes around in the bottom of the can with a stick to loosen the dried-up bits and he adds some paint thinner which has lasted better than the shellac. He stirs and as he does so he casts around for something else he can make use of. An old can of paint, some varnish, some wood preserver. He gathers it up and pours everything into an old tub that once stored flour and he concocts a cocktail of various fluids and the vapors sting his nose and his dried-out throat which feels like it's lined with tree bark. He realizes he hasn't drunk or eaten anything for hours and he wonders what the mixture in front of him might taste like. He finds a large paintbrush which has stiffened over time but hasn't rotted and he goes to work on it to try and soften it up. He scrunches the bristles and taps them on the old stone sink and one or two bristles break off but enough stay in place and then he's ready.

The boy is still wrapped in the sheet, which is now showing the camouflage grime of the journey. He lifts him and the tiny body is stiff and he's desperate that it doesn't crack and shatter into a million parts and crumble to dust and blow away on the breeze that has picked up now.

He cradles him for half a mile through thick undergrowth

and he goes up and up above the cabin where he had once lived during a previous lifetime when things were good and things were simple – until his wife died and set him on a journey into civilization and on the road which eventually led to him burying his grandson.

He comes to a small clearing where the tree canopy opens up and is mostly below his feet and the ground has a covering of grass and the hole that he has dug is so small he thinks he will have to make it bigger but when he lays the boy next to it the hole seems so large. He stands there a while and he looks around over the tops of the trees which waltz on the wind. He hears the birds now and their songs trill innocence and he thinks it's a fitting requiem. He wants to say a prayer but he isn't sure how to do it so he just speaks the word "sorry".

He sees in the distance a thin pillar of smoke – five, six, seven miles away and for a moment he thinks he's being followed but then he realizes what it is. A lightning strike from the previous night has lit the dried-out trunk of a dead pine and a fire is spreading on the wind.

He goes about his work now, tightening the sheet and tying it with the rope in a crisscross pattern. Then he dips the brush into the cocktail he has created and he begins to paint the bundle and he feels light-headed and he puts it down to the fumes.

After he has applied one coat he sits and rests. The dry wind has crusted the tears in the corners of his eyes and he doesn't cry again and he wonders if he will ever cry again.

He sits for an hour and then he paints on another coat and then he sits for another hour and he begins to feel hungry.

Gently, he lowers the boy into the grave and his hands are sticky with the mummification mixture so he rubs dirt on them and wipes them on the grass. With the spade he starts to cover the body. The dirt and stones thud against the tiny package and gradually the body is covered and the level of the soil rises as the earth swallows the boy until there is a small mound. He pats the mound with the back of the spade and then he stands up and walks away, picking up the tub and brush and making his way back to the cabin, where he leaves them and he leaves the cabin and returns to the boat and rows.

He retraces his journey on foot now and the smoke is no longer a pillar but a cloud and it's getting closer and he can smell it. He picks up his discarded flashlight on the old lumber track where he left it.

It's hours later when he reaches his truck and he sits inside it and closes his eyes but sleep doesn't come. The smoke from the fire spreads through the forest like a creeping fog now and the wind is blowing directly towards him and so he starts up the truck and he drives into the forest and when the forest blocks further entry he turns off the engine and he leaves the truck and he walks away.

He passes cotton wool pockets of thick smoke which have settled in sheltered dips and then he sees the glow of flames ahead like the glow from a huge sodium-vapor street lamp and as he gets closer the late afternoon gets warmer and he hears the voices of firefighters so he turns south and picks his way through thick plantation forest until he reaches another small track. The fire spreads west behind him and the thickening black smoke veils the sun and the sky is dried blood and he thinks that he smells like a resident of Hell.

42

Laurie didn't look at her mother when she opened the door but just squirted past her and went straight to her room. The bruising on Cherry's face had changed color and Ward regarded her with pity but she wouldn't be pitied.

"You okay?" Ward said.

"I'm alive," Cherry said, and she held his hand but he flinched as she did so. She turned the hand over in hers and a blue tinge stained the swollen knuckles.

"I told you to leave it alone," she said. "Didn't I tell you?"

Ward's face was empty and he didn't say anything.

"I said to leave it alone. Fuck, why did you get involved? I told you. Why? Answer me, why?"

Ward took a half step back as Cherry got in his face.

"You want a gratitude fuck, that it? Here. Take it. It's what men do, isn't it? Take what you want. Don't mind me." She started to lift her dress and Ward's hand stopped her. She started to sob.

"He's lucky," Ward said after a few moments and then he said, "I gotta go."

* * *

It was Newton who met Ward in the station parking lot and he said, "Go talk to Larsson."

Ward said, "I didn't think you two got on."

Newton said, "We don't but that don't make him a bad reporter."

Ward considered that for a moment and then Newton said, "It was me who tipped him off. I leaked the O'Donnell story."

"Why would you do that?"

"Why would I do that? I wanted to get some interest back in the Ryan case. I knew Larsson would help me do that."

"So, that fainting fit. That was a ruse?"

Newton didn't say anything.

"You been checked over recently?"

Newton waved the question away and said, "There's something else."

"What's going on?" Ward asked.

"There's been a complaint against you. The captain and lieutenant are waiting inside. Look, speak to Larsson. He knows this case as well as anybody, better than me maybe."

"I thought you saw the boy?"

"I don't know what I saw. I just don't know anymore. Just... none of it adds up. It don't make sense. Just speak to Larsson. Don't go causing any big ripples that are going to come back to Gammond. I don't know where we are with any of it is the truth." Newton put his hand on Ward's shoulder but Ward thought he'd done it to steady himself. Ward took a deep breath and prepared himself for the bullshit.

* * *

Troy's injuries were worse than Ward thought. The hospital report, read out to him by Captain Mumford, detailed four broken ribs, a fractured cheekbone, a broken nose, three shattered teeth which had to be removed and a perforated eardrum.

"Obviously, there will be an inquiry," Gammond said. "And obviously, you are suspended until that inquiry is done with. Dang it, son, you can't go assaulting people willy-nilly like. This ain't Texas."

Captain Mumford, a likeable old man despite his fearsome appearance – something about him reminded Ward of his grandfather – never let his eyes wander from Ward.

"What happened?" the captain asked.

Ward said, "Sir, if it sits okay with you, I would rather wait for Internal Affairs."

Captain Mumford tapped his forefinger on the desk slowly. "I want to help you, son, as much as I can, but if you don't talk to me there's not a great deal I can do."

Ward said, "I appreciate that, sir. Very much."

"The boy was a dang mess, Ward. Like a butcher's leftovers," Lieutenant Gammond said, but Ward just looked at Mumford.

Captain Mumford said, "Lieutenant Gammond will take your badge and weapon and explain the disciplinary procedure in more detail."

"Thank you, sir," Ward said.

43

Newton sat in his SUV for a half hour outside his home and tried to empty his mind. He knew she had seen him, had heard the engine ticking over, but she'd left him there and only checked through the blinds once to see who it was.

He opened the door and his wife, Maggie, was cooking dinner. He could smell it. But the smell made his stomach tumble. He tossed his keys into a porcelain bowl by the door and he took his coat off and hung it up. He thought he felt thin.

"Smells nice," he tried, and she played along.

"Aww, it's only beef casserole," Maggie said, and she giggled ticklishly as he swept her red hair to one side and kissed her on her neck.

"You say 'only' as though it isn't going to be the most spectacular culinary experience on this very planet, as it always is."

"You're just too kind. I don't deserve you," Maggie said, and she turned and looked him in the eyes and tried not to cry but a tear betrayed her. But Newton played along with the game and he ignored the tear.

"My mother said all along that I was too good for

you," Newton said.

"And my father said exactly the same thing, that I was too good for you," Maggie said, and the other eye sprang a leak. She wiped her eyes with the bottom of her apron and Newton grabbed her and held her close.

"Oh, what have I done to deserve this?" Maggie asked, and she cried and Newton's body jerked as he wept silently.

"Just hold me, please," Newton said, and they both sobbed twenty-five years of tears.

"I know it's happening again. The case of the little boy. All I ask," Maggie said, "all I've ever asked is that you leave something for me. Leave some years for me. For us." And they sobbed and they hugged and the beef casserole smelled like a fabulous last meal.

Newton had pushed the food around on his plate but had managed to eat some and Maggie didn't say anything about his appetite. They ate in silence mostly but Newton asked if his son, Phil, had been over today and Maggie said he had and he'd brought some flowers and she'd asked him what the occasion was. Phil had said there didn't have to be an occasion to buy his mother flowers and Newton nodded agreement at that. Newton asked if Phil was okay, like asking about an old acquaintance, and Maggie said that he was and was looking at a promotion soon.

His cell phone rang and he looked at the clock as he answered. It was McNeely.

"Sir, I've got something," she said.

"What is it? Did you lift some prints from the light pole?"

"I did and... well, it's interesting," McNeely said.

"Go on."

"I ran them through the database and there were no hits."

Newton sank into his chair.

"But then I checked them against the latents from the old man's windowsill. And we got a match. This is our guy," she said.

"Are you sure?"

"Hell, yeah. One hundred percent."

Newton hung up the phone. He ate a large forkful of food. The man he thought was Ryan Novak was the person who had left numerous prints on the windowsill of Bill O'Donnell's room. He had visited the old man, his grandfather, on more than one occasion judging by the number of prints. And he'd come in through the window. But Newton doubted that he had killed him. And anyway, how could a dead boy kill anyone? None of it made any sense to Newton. None of anything made any sense at the moment. He heard the knock on the door but he was swimming in his own thoughts until Mallory broke the trance.

"I let myself in."

"Percy, you don't need to say that every time you come over," Maggie said. "You are too polite sometimes."

Mallory smiled. "I forgot to stamp my feet and take off my boots," he said.

"Ain't too late," Maggie said. Mallory turned to leave the room and Maggie called him back. "You're in now. Just wipe them on that rug there."

"Hey, Dad," Mallory called over to Newton with a passing glance. Newton nodded. "Say, something smells nice."

"We just ate. There's a little left in the pot but I'm not sure Jen will appreciate me filling you up."

"Aww, I don't want to cause a fight."

"I'll get you a small plate," Maggie said, and she stood. Mallory sat at the table and shrugged his coat off over the back of the chair. He blew on his hands.

"Winter's a cold one," Mallory said.

"Ain't it just," Maggie said.

"What brings you over?" Newton said.

"I was passing."

Maggie brought the small plate of food and cutlery to the table. She took away the other plates. Mallory put his arm around his plate and shoveled a forkful of food into his mouth.

Newton watched him closely as he had watched him when he knew him as Percy, the little boy who had been a constant reminder of Ryan Novak. Jen had been in his thrall like their other school friends. The young Percy had become a school celebrity, a macabre link to the missing boy, and for a while that celebrity gave him head table status when the kids picked their play friends. When Jen had first brought him home to play, Newton had voiced concern to Maggie. There was something odd about the boy, Newton had said, and Maggie had said he was being unkind.

"He's a child and Lord knows he's gone through a lot with this whole tragic business," Maggie said. "Let them play. Innocence don't last a whole long time, the speed they grow up these days. It'll do the boy good to have a friend like Jen."

Newton lost the argument and saw the boy and his daughter growing closer as they passed into their teens and by the time he realized they were officially dating he had a sit-down chat with young Percy to warn him he must be a gentleman at all times. Percy was the most polite boy Newton had met. Always said "sir" and "ma'am" and Maggie seemed to like that and she was fond of Percy, Newton could see that. So he let it play out, expecting Jen to start seeing other boys one day. As soon as Percy became Officer Mallory the engagement was announced and Newton accepted the situation with grace. Mallory had, of course, asked Newton for Jen's hand in marriage and how could he say no? He'd let Mallory in and now Mallory just let himself in.

"Say, how's the investigation?" Mallory asked Newton through a mouthful of food.

"Not my investigation," Newton said.

"Okay," Mallory said. "You think it'll get wrapped up before you retire?"

Newton didn't say anything.

"Station won't be the same without you."

"It'll survive."

"Not sure the new guy will. He's a fancy so and so ain't he."

Newton didn't mention that Ward had a charge hanging over him. Mallory had run out of food and run out of words and he just sat there at the table like a nervous teenager waiting for his date to sweep down the stairs in her prom dress.

44

When Ward walked into the Honey Pie with Jesús he caught Cherry's eye but she turned away. The place was only a quarter busy and he hovered at the counter for a few minutes before Cherry acknowledged him.

"What can I get you?" she said.

"You okay?"

"What can I get you?" Her battered face was fixed hard.

"Ma'am, I will take a beer," Ward said, and he removed his hat and placed it on the counter.

"And a bowl of water?"

"Yes, ma'am."

Cherry went out back and returned with a bowl of water, which she placed in front of Jesús and he started to slop at it with his tongue. She snatched the top off a bottle of beer and thunked it on the counter so that froth came spilling out of the top. Ward picked up the bottle and took a long drink. Cherry hung around and watched him drink.

"Hand looks hurtful," she said.

"Hurts plenty," Ward said.

"I ain't thanking you."

"Don't want no thanks."

Cherry looked like she wanted to swing at Ward and looked broken at the same time.

"Why'd you come back here?" she said.

"Dog likes the water," Ward said, and he saw a softening in Cherry.

"It's not good for business," Cherry said after a few moments.

Ward said, "What isn't?"

"This," Cherry said, gesturing at her face. "It's scaring people off, putting them off their food. Takings are down." She winced and put her hand up to her busted lip. "So what do you do now?"

"Well, Troy made a complaint against me and there will be an investigation," Ward said.

"Will you get into trouble?"

Ward shrugged. "I guess we'll have to wait and see. It's his word against mine."

"Weren't there any witnesses?" Cherry asked.

"I guess so, but would you take the word of an addict or a whore over the word of a cop? I'll be okay. Just a bit of inconvenience is all."

"You better hope you're right."

Ward touched her arm and she pulled it away. "I would do it again."

Cherry said, "I know you would and that's what worries me."

"Don't fret about me," Ward said. "I can just about take care of myself."

"That why you're living in a motel?"

"That's just a temporary measure," Ward said. "I'm thinking of taking a look at some real estate. Might put me down some new roots."

"So you're sticking around."

Ward said, "Yes, ma'am."

A party of four entered the diner. Ward picked up his hat and put it on.

One of the new customers whispered, "Table for four," and gawked at Cherry's injuries as she directed them to a table.

Ward tipped his hat at Cherry and said, "Ma'am," and he left and he felt her eyes on his back all the way out of the Honey Pie.

45

Ward hadn't needed to call Larsson. He'd somehow got Ward's cell number. He thought Newton. They'd set up a meeting for the next morning. Ward had asked for somewhere out of town. Larsson knew a place – a truck stop on the I-15 highway.

When Ward pulled into the parking lot of the truck stop Larsson was already there, shivering and smoking a cigarette, which he took a large double draw on before tossing the butt into a puddle. Larsson held out his hand but Ward didn't take it.

"Have you had that hand looked at?" Larsson asked, and Ward ignored the question. "Could be broken."

Ward looked him up and down. He was a weasel. He might have been five ten but he stooped to five six and snowman eyes fixed Ward and asked questions before they'd even started. His gray hair was swept back and up, presumably held by hairspray, and it offered patchy coverage in places. His teeth seemed sharp and small. More gum than tooth. He made an attempt to dress for the job but his tie was loose and his top button was open. He looked like he needed a dry clean.

A tractor, minus its trailer, revved as it passed them heading towards the pumps. Larsson stepped back to avoid getting his hundred-dollar suit splashed as it drove over the winter-plowed surface, potholes filled with oily water. Ward did the same just in time and Larsson smiled hungrily.

In the direction the truck had come from Ward noticed the girl. One of the whores from the house where Troy had taken his beating. She was probably selling blowjobs to the truckers. *She starts early*, Ward thought. Probably hitched up here for the price of a blowjob too. There were plenty of trucks parked up. Ward guessed there would be some good business for her.

They entered the truckers' lounge which was just fixing to open, although a trucker had already managed to get himself a beer and sat at the counter pondering his next shave. The trucker glanced around at the two of them and then returned to his beer. Ward guessed he was Mexican.

Ward and Larsson sat and a young woman came to their table. Told them the kitchen was closed for food till twelve. Drinks only. They both ordered a coffee. Larsson's smile was still on his face. He occasionally glanced at Ward and looked everywhere else in between times. Ward's eyes didn't leave Larsson. They sat like that for a minute or two.

"It's good to see you, detective," Larsson said finally. "Can I call you detective now, since you're suspended?"

"Cute," Ward said, trying to be friendly. He took off his hat and placed it on the table and then rubbed at his head.

"I need to know what I'm getting if I can be so vulgar," Larsson said.

"Well, that depends," Ward said. "Depends on what I get."

"Well, we can go on depending till Labor Day but I got to know I'm not wasting my time here. With respect."

"You seem to have a line into the department already," Ward said.

"I do."

Ward touched his beard with his blue, swollen hand.

"That really is a nasty injury," Larsson said. "That guy was a real mess, wasn't he?"

Ward held his tongue.

"Cop on a charge of assaulting a citizen. That's a big story," Larsson said, and he grinned and he chattered his small teeth.

Ward said, "I need a few days."

"Well, let's see, I can give you a couple and then it runs," Larsson said.

Ward nodded.

"And I want the inside exclusive when you solve these homicides."

Ward nodded again. He said, "You got what you need," and the young waitress appeared with their coffees. She plonked the cups down and slipped the check under the napkin dispenser that sat in the center of the table.

Larsson said, "Thank you, missy," and he watched her all the way back to the counter, where she sat and rested her head on her hands and stared into nothing.

"Where are you at with the Bill O'Donnell case?"

"We got one or two leads we are following up. Nothing concrete. Nothing you don't already know."

"So, my next headline is 'Cops No Closer to Finding Man's Killer'? Is that how you want it to read?"

Ward felt his busted hand. "Okay, we've got a new lead. Suspect fled from the scene and left prints matching the ones on the windowsill of the old man's room at the nursing home."

"Very good," Larsson said, and he started to take notes in shorthand. "You think he's the killer?"

"He's a line of inquiry," Ward said.

"Okay. What about the little boy? How's Newton? He feeling the pressure?"

Ward didn't answer.

"Good, good," Larsson said, and he scribbled something on his pad.

Ward reached for his hat and stood up. "I'm wasting my time here."

"No, no, detective. We have a deal."

"Right now I'm wondering whether to leave you facedown in a shit-filled puddle or under the wheels of a semi."

Larsson's smile twitched and fizzled off his face. "Let's not... let's take a deep breath there, detective," Larsson said, and he moved his hands like an orchestra conductor. "We're coming to the main course. I'm just doing my job. It would be a dereliction of duty for me not to ask these questions."

Ward slowly sat again.

"Okay." Larsson took a sip of coffee. Added some sugar. "You know I covered the original case? You do. Of course you do. It was hot that summer. Hot as hell.

Hell, it was hotter than Texas." He laughed. Ward didn't. "I even bought myself air conditioning. You imagine that?" He knocked back his coffee. "Say, you not drinking that coffee?"

Ward shook his head.

"Then do you mind if I..."

Ward nodded and Larsson took the coffee and sipped at it. He poured some sugar in, stirred and took another sip.

"We had forest fires too but I'll get to that. The night the boy disappeared I was sweating over a story about corruption in City Hall. Never did like that kind of story. Wanted to cover real crime, you know? I get excited over homicides, not white-collar crime. I know that might sound wrong but I'm a reporter and... well... the boy wasn't noticed missing till the next day. Say, what do you know about his parents?"

"Only what it says in the case notes," Ward said.

"Does it say both were drunks? Eugene and Janice Novak. A model couple. Model parents."

"Janice was Bill O'Donnell's daughter, right?"

"Right. I'm sure she was a nice girl, but Eugene Novak. There was a son of a bitch if ever I saw one. Sure, he cried and made appeals for the safe return of his son. But he was down one punching bag." Larsson looked up at Ward.

Ward said, "He was abusing his son?"

"Don't it say that in the file?"

"Maybe I haven't gotten that far."

"Well, maybe you haven't or maybe it's not there. I had to do some digging to get that information. Social Services was never alerted to it but I found out."

"How?"

"Investigative journalism, see. It's what I do. What I keep telling you. The only thing is I could never go to print on that. It was hearsay and there's Eugene Novak sobbing to the cameras saying how he wants his son back and the people see him as this helpless victim. I'd say it makes me sick to think about it but I have a detached indifference to these things. I've seen it all, detective."

"Go on."

"My theory is the boy was fleeing another beating. He goes walking off never to be seen again. Why would he do that unless to get away from his abusive daddy?" He took a drink of Ward's coffee and added some more sugar.

"So you think someone took him?"

"Well, I know what Newton thinks and I reckon that that just about ruined the case for him. Early in the case he was leaning towards Bill O'Donnell, the grandpa. You want to know why?"

"Go on."

"Well, you see, it's all about timing. Way O'Donnell explains it, his truck got stolen and he took off looking for it."

"And a police report backs that up."

"Yes, it does. It's merely a coincidence that this little boy goes missing on the same weekend as his truck. But the truck got taken first. Police report shows that."

"You buy that? Or did he report the truck missing knowing that he was taking the little boy to kill him? A cover story. An alibi?"

"I see how it could sound like that but look... Bill O'Donnell was a good man. Was the janitor at the elementary school. All the kids loved him. The teachers too."

"You spoke to him?"

"I did. And his story came across as genuine. He was distraught about the boy. Totally destroyed and I believed him. I've seen people go on TV to make appeals and you kinda know straight away that they did it. Never got that with O'Donnell. Not to say he was an open book."

"How do you mean?"

"He didn't want to talk, of course he didn't. He wanted to help the case but nobody trusts a reporter, do they?" He laughed and then took out a handkerchief and wiped his mouth. "Something he said but didn't elaborate on has always stuck with me."

"What did he say?"

"Well, detective, if you don't mind I'll get to that later." He smiled and Ward suppressed the urge to wipe that smile from his face. "I told you we had forest fires that year. Had a couple up at the National Forest. Big ones. Some weeks later once the fires was put out they found the truck burned out. Some joyriders had taken it up into the hills and left it there to burn. Never got the varmints but they never do. Truck was destroyed. The heat was so intense that it was mostly melted. Thing is, Newton goes and puts two and two together and reckons that O'Donnell had taken the body into the hills to bury and left his vehicle there. Of course there was no forensic evidence left. Hell, there wasn't much left of the truck. I saw it myself. They got it towed back. And that was that. It all dried up. And a while later the FBI came on board. The captain at the time, guy called Garrett, called them in. He'd fended them off long as he could. Newton wasn't pleased. FBI thanked him for his work and waved him away. He'd had his shot and blew it."

"I don't have much background on the FBI investigation."

"Neither do I, but that's because they found nothing. They retraced Newton's steps, followed up his leads, basically did the same job as he had done and they got the same result. They took it nationwide so I guess they did something. I guess that's what finished the case. Soon as the FBI pulled out, Captain Garrett wasn't inclined to put any more hours into it. Of course, they tell the media that the case is still open and that manpower will still be allocated to the case but that means zip. They called it off and gradually people forgot about it. Newton took it hard. He got a bad press and I guess that's down to me." He smiled broadly and Ward wanted to knock his weasel teeth through the back of his neck.

"Did the bureau like O'Donnell for it?" Ward said eventually.

"Well, let's say they weren't as enamored as Newton was. They spoke to him but they bought his story about the truck and so on and so forth."

"Did anyone like the parents for it?"

"Not really. They were just drunks."

"But you say the father was abusive."

"He was. Nobody was convinced that he had it in him to kill the boy though. The boy was his favorite sport. And besides, his story that he was in a drunken coma at the time the boy walked off didn't take much convincing. Not to say they didn't look at the father, they did, but that line wasn't going anywhere."

"So, what happened to the parents?"

"Janice got herself impregnated again and had another child a year later. Child died. She died a few days after."

Ward sat up at that. He thought of Alice White and her book of dead babies and wondered if the child was in there.

"Eugene Novak got tangled up in the back wheels of a trailer. Killed instantly. Shame. Would've liked to have seen him drink himself to a painful death."

Ward nodded and instantly hated himself for agreeing with this man.

"You mentioned something about O'Donnell said something interesting."

"I'm coming to that. Patience, detective. Can we get another coffee?" He gestured to the waitress and shouted, "Can we get a freshen-up here?"

The waitress nodded and wrenched herself off the counter as Larsson finished Ward's coffee.

"I can't function without caffeine," Larsson said. "So, where were we? Ah, yes. You will have noticed from the case notes that there were no eyewitnesses. Well, there was one but he was ruled out as being an imbecile. Which, to be fair, he was. You read what he said? At the time? He said the boy was abducted by aliens! How about that? Who would take seriously a witness who says such a thing?"

"You, right?"

"Ah, you're one step ahead of me. You gotta slow down there, detective. I'm telling the story. Don't you go taking my punch line now. I won't abide that."

"Go on."

"You might want to effect a drum roll now. Bang a

couple of spoons on the table or something. We're getting to the best part."

Ward ignored him and was close to putting his good fist through his face as the edges of his patience began to fray.

"I interviewed Bill O'Donnell, God rest his soul. I told you he was really cut up with the whole thing. He'd helped with the search himself. Didn't sleep or eat for days or so it seemed. Got a search party up and the whole town turned out. They did it for him more than the parents. Everybody knew they were drunks and probably not suitable parents. Searched high and low. If the police couldn't find him then he sure as hell would. He didn't, of course."

"About this interview."

"Okay, you've waited long enough," Larsson said, and then the goddamn waitress came over with the coffee pot and she poured. Larsson checked her out again and thanked her in the same condescending manner as before.

"Sometimes I wish I wasn't such a family man," Larsson said. "Wouldn't you like a piece of that skanky ass there?" He sucked his lips. "So, where were we?"

"You goddamn know where we were," Ward said, and the threat seemed to do the trick.

"Okay," Larsson said with hands up in surrender. "I asked him if he thought that the cops had done enough. An innocent question and a straightforward answer came forth. Didn't think nothing of it back then but it's kinda been grinding away at me in the years since. No, to be totally honest, I hadn't given it a second thought until the case resurfaced and then it came back to me. So O'Donnell says maybe they did too much. How about that? A satisfied customer. You should be proud of your department, detective. The cops didn't just do enough, they did too much."

Ward shifted in his seat.

"Thing is, Newton had this guy down for the kid's disappearance so maybe it was a reference to the harassment that Newton gave him. He did too much. Or maybe they did so much to find the boy it was meant as genuine praise. But this is where it got interesting for me. The only eyewitness, old Mitch Filmore, said that the boy was taken by aliens. He said he saw lights." Larsson's eyes glistened and he wanted Ward to catch up. "You see where I'm going with this?"

"Not really, but carry on."

"Detective, he saw lights. Don't you see? Maybe flashing lights?" He gave Ward a few beats.

"You're not saying what I think you're saying."

"I'm not saying anything, detective. Man saw lights is all I'm saying. And O'Donnell says the cops did too much. Two and two." He did a magician's reveal gesture and Ward expected him to produce some flowers from his sleeve.

"You think the cops were involved? You gotta be kidding me. All that for this? You gotta be kidding."

"No, sir. I'm an investigative journalist. That's my job. I see things that others might not. Not to blow my own horn too much." He grinned.

Ward stood and picked up his hat. "Well, thank you for your time."

Larsson quickly drank his third coffee and followed Ward into the parking lot.

"We've still got a deal. Don't forget about our deal."

"I said it depends," Ward said.

"Aw, come on detective. A deal's a deal. Don't go welshing on me now."

Ward was walking towards his car and he paused to let a semi pass. Larsson hurried past him and nearly got wiped out by the truck. A tire clipped a puddle and shit-colored water splashed up the back of his pants.

"Fucking shit," he said, and Ward continued to his car. "We have a deal."

Ward stopped, turned to Larsson.

"Just out of interest, what happened to the corruption piece?"

Larsson perked up. Smiled at Ward. "That got pulled."

"Any reason?"

"Who can say? As I understand it they couldn't make anything stick anyway."

"Who was involved?"

"A few people in City Hall. A property developer."

"Who was the property developer?"

"James Kenny."

Ward's eyebrows raised.

"He pay off your superiors to get the story killed?"

"Couldn't possibly say."

Ward turned and started walking away.

Larsson called out, "Hey!"

The waitress appeared at the door of the truckers' lounge waving the check. Larsson looked at the stain on the back of his pants and cursed.

Ward called back, "You got your deal," and he got in his car.

46

Ward drove to his motel. Jesús came striding over to him as he opened the door and Ward rubbed the dog's head and play-fought with him. Jesús had Ward's hand in his mouth in a mock bite but he didn't apply any pressure. Probably didn't have a whole lot of pressure left in his jaws anyhow. Ward went over to the kitchenette and took a box from a cupboard. A high cupboard. He tossed a biscuit to Jesús, who attempted to swallow it in one go and then coughed it back up and decided to chomp it into smaller pieces. He made contented little growling noises as he ate.

Ward thought about what Larsson had said. Cops might have been involved. That seemed unlikely. But could O'Donnell have been hinting at that? And how would he know unless he was involved too? O'Donnell's possible involvement matched up with Newton's train of thought. But everybody said O'Donnell was a good man. Was he that good an actor? And all the time this was going through his mind Ward couldn't stop thinking about James Kenny. Corrupt property developer with a habit of paying people large sums of money to get out of a tight spot.

47

Ward called Newton. He had decided he wouldn't tell him everything Larsson had said.

"I spoke to Larsson."

"Okay."

"He's some shyster."

"He tell you anything you can use?"

"Oh, you know. He went over the case. Pretty much what's in the file."

Newton remained silent for a few moments. Ward thought he was waiting for more. He didn't give him anything.

"I need to work one or two angles. Off the radar."

"Okay. You keep me updated?"

"I will." And Ward thought if there was police involvement in the disappearance of Ryan Novak maybe he should keep that to himself for a while until he'd had time to mull it over. "Say, what's the latest on the old guy?"

"We look for the man who left the prints. I'm getting a facial composite of the guy and I'll send out all units with it. See if we get a hit."

"Good. Progress."

"We'll call it progress. Internal Affairs is scheduled for next week. You might want to work on that too."

"Okay. Thanks for the heads up." And Ward hung up.

Back at the station Newton was slumped in his chair. He popped a pill, threw his head back to dry swallow it, and he closed his eyes.

Over on the other side of the office Mallory was hanging about like a bad odor. He sidled up to McNeely, who tapped away at her keyboard with one hand, the other feeding her mouth. She tried to ignore him.

"I dreamed about you last night," he said.

"Nice," McNeely said through her chewing.

"You gave me the sweetest blowjob." His grin made her next swallow impossible. "Woke up in love with you."

"Have you told your father-in-law that yet? He's right behind you. Tell him now."

Mallory whipped around like a rattlesnake. Newton wasn't there. Mallory's lips pinched the smile from his face.

"You're cute, I'll give you that," he said, and he walked. McNeely spat out a mouthful of chewed raisins into her hand and tossed them into the trashcan.

48

Marcelo was to be Bill O'Donnell's ride back into town. O'Donnell had carefully chosen a rig that looked like it was from way out of town. Marcelo had obliged by advertising his Florida credentials all over the front of his truck. 'I heart the Sunshine State'. 'Go Dolphins!' O'Donnell had gotten a hit with his first thumb. Marcelo hadn't commented on his appearance or his smell. O'Donnell had been unaware of how dead he looked and reeked and Marcelo hadn't mentioned it.

He asks his name and O'Donnell says it's Mike. Says he's been fighting the fire and has missed his ride back. Says he's grateful for Marcelo stopping. Says nothing else. Marcelo does a little talking in something of a Spanish accent, O'Donnell thinks. O'Donnell counts the crucifixes that Marcelo has in his cab and then his eyes land on the most ornate one and his gaze lingers there for the rest of the ride. The intricate silverwork, or maybe pewter or some such alloy, weaved into a cross upon which a depiction of Christ, detailed in divine pain, suffers for man's sins. He wants to take it and plunge it into his own heart but knows he doesn't have the strength.

Marcelo drops O'Donnell five miles from town and sounds his horn as he pulls away off the shoulder. The truck driver pulls into a truck stop a few miles further on and has a beer. He will pull into the same truck stop twenty-odd years later, where a cop who doesn't believe in coincidences will be talking to an invertebrate journalist who drinks too much coffee.

O'Donnell walks the five miles into town. His sweat streaks the grime on his face so he looks like a soldier with face camouflage. He passes a church and he pauses. He hears muted singing inside. He carries on. He passes another church and a few yards past it he stops and turns back and goes up to the door, which is open. He pushes through the inner door and the congregation is singing a song so sweet that his heart throws a roll and he wants to fall to his knees but he stays upright. He stands at the back of the church and he stares at Jesus on the cross and he gulps in air and he gulps in the spirit of the people, which he imagines he can see swirling around above their heads as they stand and sing at the top of their voices, and it's lovely and he feels at home and he feels like an alien at the same time.

The preacher has a microphone and he is called Reverend Adrien Baptiste and he sings the loudest.

Bill O'Donnell stands there at the back of the church and when the congregation sits he remains standing and one or two people cast looks over their shoulders to look at him and he thinks he will be judged but they just smile and he resents their gift at first.

But he stands there and, when the service is over, every person who passes him on their way out of the church smiles at him and the preacher, who stands an arm's length away from Bill O'Donnell, shakes their hands and they leave money on a silver plate by the door - notes and coins. The preacher looks him up and down and he smiles the entire height of him and Bill O'Donnell shakes his hand but he doesn't leave and he has no money to put on the plate but the preacher understands that he hasn't any and he just nods at him and says something which Bill O'Donnell doesn't hear and then the preacher turns and walks towards the altar and he disappears through a door at the side and then there is just Bill O'Donnell and God. And Jesus there on the cross. Sweet, lovely Jesus who is a stranger to him.

And then he notices the woman who's doing something with the flowers. She doesn't seem to have seen him and he walks to the front of the church where the altar is and he stands and stares at Jesus and he thinks he feels something but decides he doesn't. He stands there for a hundred years and tries to pray and then he stands for a hundred years more and still he can't pray and he can't hear nothing coming back from Jesus neither. Then he hears the woman say something but he doesn't hear it, he feels it, and he spins around and she's there standing and staring at him and she seems surprised for a millionth of a moment and then she smiles like the others had. He says "I wanted to get closer," and then he strides out of the church and doesn't look back at Jesus but he doesn't feel so wretchedly filthy no more. He stops outside and for a moment doesn't know where he's going and the woman comes to him.

She says, "You need to get washed and out of those clothes." And she knows that if anybody asks her later, and they will, she won't tell this fragment of history. The Lord will be all right with that. She knows that for sure.

Bill O'Donnell doesn't put up an argument. She introduces herself as Alice White and she takes him home in her car very slowly and when they reach her house she runs him a bath.

"I got some old clothes you can wear. We'll get rid of those filthy ones." And Alice White smiles at him and he *feels different but he can't tell how he feels but just knows things will be okay.*

After his bath and change of clothes he thanks the woman. He walks home and Alice burns the clothes that smell of hellfire when he has gone.

He lives with his daughter and son-in-law in the least salubrious side of town. The house is on one level and everything about it begs for repair. When he turns the end of the street he can see the house and there is activity he hadn't been expecting. His labored walk becomes a frantic shuffle. His son-in-law, Eugene Novak, asks him where the hell he's been and Bill O'Donnell asks what's going on.

"Ryan's gone," Eugene Novak says.

"Gone? Where? How do you mean gone?" O'Donnell says, and in his confusion he is genuinely shocked that the little boy is missing.

"He's up and run off." *Novak smells of booze but he seems stone cold sober.*

O'Donnell's daughter Janice had been talking to a man who looked like a cop and she runs over when she sees her father. She hugs him and her deep sobs inhale his soapy smell. She smells of booze like her husband. Both too drunk to notice the clothes O'Donnell wears are not his own.

"What's happened, Daddy?"

"What's this about Ryan? He up and went? When? Why?"

"He's been taken," Janice says.

"Noticed that he wasn't there," Novak says.

"Noticed when?" *O'Donnell asks and Eugene Novak steps back and he snarls at O'Donnell.*

"Where the hell have you been? We thought he was with

you. How could we goddamn know he wasn't?"

Bill O'Donnell says, "How long has he been gone?" And then the lanky cop is there and he eyes O'Donnell like prey.

"Detective Newton. You must be the grandfather? William?"

"Bill."

"We're just trying to ascertain when Ryan went missing. To help us find him and bring him on home."

"Okay."

"When did you last see him?"

"Yesterday."

"What time?"

"Afternoon, I reckon. I'd seen him and then gone back to the school to take care of something."

"Where have you been? Your folks have been looking for you."

"I've been looking for my truck. It got stolen."

Detective Newton doesn't show any emotion and says, "What time did you report it missing?"

O'Donnell feels panic rise inside him. He hadn't reported it. The man had said he would take care of it. That was their story. And when O'Donnell got back from burying the boy he would raise the alarm that the boy was missing. He knew Eugene and Janice Novak wouldn't notice Ryan wasn't there. He was mainly invisible to them. But they had noticed.

He takes a guess and trusts that the man wouldn't let him down. "Last night sometime. I don't know the exact time. I'm sorry. I'm in a bit of shock."

"I understand sir. I just got to ask these questions. I'll check our records for the exact time. You see anybody take it? Could the boy have taken it?"

Eugene Novak jumps in. "He's seven years old, for

Christ's sake. His feet wouldn't reach the damn pedals. Wouldn't have gotten more than ten yards and then crash it. Damn it, what are you doing to find my son? We ain't got all day to talk. It's getting on dark. Get on looking for him."

Janice says, "He doesn't like the dark. Always sleeps with the light on. Oh, I'm a terrible mother. We should get some flyers done. Yes, we'll get some flyers and posters done."

O'Donnell's heart stutters over the futility of what his daughter has said.

Newton appears calm and reassuring. "We need to collect some information. I've already got patrols looking out for him. Can't have gotten far."

"He wouldn't have took the truck," Bill O'Donnell says. "Got to be some youths. They been at it before."

"You reported it before?" Newton asks.

"No, sir. They didn't take it before. I stopped them."

"You stopped them? You saw them? You could give me a description?"

"No. I didn't see them properly. It was dark. I heard them and ran them off."

"How many were they?"

O'Donnell pauses and feels rushed and he wants to run away from his answers. "They were three or four. Like I said, it was dark and they run off. Maybe they took the truck and took the boy." He feels like he's freefalling now and he desperately tries not to show his fear which will expose his lies.

Newton stares at the man in front of him and O'Donnell feels accused and trapped in his own nightmare. O'Donnell glances over at the small cherry tree sapling which he had helped Ryan plant days earlier and he bites hard onto his first knuckle, right hand.

"You live here also, correct?"

"Yes, sir."

"You didn't notice he wasn't here?"

"I didn't. I had to go to the school and then when I got back I didn't see him. I would have thought he was in his bed."

"Would have?"

"What do you mean?"

"You said 'would have' as if you're not sure what you thought."

"Heck, I didn't know he was missing."

"You reported your truck stolen at what time?"

"Like I said, I can't remember. It was last night."

"And you didn't notice that the boy wasn't at home?"

"This is difficult for me. I can't remember about last night. I just had my truck taken, and… well, this is just… I'm upset is what I am."

"I know and I have to ask these here questions so's we can get to finding him." Bill O'Donnell looks at the cop, who says, "You been gone best part of a day. Looking for your truck, that right?"

"That's right, sir."

"All through the night and the most part of today?"

"Had a fair few places to look. Say, are you suspecting me because if you are… it ain't right."

"Just asking questions, sir. We have a serious situation here and time is against us."

"I understand."

"Maybe we can help you find your truck. Where have you looked?"

"Oh, I looked just about everywhere in town."

"You see many people out and about?"

"Well, it was nighttime and they weren't many folks out."

"What about today?"

"I saw people, yes."

"Anyone you know? Anyone can say they saw you?"

"Not mostly."

"Not mostly?"

"Not anybody, no. I don't know why you're asking that to help find my truck."

"I'm a detective, Mr. O'Donnell. It's my job to ask questions."

"Okay."

"Did you stop anywhere, maybe for something to eat?"

"No, sir. I ain't eaten. And if I had or I hadn't it ain't making no difference to finding my truck."

"Okay. You look anywhere else? Outside of town?"

"No, sir."

A marked police car pulls up and a short cop in uniform, packing a few pounds over, steps out. Newton asks Bill O'Donnell to excuse him and walks over to the cop. He nods and speaks the cop's name in greeting and then says quietly, "The grandfather took him."

Officer Gammond says, "He did? Dang."

"Sure he did. He's lying. He's lying about his truck being taken. Check to see if it was stolen and what time it was reported."

Gammond's head snaps up. "No need to check. I done took that call. He reported it around nine last night. I took a statement. He said he was going to go off and look for it and I said not to but I guess he did anyways."

Newton feels a spasm scrunch his lower back. "Don't change anything. I know he took him. Get me that truck."

"Yes, sir," Gammond says and he reaches into his car and grabs the radio.

Out front of the Novak household Eugene Novak is

jabbing his finger at the broken man and shouting something. O'Donnell pushes him in his chest and Novak staggers back and looks like he's going to come in swinging at his father-in-law but doesn't. Janice Novak stands there sobbing.

Before Gammond can speak into the radio, Detective Newton says, "The boy's probably dead already. I'm going to take the guy in. I'll get his agreement to do some tests on his clothes. I think we'll find blood traces and we'll get a confession. I'll have this case closed within days. You'll see."

Officer Gammond nods and clicks on the radio.

49

Newton stared at the evidence board for the O'Donnell homicide case. McNeely appeared by his side and stood there with her hands on her hips, head tilted as if trying to view the board sideways. Various photographs were attached to the whiteboard with small round magnetic holders. There were two photographs of the old man – one alive, taken a year or two ago at a church event, which Alice White had given to them, and the other deceased, on the slab in the mortuary, his chest bearing an ugly sutured autopsy scar. There was another image of just his foot, showing the point of entry of the hypodermic needle where the fatal dose of morphine had been administered. There was a copy of the photograph of the little boy which they had discovered in O'Donnell's Bible. There was a photograph of the windowsill where the prints were found by McNeely during the crime scene investigation. There were various words, phrases written in a kind of word cloud – 'clean scene', 'prints on windowsill', 'morphine', 'photograph of boy', 'confession?', 'Ryan Novak', 'Alice White', 'MONEY' in uppercase letters. There was a photo of the newspaper that Penny Gilfoyle had been reading to Bill O'Donnell on the night the old man had flipped. And there was a photograph of Doctor Brookline, postmortem, and a circle around that with a BIG question mark by the side of it.

"More I stare at it the less it makes sense," Newton said. McNeely placed a hand on his shoulder.

"You okay, sir?"

"I'm fine, Helen. Thanks. It's just… I need to finish."

McNeely said, "Finish the case?"

Newton said, "Just finish. I don't know."

"We'll catch this guy. Don't we always?" And McNeely realized what she had said a moment too late. She cringed inside and looked at Newton, who just stared at the board and said nothing. McNeely said "fuck it" over and over in her head. And then Newton turned to McNeely and said, "Yes, we will," and he walked over to the door, grabbed his coat from the stand, and strode out of the station, leaving McNeely standing there, searching the evidence board for something. Anything.

50

Ward read his notebook and scratched at his head with his good hand. The swelling on his Troy-damaged hand had gone down but the bruising was coming out and Ward grimaced when he noticed it as he turned pages. He had scribbled notes down from his meeting with Larsson and he looked for his next move. Decided it would be to talk to the crazy old man who'd witnessed something. Something strange. It was a long time ago and he didn't expect to get anything from him but he hadn't a great deal else to do and his suspension meant he had to follow the quiet leads that wouldn't get noticed.

He called Newton and got the address. Newton had the case memorized and knew everyone who had provided a statement by name and address. He gave him the Novak address too. Newton was on his way driving somewhere but he didn't say where. Ward didn't press him. He just grabbed his hat and coat and hurried out to his car. They'd taken his badge and weapon but the car was his own. He was grateful for that.

He drove the few miles out to where Ryan Novak

had lived unhappily with his parents and grandpa. He stopped in front of the house and a gust of wind blew a spiral of tiny snow crystals around the car and up into the sky, which was so low it seemed to crowd out daylight. A decent snowfall would lighten things a little from the ground upwards at least. The car's headlights shone upon the house and showed it to be empty and the wooden shell was bleached out like a skeleton left out in the desert. The place looked bandaged up in parts and the front screen door slapped sluggishly at its frame. An ancient realtor's sign leaned untidily against a cherry tree which had forgotten its leaves and looked like it yearned for sunlight and warmth. The screeching sound of the tree's trunk rubbing against the signpost seemed like a keen for the little boy who had planted it.

Then Ward thought he saw someone looking through one of the windows and he straightened up in his seat. But as soon as he had seen them they disappeared. He stepped out of the car and opened the scabbed front gate to the property and he walked up to the house. A gust of wind tried to take his hat but he hung on to it and peered through the window where he thought he'd seen somebody but the room was empty save for dusty memories of the previous occupants. He walked around the outside of the house and looked through all the windows but saw nothing. Then, from inside the house, he heard a bang. Sounded like a door slamming shut. He scuttled around to where he thought the sound had come from but the door was open. Again he checked all the rooms but all the doors were open. He shook out a shiver and returned to the car.

* * *

The crazy man's house was a half mile away – four streets and a couple of acres of scrub wasteland and scattered pines. The house stood alone on the quiet street, set back from the roadside and a thicker collection of planted trees shielded it left and right but opened up to the road at the front like a theater curtain. The field of vision to the road was narrow but somebody positioned in one of the two front windows would get a good view of any activity outside the house even when the deciduous trees were in full leaf. And somebody did today. Ward saw a figure at the window. He climbed out of the car and walked past the realtor's sign that told that the house had been sold and he stepped slowly up to the front door. Before he could knock, a woman of forty or some years appeared at the door.

The woman said, "Can I help you there?" Her voice was snatchy but amiable.

Ward said, "Well, maybe you can and I appreciate any help you can give me. I'm looking for a Mitch—" Before he could say the last name she said it for him.

"Filmore. That's my father."

"Would Mr. Filmore be—"

"Should say *was* my father. He passed this last year."

"Oh, I'm sorry to hear that."

"Thank you, sir. Say, who are you?"

"Sorry, I'm Ward. Detective. And this sure was a long shot and I'm sorry to have taken your time. Again, condolences for your loss." He turned to walk back towards his car.

"Only time police have been to this house was when the little boy was missing."

Ward turned.

"Come in, detective."

He followed her into the house and he saw that her stay was coming to an end. Open, half-packed boxes. Black garbage bags full and tied off and piled up in a corner in the hallway and spilling into another room.

"Just getting rid of a few things. Now it's sold I got to clean it out. House has been empty since Dad died. Empty apart from all this. He kept things you and me would consider unnecessary clutter."

In the main living room the old furniture was covered with dust sheets and she pulled back one which concealed a sofa and invited Ward to sit. She sat next to him.

"I lived with him back then. I was his caregiver, you might say. But I had to move away. Heartless as it sounds I couldn't cope no longer. He was difficult. A handful. You might say crazy. I bet that's how Detective... Newton described him to you." She smiled at that and Ward smiled an apology on Newton's behalf. "I guess you're looking at the case again. I saw his grandfather died."

"Yes, we're taking a fresh look."

"Well, if I can help, then I will."

"Do you recall what your father saw that day? I know what it says in the report but I wondered if—"

"I can. In fact, I can do better than just tell you." She got up and walked over to the pile of garbage bags. "I only just threw them away. Now, which bag was it?" She untied the knot in the top of one of the bags and she fished around inside. "Not this one." But the second one yielded what she was looking for. A handful of papers. She handed them to Ward and he turned them over one by one. There were drawings on all of them.

"You ask me if he drank, I'd say he favored whiskey, cheaper the better. You ask me if he'd been drinking that night I'd say most likely definitely. Can't recall a day he didn't. You ask me if these drawings are the work of a crazy man, I'd have to agree with Detective Newton on that score. All I can do is show you and you make your own mind up."

Each drawing was a depiction of the same event. The old man, Filmore, had drawn stick figures for people and one of the figures was small and was carried by a taller figure. There were three other figures standing watching. Maybe talking. They were all tall and the old crazy man had drawn them with large heads. Typical alien shape with large eyes. They were standing beside two interstellar vehicles. Spaceships. He had taken colored pens to draw on lights around and underneath the spacecraft. What struck Ward was that neither were in the air, flying. Ward turned to the woman and he smiled.

She said, "Crazy, huh."

Ward flicked through the pictures. They were all variations on a theme.

"He'd draw them pictures for years after the boy had gone. I would find them and throw them away but I guess he stashed a few."

Ward said, "These seem to back up his statement at least."

"Nobody paid him no heed. Probably rightly so. But he was adamant he'd seen what he saw. He would sit in the window and look out most nights while knocking back his drink and he'd fall asleep there and once he was asleep there was no shifting him. He had a big middle and was heavy." She laughed and Ward laughed with her. "I'd be pleased to help you more but that's about all there is."

"No, that's fine. Really helpful, ma'am."

"You're from somewhere down in the South, aren't you?"

"Texas."

"Don't you mind the cold?"

"No, ma'am. It's mostly manageable."

She nodded. "It mostly is I guess." She stood and Ward did too.

"Thank you again for your help. Do you mind if I…"

She waved a hand and said, "Take them. They're yours. If I come across anything more I'll send them on to you. You can take the rest of these bags while you're at it if you want."

Ward smiled and reached into his pocket and pulled out his notepad and a pen. He scribbled his phone number down and tore the page and handed it to the woman. "You can get me here."

She studied the piece of paper. "You have a first name?"

Ward said, "Ward will do. It's what everybody calls me."

"Well, Ward, it was nice to meet you." She held out her hand to shake. Ward shook it gently and his hand passed the test.

"You too."

As he went back out into the cold her last words

followed him.

"He wasn't loco perdido, you know. He held down a hundred and one jobs. Some for days at a time." Her smile was infectious and Ward returned to his car with the makings of a grin.

In the car Ward turned the heat on full blast and studied the drawings. Drawings from a crazy old man of an alien abduction. And he got the feeling that this was probably the most significant evidence in the entire case. The only eyewitness account from a crazy old man. He just had to figure out what the hell it meant.

51

Newton pulled up outside Alice White's house. The place glowed with lights lit in all rooms. He sat there in his vehicle a while and then got out and walked up to the door. He paused. Didn't want to knock. But he knocked.

It took a few moments for Alice to answer, but when she did there was no surprise on her face. She asked him in.

In the living room there were two cups set out for tea and a plate piled high with cookies. Her own. The house smelled of baking. She poured two cups of tea and Newton took one and sipped. He reached for a cookie and Alice smiled at him. He noticed the tear on her cheek and he wanted to wipe it.

The tea was hot but he knocked back a pill and took a gulp of hot liquid, which seared his throat.

"You seen a back prodder?" Alice White said.

Newton said, "I've seen two."

"Maybe it's time to try something else. Something more spiritual. I can recommend someone."

"Maybe some other time. Thank you."

He sipped the tea and chomped on a cookie and it

tasted as sweet as any cookie he'd ever tasted.

"Snow's coming," Alice White said.

"I see it," Newton said.

"It sure is cold."

"It sure is."

They sat there without speaking any more words for five minutes. Newton looked at his hands. He looked out the window. Alice sat there and hummed a tune, almost inaudibly. Newton felt he could fall asleep. Alice smiled at him. He smiled back. He took another cookie and ate it in two bites. Alice smiled bigger. Newton stood and went over to the dresser where there were a dozen pictures of children. He picked one up and studied it. He put it down and picked up the photograph album which sat on the bookcase. He flicked through it. He sat down again. Finished off his tea. Alice made to pour some more but Newton held his hand up and he stood.

"Wisht my husband had made your age," Alice said. "The Lord had other plans for him unfortunately. Your wife is a lucky lady. She knows it. Do you?"

Newton was in the doorway with his back to her. He paused and then turned to briefly look into Alice's watery eyes and then he left.

Tommy's Bar was empty apart from two men who looked like they'd been at work but probably hadn't. Newton ordered a beer and immediately made a call on his cell phone.

The big bear of a man with the full salt-and-pepper beard arrived thirty minutes later after telephone negotiation had failed. Newton hadn't touched the beer. He'd swiveled the bottle a thousand times and peeled back the label and scrunched it into a perfect ball. And then he'd shaped it into a cube and continued to work at it until his sponsor arrived. But he hadn't taken a solitary swig. The bartender had eyed him peripherally once or twice. Newton left the bar with the man and then he got in his car and drove off.

The call he got from the warden at the Montana State Prison came as he was driving to nowhere.

52

Ward was surprised that School Principal Leon Taylor at Meriwether Elementary School hadn't retired or moved on. He was even more surprised to see that he was only in his midfifties. He had taken up the position at the age of twenty-five – the youngest school principal in the county at the time. He greeted Ward with an open hand and an open face. His mop of runaway black hair still strangled out any attempts at grayness. Ward was impressed. He guessed that came from working with kids. Detectives were mainly gray or bald or both by that age. Or dead.

Ward thought he'd seen him before but couldn't place where.

He heard a classroom singing discordantly as the principal led him down corridors which seemed designed for fairytale dwarves. A miniature world decorated with children's drawings. A nostalgic smell of crayons colored the air. They passed another classroom and Ward couldn't help but look inside and he saw small groups of children gathered around tables, all seemingly enthralled by something he couldn't see. He instinctively placed a hand on his chest, where the tattoo of the little girl sat amongst dragons.

The principal had been in a hurry to talk as fast as he walked.

"In fact we both started here 'round about the same time," Principal Taylor said. "I'd been here a matter of weeks before. I was on the interview panel. In case you're wondering we did all the proper checks. I know the history behind the Ryan Novak case and the interest that the police paid to Bill. We knew it was all baloney. Knew it was. Bill was a very popular member of our staff. We got lucky with him, certainly."

"What can you tell me about him?"

"He was a good man. More than a janitor. He kept this school running through thick and thin. Never complained. No job was ever too much for him. He was very good with his hands. The place would have fallen apart were it not for Bill. But he was more than that, as I say. He was a part of the school. How can I explain?" He stopped walking and tapped a finger on his lips. "He was always there. First to arrive in the morning. Last to leave at night, no matter how late someone was working. The school really is a community and he was the center of our little universe. It might sound trite but that's how it was. I wish he was still with us. We all do."

"Was there anything in his character that might make you uncomfortable about him being around children?"

Principal Taylor stiffened. He got that "now look here" stance but Ward headed him off.

"I'm sorry, but I have to ask these questions. I mean no offense to Mr. O'Donnell's memory."

"He was fine around children and never gave off any signals that would make anybody doubt that he was suitable to work with them. It's a ludicrous suggestion." Ward had managed to take the venom out of that last sentence.

"I understand," Ward said, and the principal reverted to his demeanor at their initial handshake. The handshake that had made Ward wince.

"He didn't have any formal education himself. You know he was a woodsman?"

Ward nodded.

"His wife died and he walked out of the woods with his daughter." And then the principal laughed. "You know, he would take home books. Children's textbooks. He never asked, just took them. Maybe he was embarrassed. I think he took them to practice his reading and his math."

Ward said, "How many did he take?"

The principal said, "He took lots. Over a period of three or four years, I guess. Like I said, he always brought them back. I wish he was still here. We could use a man like that with all the building work."

"A new science wing, right?"

"That's right. We want to introduce science and computing to our pupils at an earlier age. The new facility will be splendid. At the moment it just seems like demolition rather than building."

"That I see. When do you expect to open the new wing?"

"Next school year, all being well."

"Did you know Ryan well?"

Principal Taylor's face slid. "I knew him well. He gave cause for some concern."

"Concern how?"

"He was a very withdrawn and quiet child."

"Quiet enough for Social Services to be called?"

"We considered it. But it's always a tricky business. We try to engage the parents in most cases. Try to get to the bottom of what's troubling the child. It was always difficult with Ryan's parents. They were boozers, both. Gee, I feel like I'm speaking ill of the dead here. Let's just say they didn't come across as model parents."

"Okay."

"It's hard to know what to say."

"I think what you've said is very helpful."

"Well, I only hope so. I only hope so."

Ward wanted to ignore his cell phone and ask a few more questions. Didn't think he was done. But when he looked he saw that it was Newton, and he excused himself from the principal like a naughty schoolboy and answered.

His farewell to the principal was a nod and then he was almost running to his car as he took Newton's news.

53

It was a fifty-minute drive and Newton drove.

"I'm suspended. I shouldn't be here," Ward said.

"To hell with that," Newton said. "You're here as my guest."

The deputy warden met them and got them signed in. Newton checked in his weapon and took a voucher.

"He spoke to me. Said he had something he'd been meaning to get off his chest for a while. Twenty-five years, in fact. Kinda unusual to get a confession so long after the crime."

"He ask for anything? Special treatment?" Ward asked.

"No sir, he didn't. Didn't ask for a thing. Just asked to see the detective in charge of the case. So I called your station and got your number and here you are."

"Who'd you speak to at the station?"

"The lieutenant."

"Gammond?"

"That's the one."

Ward turned to Newton and said quietly, "Didn't

think Gammond wanted you anywhere near this case."

"It's what I thought," Newton said.

"He had any visitors recently?"

"He's not the kind that gets visitors."

Ward nodded.

The deputy warden pressed a button. Moments later a lock was broken and bars slid to the sound of a loud buzzer. The operator of the security system was behind plexiglass and he studied Ward and Newton like a cat watching two birds.

Two more sets of security gates unlocked and they went through. The corridor they entered smelled of a cross between cabbage and festering corpses. With a splash of cleaning fluids. They walked to the end and turned right. The bright lights above them buzzed a high-pitched note and one flickered. On. Off. An old man in prison threads was mopping the floor and he nodded a respectful acknowledgment and Ward and Newton returned it. At the end of the corridor was a door leading to a room. A guard sat on a chair outside and he stood as the three men approached.

Eric Lafayette sat inside the windowless room grinning but his smile was crooked on account of the big prison scar that streaked up from his cheek and finished in an empty eye socket that was closed and looked stuck with crusted glue. His good eye was topaz blue and bright as a flashlight. The sparse teeth that were there were unevenly spaced and mostly rotten. He managed to stroke his greasy hair back in spite of his cuffed wrists. His bones had a covering of pasty, wrinkled skin. Like wadded-up paper had been plastered onto his skeleton. His throat crackled phlegm as he breathed heavily.

"You came in the plural. Only expected one. Two's even better. Should I feel honored? I should feel honored." He watched them both sit and the grin never left his face. "I guess it's only polite to do introductions. I'll go first. I'm Eric. Very pleased to meet you." He held out his hand to Newton, who didn't move. Then to Ward. The same reaction.

"Aww, come on, gentlemen. We're all gentlemen, aren't we? Well, please yourself. I do it all the time. Please myself. You should try it." He launched into a fit of laughter ending in a coughing fit which turned the gray skin on his face a dirty pink and nearly popped out his good eye. He swallowed phlegm and seemed to enjoy it. The grin returned like some oily residue.

Ward spoke. "I'm Detective Ward and this here is Detective Newton. We've come to discuss what you said to the deputy warden. It's an informal interview at this stage. You can request a lawyer to be present if you'd prefer."

"Don't need no lawyer. Didn't do me no good before." He wheezed.

"Do you want to tell us what you told the deputy warden?" Ward said.

"It would be my pleasure, detective. I killed your little boy." He grinned and his one good eye darted from Ward to Newton and back. "How's that?"

Ward noticed Newton twitch in his chair.

"Oh, you want more details? Okay, but it ain't

pretty. Kinda grisly."

Ward noticed Newton flinch and he saw his hand form a fist.

"Go ahead," Ward said.

"Well. Once upon a time there was a little boy and then there wasn't. How's that? Or do you want more?"

Ward noticed Newton stand to his full height and noticed that he was about to snap Lafayette like a bunch of twigs. Noticed just in time to grab him and put himself in between Newton and the table, which got shunted into Lafayette's midriff and pushed out a gasp and a cough. Lafayette's grin morphed into something more sinister.

"I got your attention, then."

"You son of a bitch," Newton shouted, and the door opened.

The guard studied the situation.

"It's okay. We got it under control," Ward said, and he managed to get Newton seated.

The guard nodded and he left the room and closed the door.

"If you come for a happy ending I can tell you now you're gonna be mighty disappointed."

Ward said, "Look, we're not here to play games. We can leave now."

For a moment Lafayette's grin faded under the bleaching intensity of Ward's scowl.

"Okay, okay. I'm done playing with you. We're all gentlemen here. All friends. Okay. It was a hot day. So I took off in search of something to keep me occupied." He winked at them both but tried it with his missing eye and it lost its effect.

"Sometimes you drive forever and don't find a morsel. On this occasion, though, the Lord himself was smiling down on me and he handed me this little gift straight from heaven itself. He was walking down the street. Little boy lost. So I pulled up my vehicle and I asked him 'is you lost, little 'un?' And he cried at me and I said not to cry, I'd get him back to his parents in no time at all. And I scooped him up like his daddy might and I put him in the car. We drove a while and he starts crying again and I said not to worry, we going the scenic route and I'd have him back with his parents before dinner. Right after I'd taken him for ice cream. And he stops crying again. All young 'uns, they like ice cream. That itself is a blessing 'cause it shut him up a whiles longer. I think it was when he sees the woods that he set to crying again."

Ward saw that Newton was winding up for another crack at him. He looked over at Newton and caught his eye and Newton breathed out heavily through his nose.

"I have to warn you, while this is my personal favorite part, it might not be to everybody's taste."

Ward said, "Go on."

"Okay, you asked me to go on and I will go on."

Ward started tapping his foot as Lafayette went into more detail. He nipped his own leg to distract himself from what he was hearing. Newton just stared straight at Lafayette and didn't move a muscle. And all the while Lafayette's grin grew and Ward wanted to knock his remaining teeth out. In his head Ward hummed. He tried to take his mind out of the room but he heard every word and he wanted to kill the son of a bitch.

Lafayette let out a sigh. "And that's that. You can't write that shit."

Ward and Newton were silent for a few moments and then Ward said, "What did you do with the body?"

"Well, I buried it of course. Out there in the woods."

"Could you tell us where?"

"I could not do that. I can show but not tell. I reckon I can take you right to the spot. Could do with the fresh air, truth be told. And it'll bring back such sweet memories." He laughed.

Newton launched himself at him and Lafayette crashed heavily on the floor, his head clanging as it hit. The door was quickly opened and the guard was in. He said "whatthefuck?" and he dragged Newton off. Ward was on his feet but he was slow to react. He didn't know whether that was a conscious thing. He hoped it was.

Lafayette was dazed and he breathed heavily and then went into another coughing fit and this one dislodged a tooth and it sounded like a tiny pebble when it hit the floor. The guard sat him upright again and a single drop of blood fell from Lafayette's mouth onto the table. His grin returned and the extra gap took the grin to another level of sinister. His tongue examined the new gap.

"I'll take that for the tooth fairy," Lafayette said, looking on the floor for the tooth.

The guard guided Newton out the door and Ward

stood and stared at the bag of bones in front of him.

"Is there anything you want for this information?"

"I don't want nothing. Just doing my civic duty."

Ward followed Newton out. In the corridor, as the guard shuffled Lafayette out of the room, the old man shouted, "You ain't taken my confession."

Ward called back, "Go see the chaplain."

"Hey, hey! You didn't write it down. I ain't signed nothing. This is my kill. I want my kill."

"He said he didn't want anything. Does that sound right to you?"

Newton was still shaken. He heard Ward speaking with a slight time delay. "He didn't do it."

"What I was thinking. Why would he confess now after all this time and not want some kind of privileges?"

"He didn't do it."

"You still think O'Donnell did it?"

"Spent twenty-five years thinking he did. Knowing he did."

"And now?"

Newton clenched both fists and studied them for a few seconds. "Hold on a minute while I get my head around twenty-five years of being wrong."

"Don't mean you're wrong."

Newton turned his head to face Ward. "You know it does. Someone put Lafayette up to this."

"You think?"

"I know, son."

"Who?"

"Well, it sure as hell wasn't O'Donnell. But it's not just the who, it's the why that concerns me."

"Somebody wants the Ryan case to go away."

"I know it. But the deputy warden said Lafayette's had no visitors."

"My guess is somebody got a note slipped to him. Asking him to kindly confess to a crime he didn't commit. Somebody with connections inside the prison. Could be anybody." Could be a cop, Ward thought, but he kept the thought to himself. Larsson had as good as said that there was police involvement in Ryan's disappearance. But Ward didn't want to air that thinking just yet.

Newton said, "Who has something to lose by the truth coming out about what happened to Ryan?"

"Whoever took him."

"Don't you get the feeling there's more to it than that?"

"And we come back to the question of whether the two cases are linked."

Newton took a breath. "We solve one, we solve the other."

"Let's see. Little boy disappears. Grandpa gets killed twenty-five years later. Why now? Maybe he knew something and was about to tell. He mentioned a confession. Somebody got wind of that. O'Donnell knew who did it. He knew what happened to Ryan. That was what he wanted to confess to. So person unknown kills the boy and all these years later kills O'Donnell because he thinks that suddenly O'Donnell is going to confess to keeping his silence about what happened. Who would know about what went on that night in Sunny Glade? What O'Donnell said about confessing to something? Who then went and killed Doctor Brookline because he thought O'Donnell had maybe said something to the good doctor? O'Donnell only said two things when he blew up according to the girl. He mentioned a confession and he also mentioned Doctor Brookline. That got somebody spooked enough to kill the old man. And the doctor."

"I know who you're thinking."

Ward said, "Kenny."

"You still think Kenny's involved?" There wasn't really a question in Newton's voice. Sounded like a man coming to terms with an inevitable truth.

"Don't you?"

"I still think we have to tread careful with him."

"But you think—"

Newton cut him off. "What I think is that we've just been given a bit more to go on. And I mean it about treading carefully. If Kenny's involved, this thing could get dangerous."

"Look, Kenny was there that night. He has access to the pharmacy to get to the morphine that killed O'Donnell and Brookline. He has connections. Could've got Lafayette to confess to killing Ryan. If we agree that the two cases are linked it would do him good to pin the Ryan murder on somebody else. If we can't link the Ryan case with the O'Donnell case it weakens the O'Donnell case. Takes away motive."

"But no morphine was missing from the pharmacy."

"And that's a problem."

"A big problem."

"And what about the guy you say you saw? You thought he was Ryan."

"Could've been mistaken. I was mistaken twenty-five years about O'Donnell."

"We don't like him for O'Donnell? His prints were found on the windowsill of O'Donnell's room. But everything else about both scenes was clean. No prints anywhere else. So he's not our killer."

"But we still need to find him. Rule him out."

"And find out what the hell he's been doing going in and out of O'Donnell's room."

Newton turned the engine over and revved loudly. "All we know for certain is that piece of shit Lafayette didn't take Ryan."

"He really got to you."

"That thing in there?" Newton set the vehicle rolling. "There was some truth in it. He was describing another homicide he committed. He's down for two. Son of a bitch was describing one of those. 1987. A year after Ryan went missing. He was getting off on the memory. And I won't tolerate that."

54

"You take his confession?" Gammond was more animated than normal. His cheeks were sherry red. His thick mustache, gray for the most part, twitched on his lip as he chewed on an imaginary tidbit.

"He didn't do it."

"Come again?"

"He didn't do it."

"The heck he didn't."

"Lieutenant, he did not murder Ryan Novak."

"The heck he didn't. You want to go tell the captain that? The heck he didn't do it. I spoke to the dang deppity warden myself. Heard what the man said. He's our man. It all fits."

"You ask me, it all fits a bit too neatly."

"Too neatly my backsides, Newton. The guy made a convincing confession. You took his confession, right?"

"No, sir, I didn't. Because he didn't do it."

"Son of a gun. You get back there and take his dang confession in writing. He wants to claim a murder death, we let him."

"That's just it, though. He wants to claim it. Another trophy. Why now? Why wait? He didn't do it. I'm not taking no confession. You want his confession, you go get it. With the greatest respect. Sir. I have another homicide to investigate. The Ryan case is in the past."

Newton stood up as straight as his body would let him and he walked to the door. Gammond's face was nuclear but all he managed was to sputter a few sounds that approximated curse words.

55

His skin itched to the tune of jazz piano. Worms poked at every pore. His skin felt hot and tight and it hummed underneath the surface like a swarm of bees. He wanted to scream but the scream would have to come out of his pores and the worms were blocking them. He saw two tubes snaking over his stomach. One carrying blood and the other carrying something that looked like strawberry milkshake. He figured it was some kind of filtration system and he thought he saw insects in the milkshake. He counted – one, two, three, ten, nine, eight – over and over again and he paced in the room. He hugged himself but the hug took his breath as his broken ribs bent like rubber and then he thought he was his own prom date and he kissed his arm and then bit it and almost drew blood with his remaining teeth. He wanted to shit and so he tried to do it in his pants. But he didn't shit but he definitely pissed. Fuck, fuck, FUCK! No, no, no, no, no, no, no…

He smacked himself about the head with his fist. He screamed at the pain as the impact reverberated like a broken cymbal and his cracked cheekbone exploded into purple flame. And the scream came from the worms and they all stood off his skin like fat hairs and they swayed in a nonexistent wind. He fell to his knees. Scrabbled frantically in the debris on the floor and came up with nothing. There was just the gun. He knocked it aside and found an empty pill bottle, which he shook and shook but it made no noise. He'd done a dumb trade. He knew it. And he hurt. And he gasped. And he wished he was still in the hospital. And the worms screamed.

56

Larsson answered. Ward asked him one question. Asked if the FBI investigated Kenny. He got his answer and hung up the phone. He called his friend in the FBI's San Antonio field office.

Ward said, "Hi, Jake. It's Ward."

"Hey, Ward. How's it going there, my friend? More to the point, where the hell are you?"

"In Montana."

"Fuck. Are you crazy? It's fucking cold up there."

"I know. But it's mainly manageable."

"Rather you than me. I guess you're running? You hear anything from her now?"

"No, I don't."

"So, what is it you want? You want something, right?"

"I need some information. Public corruption case back in 1985, 1986. Name's James Kenny. Westmoreland, Montana. The case got canned but I wondered if you could get your hands on some bank details."

"What kind of investigation we talking about?"

"City Hall kickbacks. He's a property developer."

"You got something new on him?"

"No. It's unconnected. Another investigation. Homicide."

"Bro, I'll do my best for you. What is it you're looking for specifically?"

"I need his bank statements. Say for the entirety of 1986. I would expect the Bureau investigation would have that."

"That's if they haven't been destroyed. In any case, it might take some time. What's your urgency?"

"Ten."

"Okay. I'll see what I can do. Leave it with me."

"Do your best."

"You know it, bro."

57

Newton was sitting at his desk. He didn't focus on much. Just sat. Gammond walked over to him. He'd calmed down. He eyed Newton with concern.

"You want to finish early, I'd understand that. You don't need this."

Newton glanced at Gammond. "What about the investigation? Ward's out of the picture. Who's going to run that?"

"We can cover it. I don't want you to go overstretch yourself. This thing might run for a few weeks and you ain't got that time."

"I got all the time in the world." He drew himself up in his chair and tried for a resilient look. "We're getting closer anyways."

Gammond's calm expression threatened to crack like old paint but his voice remained quiet and full of concern. "You're getting old, Adam. You know you don't have nothing to prove. Not to me, not to nobody. Heck, I'm getting old myself."

Newton didn't say anything more.

Gammond said, "Internal Affairs going to be here tomorrow. For Ward."

Newton nodded. Gammond hung around for a spell and then retreated.

58

He still thought she looked beautiful even with her bruised face. Cherry was as busy as ever, taking orders from customers who tried not to look as if they were staring and wondering where she got those big purple trophies. Her confidence had returned a little and she seemed to enjoy the intrigue she was creating. She was wrong about one thing. It hadn't damaged her business. The place was busier than Ward had seen it.

She saw him walk in and her face brightened and a smile nearly broke on her face. She stifled the smile to avoid cracking open her split lip.

Ward took a seat. He had to settle for a table tucked away in the back wilderness of the diner beneath a half canoe that had been fixed to the wall. He sat for a while before Cherry came over. Ward took off his hat and tipped his head politely.

"What, no pooch?" Cherry said.

"I'm working. He's sleeping."

Cherry looked at him for a long while without saying anything.

"Working unofficially." He said it with a smile and he wanted to give her a hug but didn't.

"So, what can I get ya?"

"Can we start again?"

"That's exactly what we're doing." And Cherry smiled the half smile of someone with a cracked lip and she tilted her head to one side, waiting.

Ward said, "Well, ma'am, I'm feeling kinda partial to some cherry pie if you got some."

"Certainly, sir. And how would you like that? With whipped cream? Ice cream? Both?"

"I'd just as soon take it dry, ma'am."

"You got it, mister. Coming right up." Her hands were in the pocket on the front of her apron and she bent down and kissed him on his cheek. He held her hand.

"Do all your customers get a kiss?"

"Most of 'em. Yes." A laugh escaped her lips.

59

It's hot outside and in the station. There are two interview rooms and Newton has picked the starkest. It also happens to be the coolest room in the building but that hasn't suited Newton so he's had a portable heater brought in and now the room smells of scorched dust. Paint of an indeterminate color flakes off the walls like sunburnt skin. A light in the middle of the room flickers. There are dead insects – flies mainly, but not exclusively – in the yellowed plastic light enclosure.

The old police station had been falling apart at the seams for as long as Newton could remember. A new one had been promised from City funds a million times but they hadn't started building it yet. Probably wait until some masonry falls on some suspect, Newton thinks. Hell, they probably wouldn't worry if some masonry was to fall on him or his colleagues.

He'd been friendly enough when O'Donnell had entered the station. He'd led him to the interview room and had asked if he would like a coffee. O'Donnell had declined. Newton had said he'd get himself one and had left O'Donnell alone in the room.

He observes O'Donnell through the one-way glass. He

tries to gauge his demeanor. Tries to look for the usual signs of a guilty man. But he just sees a man sitting, looking at his hands, which are placed flat on the table. O'Donnell shows no emotion. Looks calm if anything. Newton goes toward the door and then remembers the coffee he had gone to get. He snatches a Styrofoam cup off somebody's desk. The somebody complains. Newton takes a sip as he enters the room. The coffee is awful. Bitter. Tepid. He suppresses the urge to spit it out but instead sips contentedly.

"You sure I can't get you one?"

"I'm fine, thank you." O'Donnell is clean shaven. He wears a neat check shirt and light cotton jacket. Newton had observed him during the searches and he had looked like a wild man of the woods then. And now he looks smart. A different shirt from the one he'd worn during the televised appeal for Ryan's safe return. Newton had studied the tape over and over again. He'd gotten a body language expert to watch it. And then he'd gotten them to watch it again but there was nothing there. No telltale signs of guilt. So he'd finally brought him in.

"Firstly, let me say we are still looking twenty-four hours a day for Ryan. The operation has brought in extra men from neighboring counties as well as the Sheriff's office. The searches are continuing and we have cast the net farther afield. Currently, we are following up on various sightings from members of the public and we are still hopeful of a resolution."

"You expect to find him alive?"

"We hope so, sir. We very much hope so."

O'Donnell nods. "It's been four days now. Don't they say you find them in forty-eight hours or not at all?"

"We'll keep looking. And we'll keep following up the leads. The trail isn't cold yet. Do you have anything else you would like to ask me?"

"No, sir. I guess you got me down here to do the asking yourself."

"Well, I've got a few questions."

Bill O'Donnell says, "When will I get my clothes back?"

"We'll get them back to you as soon as we can."

"Okay."

"I should make it clear, this is not an arrest situation. You have chosen not to request that a lawyer is present. Okay?"

"That's okay. Ain't got nothing to hide."

Newton takes a wander around the small room. He doesn't look at O'Donnell but O'Donnell's eyes follow him around.

"Are you and Ryan close?"

"Yes, sir, we was. We are."

"You say you was. In the past tense there."

"We are. We are close."

"You spend a lot of time together?"

"Whatever time I can manage, yes. I lived in the same house so I saw him a deal outside of work. Before his bedtime."

"You used the past tense again there."

"Sir, I don't mean to. I'm a little shaken is all."

"Of course. I understand." Newton takes another sip of the awful coffee. "But you didn't see him before his bedtime the night he went missing?"

"No, sir. I had to take care of something at the school."

"Oh? What something?"

"There was a water leak in one of the bathrooms. You can check. I was seen there."

"We will. And when you came home you assumed Ryan was in bed, that right?"

"That's right."

"And then your truck gets stolen and you take off after the people who took it."

"Correct, sir."

"Not knowing that Ryan was missing. His bed wasn't slept in."

"I didn't look in on him."

"You usually look in on him?"

"No, sir. Not always."

"But you were close."

"Yes, sir, but I don't always look in on him."

"Okay." He takes a slow breath. *"Is Ryan a little wild at times?"*

"Just a usual kid. Not overly rambunctious but occasionally... You know."

"He's a normal kid." Newton smiles. *"They get into things, don't they?"*

"He gets into things, yes. But he's mostly a good boy."

"Wouldn't run away? Isn't the type to up and wander off on his own?"

"Not the Ryan I know. No. Wouldn't normally do that."

"Any reason recently why he might feel the need to do that?"

"I don't know what you mean."

"You know. Is he happy? At home?"

"He was happy as I saw it. Like I said, he's a usual kid."

"Yes. Yes. He ever get into a sulk? When you had to chastise him?"

"Didn't need to chastise him, mostly. Again, like I said. He's a good boy."

Newton nods and smiles. "I'm not surprised to hear that. It's what everybody is saying." Newton suddenly sits down and looks directly into O'Donnell's eyes. He sees now that they're bloodshot. His heavy lids seem to cast shadows that sit below the eyes. "So you never had to raise your voice to him?"

O'Donnell's gaze has become stuck to Newton's. "Can't ever recall, sir. No."

"How about his parents? They ever raise their voices at Ryan? They ever need to discipline him?"

"That's something maybe you should ask them."

Newton smiles. "I'm asking you."

"They've done their best, I'm sure about that."

"His father ever raise a hand to him?"

"No, sir. Not outside of the usual."

"The usual?"

"Sir, I can't recall ever seeing anything. Would tell you if I had."

"No, no, that's fine. We have to ask these questions. Sometimes they seem pointless but it helps build up a picture of Ryan and his home life. Anything. Any little thing might help us to find him. You understand that?"

"Yes."

"So, this truck of yours. You reported it missing the night before Ryan was discovered missing."

"That's right." Bill O'Donnell moves for the first time. Adjusts his seating position. Then returns to the calm, almost serene stare.

"You said some young boys took it."

"That's right, sir. I saw 'em."

"Oh. I thought you said you didn't see them."

"I meant I saw 'em before. Ran 'em off. I'm guessing it was the same lot."

"And you can't give me a description of them."

"It would've been dark. My eyes ain't what they was."

Newton smiles again. "You wear glasses for that?"

"No, sir. I manage."

Newton turns the coffee cup in his hands. O'Donnell's eyes focus on Newton's hands. When Newton looks up, so O'Donnell looks up. As if coming out of a trance, Newton thinks.

"You went to church. We have people say they saw you."
"You been asking questions about me?"
"You went to church."
"I did."
"To pray for the return of your grandson?"
"No. I went before I knew Ryan was missing."
"To pray for the return of your truck?"
"No, sir."
"You a regular churchgoer?"
"No, sir, I was passing."
"You were passing and you suddenly felt the urge to go in? It was a black church, no?"
"Yes, sir. They was mainly negroes."
"So, suddenly you go to church for the first time in what, ever?"
"I been to church before."
"But not for a while."
"No, sir."
"And you chose a black church."
"That's right."
"Why did you suddenly get the urge to go to church?"
"I was passing."
"That it? You were passing. No other reason?"
"No, sir. I was passing."
"Can you understand how that might look a bit odd to me?"
"I can, sir. But I went in and that's all there is to it. Nothing more."

"Do you know what's happened to Ryan?"

The question wakes O'Donnell's eyes. "Seems to me you could've asked me that question to start with."

"Well, I'm asking you now, Bill. Do you know where Ryan is? If you do know anything you should tell me now. Were you in that church praying for your mortal soul for what you did?"

O'Donnell closes his eyes. He opens them and stands up. His eyes settle on Newton's. "Sir, I appreciate what you're doing to find Ryan. I genuinely am appreciative of that." And then he opens the door. He stands in the doorway with his back to Newton for a few seconds.

"Where is he, Bill? Where's the boy, Bill?"

And then Bill O'Donnell leaves. Newton remains seated and he drums his fingers slowly on the table, sweat bathing his face.

60

He shoved the gun down the front of his baggy sweatpants and put on his jacket over his hoodie. He pulled the hood over his head and zipped it up as far as it would go, and then he left his room. On the stairs he passed an old man with a long gray beard and the man said something to Troy which Troy didn't quite catch and he took the gun from his pants and waved it in front of the man's face. The man spun around and fell back onto the stairs and he put his hands over his face. Troy smiled and said, "Yeah, you see. You see!" And he hopped down the stairs and scurried out into the freezing cold and all the while he was smiling and muttering to himself.

Ward couldn't see the door from where he sat. Couldn't see much through the windows either, past heads that bobbed up and down like cattle feeding from a trough. Couldn't see Cherry but she was probably in back picking up orders. He saw a couple of heads turn to the door and he moved in his seat to get a better view. He couldn't see at first and then he saw

Cherry emerge from the kitchen and she dropped the tray she was carrying, the order spilling over the floor. Ward was on his feet and he banged into the table where he sat and nearly fell as he twisted himself out of the booth, almost wrenching the table from the bolts that held it down. He heard gasps and cutlery falling to the floor and people shrunk back away from Troy, whose head Ward could just see. The first thing Ward noticed were the bruises he had decorated Troy's face with. The broken nose. The grin with gaps where three teeth used to be but had been pulled. And then Troy came into full view and Ward saw the gun which Troy still had shoved down the front of his pants. He'd pulled open his jacket and flashed the gun to the diners and to Cherry. Ward reached for his gun but it wasn't there.

Troy shouted, "Draw," and he pulled out the gun and waved it in Ward's direction and he grinned. He scratched his head like a dog with a flea.

Cherry was frozen to the spot and Ward noticed that she was trembling. He looked at her and willed her to look at him and she did. He nodded the smallest of nods to say "it's okay" and he was desperate that she remain calm.

"If you ain't gonna draw I might have to shoot you down dead cold-blooded," Troy said. His speech had a slight lisp now where his tongue poked through the gap in his teeth.

"I'm unarmed," Ward said, and he held his hands out at his sides.

"Let's see," Troy said.

Ward slowly opened his jacket to show there was nothing there.

"Turn around. You ain't got something shoved down the back of your pants, have you?"

Ward turned around and lifted his jacket.

"Oh, well, that's just too bad. Seems I got the upper hand this time," Troy said, and he laughed and he scratched. Ward could see that he was shaking and his pupils were wide and wild. And he stank like something old and rotten.

Someone by the window, an old man with a long journey etched onto his dark brown face, said, "Now calm down, son," and Troy spun around and pointed the gun at him and then swung back quickly to point it back at Ward.

"Let these people go," Ward said. "You don't need them here."

Troy gave Ward a puzzled look. "Oh? Are you in charge here, huh? That right, huh?"

"No, you are. And I'm asking you to let these people go if you wouldn't mind."

"If I wouldn't mind? If I wouldn't mind. If I wouldn't mind."

"It's your call but how do you know one of them hasn't got a gun of their own concealed on them and about to blow your head off?"

Troy looked around the diner. "Anybody got a gun?"

A few people mumbled "no" and a woman screamed and grabbed her young daughter and pulled her close and said, "Please don't hurt us."

Troy laughed. "Have you got a gun, missus?"

The woman shrunk back and cried, "No."

"Well, then, be fucking quiet if, you, wouldn't, mind."

237

Ward said, "It's okay, ma'am, I'm a police officer," but it made no difference to the woman, who sobbed along with her daughter.

"Troy, I'm asking you as the person who's running this show to let these people go," Ward said. "You don't need them here. I'm here and not going anywhere. Simplify things for yourself. Makes no sense keeping them here."

Troy seemed to mull it over. He tilted his head from one side to the other with an exaggerated puzzled look on his face. He waved the gun around at the people and they variously ducked, gasped and screamed. "The man in charge, me, says you all can go. Please do so in an orderly fashion. If you wouldn't mind." Troy was smiling at his new favorite phrase. "Nice and orderly if you wouldn't mind."

The door swung open and the cold wind blew in and people filed out quickly, keeping as much distance as they could between themselves and Troy. The diner was empty in seconds. Empty save for Troy, Ward and Cherry. Cherry, who all the while had not said a word and had stood statue-still just to the side of Troy.

Troy took a step to his left and, without taking his eyes off Ward, he scooped up a couple of chicken wings from a plate. He dropped one and started to chew on the other, getting the sauce smeared around his mouth. Ward and Cherry watched him eat. Troy tossed the half-eaten chicken wing on the floor, licked his fingers and then wiped them on his pants.

"Ain't so easy to eat with these missing." He gestured toward his mouth.

"What do you want?" Cherry said.

"I want what's due to me."

"What's that?"

"A slice of the profits."

Ward said, "If you want money, Cherry here will get you some."

"The fuck I will," Cherry said. "We're not doing this anymore, Troy. It stops here."

Ward looked at Cherry but she wouldn't look at him. She stared straight into Troy's bloodshot eyes.

"If you want money you'll have to fucking shoot me first."

Ward kept quiet. Just watched to try and judge what Troy might do. Waited for an opportunity. Maybe Cherry's stubbornness might give him that opportunity. Or maybe it would get them both killed.

"Whatever it takes," Troy said.

They all heard the sirens and they all turned to look out of the window.

"Looks like you're out of luck," Cherry said.

Troy grabbed at his matted hair. "I still got me a couple hostages. But I ain't leaving without what's my due." He turned to Ward as cars screeched to a halt and the guy Ward had never seen before who worked in the kitchen came into view and ran out to meet them. He ducked behind one of the cars. The one which Newton climbed out of.

"You. Get the takings," Troy said to Ward.

Ward turned to Cherry.

"If you do I'll have that gun off him and kill the both of you," Cherry said.

Ward played for time. He could see them outside taking positions. Newton, Mallory, Poynter and two other guys he couldn't make out. "Look. He's got a gun and he's asking for money. I think we should give him what he wants and then he can leave." Ward knew that would get a reaction.

"He gets nothing. Everything here is mine. I've worked my ass off to make this work. You've seen what he did to me." She pointed at her face. "This. Remember? Remember?"

"Hey, whoa, whoa," Troy said. "We don't want a lovers' tiff here." And then he spoke to Ward through his teeth. "I'll tell you once more. Get me the fucking money, pig."

Ward held up his hands. "Okay, okay." He looked at Cherry. "Listen to me. This is how it goes. We let him have the money, he leaves, the officers outside shoot him dead. You get your money back. How's that sound?"

"How about I shoot you dead?" Troy waved he gun in front of Ward's face and Ward hoped his finger wasn't as twitchy as the rest of him.

Cherry looked at Ward and then at Troy, who both looked outside. She looked at the cops taking aim. She heard Newton shout something but the wind took his words.

Ward heard Newton's words though. He had told Troy that there were armed police outside.

"Okay. Get him the money from the register," Cherry said.

The short order cook from the Honey Pie Diner had called. Someone with a gun was there. The caller had managed to sneak out back. Newton called him back on his cell. The guy identified himself as Richard. He told Newton it was Troy with the gun. Newton knew.

He was already in his SUV and tearing down the street. Mallory and three others followed in two cars which lit up the town with sirens and lights. Mallory had taken the SPR sniper rifle from the gun cabinet.

They pulled up on the opposite side of the road to the diner and parked in a three-vehicle V formation. By then Newton had been told that there were only three people left inside: Ward, Cherry and Troy. Still a few of the other customers stood around at a safe distance. Poynter ushered them back to a safer one.

"Don't shoot," Newton said to Mallory, who was checking his rifle. Mallory clicked off the safety and took aim from behind his car door. He loosened his jacket. The other two officers, Davenport and Wheeler, had their pistols drawn and pointed at the diner.

"You listening to me? Don't shoot. He's too close to Ward."

"I'm just taking aim, sir," Mallory said, and he stroked his greasy hair back and adjusted his sights. "I have a shot, sir."

"Well, don't be taking it but on my say-so."

"Yes, sir."

Newton cupped his hands and called out across the street. "Armed police officers. Drop your weapon." The cold wind pinched at his cheeks. He saw the three figures looking his way. He'd made contact.

"Okay, easy. Easy," he said to his men. "We've got Ward and the owner in there."

Mallory licked his thin lips and smiled.

Ward moved slowly.

"No funny business," Troy said. "Just get me my

money and then we'll all leave."

"Okay," Ward said, and he went behind the counter. The cash register was at one end and Troy kept the gun trained on him all the way.

"Keep your hands above the counter where I can see them."

Ward held his hands above shoulder height. When he reached the cash register he wasn't sure how to open it. Cherry reached into her pocket and Troy saw the movement and he spun around.

"Hey, hey. What you doing?"

"He needs a card. To get your money." The electronic card was fastened to a retractable cord fixed to a belt loop on her pants. She unclipped it and tossed it to Ward. Ward caught it. Troy seemed even more twitchy. He switched the gun to his other hand and then switched it back. Ward could see that he was sweating and a smell of fresh piss wafted towards his nostrils. There was a stain on Troy's gray sweatpants. Ward figured it wasn't sweat. He tried to slow things down.

"Okay, I'm going to open the register and get you your money." He swiped the card. Nothing happened.

"Is this a trick?" Troy moved over to Ward and he craned over to see the closed register.

"You need a code," Cherry said. "3, 8, 4, 9. Swipe and then 3, 8, 4, 9. That opens it."

"Okay, do it," Troy said. Ward did. The cash register opened. Ward levered the clips that held the notes down and took everything out. He handed it over to Troy.

"There's the money."

Cherry said, "My fucking money," and Ward could

see the anger in her red cheeks.

Troy took the money with his left hand and tried a quick count with his gun hand. Ward could see he was trembling worse now. He saw the gun fall out of Troy's hand. He saw Cherry's eyes flash down. He saw her go to pick up the gun. He saw Troy shove her back. He saw the money flutter to the ground. He saw it all in slow motion. But he was the wrong side of the counter. And then he saw Troy bend and come back up with the gun. He saw the barrel point at him. And then he heard the shot.

Newton opened the back door of his SUV. He searched for a megaphone. Wanted to set up a dialogue with Troy. He knew Troy and he knew the boy wasn't right. Convictions on drug charges were one thing. Waving a gun around in a public place was a big step up. He lifted a road sign but the loud hailer wasn't there. He moved a box to one side but it wasn't there. And then he heard the shot.

Ward thought he was dead for a moment. He felt something like a tap on his shoulder as if someone was trying to get his attention. He heard glass breaking somewhere and he looked behind him and the mirror behind the counter was shattered. He saw the hole in the diner's front window and knew that a colleague outside had taken a shot. He realized then that the bullet had grazed his jacket but missed his flesh. He saw Troy holding his hand and saw blood and he heard the clunk of the gun hitting the floor. He saw

Cherry make a move towards the gun.

Newton screamed, "Mallory!" Mallory was taking aim for another shot and Newton lurched over and kicked his arms. The gun fell to the ground. "Goddamn it, Mallory, I said not to shoot!" Newton raced into the middle of the street and he could see Troy holding his hand and he saw the surprise on his face. He couldn't see the gun in Troy's hand. He saw Cherry move quickly and pick something up from the floor.

She had the gun. She held it with both hands and pointed it at Troy. She kicked him in the leg and he came out of his shock. He even said "ouch". When he saw the gun he flinched and held his hands up to his face. Blood dripped from a gash on the heel of his right hand.

"Cherry," Ward said. "Hand me the gun."

"How does this feel, huh? How does it fucking feel?" Cherry screamed into Troy's ear. Troy cowered.

"Don't shoot. Please. Don't hurt me."

"Cherry. Give me the gun." Ward was out from behind the counter now and he held out both hands as he walked slowly towards Cherry.

"Don't come no closer," she said. She was crying. "Don't come no closer."

"Cherry. Listen to me. You don't want to do this. This is not the way this ends. Come on. Hand me the gun."

"Hand him the gun," Troy said.

Cherry sniffled. She said, "This is the last time you

do this to me." She looked at Ward and Ward thought there was an apology in her eyes. She put the gun to Troy's head. Troy whimpered. Cherry pulled the trigger. Her eyes were closed. Ward leapt at her, knocking Troy out of the way. He snatched the gun from Cherry's hand.

"The safety was on," he said.

"I know how to use a gun," Cherry said. "I wanted him to fear me." She turned and walked towards the door.

Troy was on his knees. Cherry passed Newton and one of the other officers on her way out. Poynter grabbed her as she exited and she hugged him and she sobbed.

Ward kicked Troy onto his front and Newton said, "You okay?"

The officer cuffed Troy and started to pull him to his feet, blood dripping from the gash on Troy's hand.

"I got him," Newton said. "Wait outside."

The officer seemed confused.

"I said I got it. Tell Mallory and the others they speak to me before filing any reports on this."

"Yes, sir," said the officer and he let Troy drop to his knees and he left the diner.

Newton grabbed Troy's hair and he pulled his face towards his. Troy saw Newton's face upside down.

"Have you got your faculties intact, son?" Newton said to Troy. Troy didn't react. Newton cuffed him across his head and came around and crouched down in front of him.

"Okay, okay," Troy said.

"Good. Ordinarily I don't cut deals with punk-ass little bastards like you but I'm gonna cut you one so listen up and listen up good. You're going to sign me a statement that says Ward didn't assault you and it was one of your junkie cohorts who took offense at you owing him money. And then you're going to leave this town and you're never going to come back. Because if you do, and know this for a goddamn certain fact as sure as Christmas, I will put a bullet in your head myself and call it an unfortunate accident while you was resisting arrest. You got that?"

Troy stared at Newton. His nose started to bleed a little. And then he nodded and a speck of blood dripped onto his jacket.

Newton said, "I ought to kill you right here and now, you son of a bitch."

"You could've killed me." Ward was in Mallory's face. He pointed to the scuff mark on the shoulder of his jacket where the bullet had grazed it.

Mallory smiled. "Didn't, though. Maybe I'm not as good a shot as I thought."

Ward punched him and he felt something crunch in his hand, a lightning bolt of pain shooting up his arm. Mallory's knees buckled and he fell to the ground. Newton pulled Ward away. Ward shook out the pain but it wouldn't go. Might have been broken already from Troy's beating. Now it was definitely broken.

"Mallory. Stay down, son. You heard my orders. You got it coming a long time."

Mallory wiped the blood from his nose and spat a pink gooey spit on the pavement. Ward thought the red paintwork on his picket fence teeth suited him. He turned and walked towards Cherry.

61

The little boy, Percy, sits on a chair next to Newton's desk. He has a can of Coca-Cola in his hand and he looks around the station with wide eyes. His father is standing next to him and he stares sternly at the detective, who is leaning forward in his chair.

"Just tell me what happened," Newton says. "You saw Ryan, right?"

The little boy looks at his father, who nods.

"I saw him in the street. He seemed kinda upset so I asked him if he was okay and he didn't say nothing. I put my arm around him to try to cheer him up but he wasn't in no mood for talking. I let him be and he walked off."

"Did he say anything at all? Did he say where he was headed?"

"Didn't say nothing. He was sniveling."

"Was he hurt, you think?"

"Didn't seem it. Just sniveling."

"Did you see anybody else or was he on his own?"

"I didn't see nobody else apart from Mister Parrish, who drove past and I waved at him."

Percy's father says, "Ray Parrish."

Newton nods without taking his eyes off Percy. "So, did

you see which way Ryan went?"

"He just carried on walking up the street."

"And you..."

"I just doubled back," Percy says and then tears appear in his eyes. "I just wish I'd stayed with him and then maybe he wouldn't be missing and maybe..."

"It's okay, son," his father says, and he puts a hand on Percy's shoulder. "Say, can we wrap this up now? Boy's getting tired."

"Of course," Newton says, and he puts a hand on the boy's knee and squeezes gently. "You've been a great help. Hey, how about you come back in sometime and we'll give you a full tour of the station. Show you everything. You like that?"

Percy nods and his father smiles.

"Thanks for coming in," Newton says to Percy's father.

"No problem. And if there's anything I can do to help. I guess times like these we all pull together as a town and do what we can."

"That's what we do."

He watches them stand and leave and he stares at the skittish boy, whose legs move quickly at the side of his father's long stride. Something about the boy. He shakes the thought out of his head.

62

"Funeral's tomorrow. You'll be there?" Newton said.

"I didn't realize they'd released the old man's body. And I'm still suspended."

"Not for long. I got that in hand." Newton touched Ward's arm. "Good work back there."

"Thanks. Mallory takes a good shot."

"He does. Even if he is slow-minded. Go get that hand seen to. It's met too many chins recently. Probably broken."

"I know it."

63

Everybody was gathered around the whiteboard, which had various pieces of evidence from the case and Ward's scribblings. Newton stared at the board as Ward walked into the station. Mallory offered him a glare and Ward ignored it as he drew up alongside Newton. His hand was strapped up lightly. Looked like a homemade solution.

"Okay?" Ward asked. Newton didn't reply at first. Just stared at the board.

"I'm looking but not seeing," Newton said, and he rubbed the base of his back.

"You want to take this?" Ward said. Newton nodded and then he turned to the gathered police. "Okay, we'll keep this brief. We got pressure to get a result. I know you've already done it but I want everybody to take a look at what we've got. Go over things again. Ask each other questions. The victim is being buried today at Gabriel Heights. I want Mallory and Poynter there but at a respectful distance. Take an unmarked car. Park on the cemetery road where we have eye contact. Myself and Ward will be there too. We keep an eye out for anyone who stands out. Our perpetrator could be there so keep vigilant. Anyone raises any suspicions, we take them after the funeral. You got that?"

Mallory grunted and Poynter nodded. Newton handed out the facial composite he had had made up of the man he thought was Ryan Novak.

"This man is a person of interest. Extreme interest. If you see this person you let me or Ward know. Don't spook him. You listening, Mallory? No fuck ups."

"Yes, sir," Mallory said in a low rumble, the left side of his face sporting fresh bruising.

Newton said, "Okay. That's it. Any questions?"

Nobody said a word.

"Okay, good, then." And then Newton walked to his desk. Poynter took his usual place by McNeely's desk and admired her as she ate. Mallory loped away like a coyote, nervously looking at Ward as he walked past him.

Ward was about to follow Newton to his desk when Newton suddenly spun around and pushed past Ward. He looked at the evidence board.

"Son of a bitch," he said.

"What is it?" Ward said.

Newton unpinned the copy of the photo of Ryan Novak from the board. "Look."

Ward looked at the photo. "You're going to have to give me a clue."

"Son of a goddamned bitch. 1985. That's when Ryan disappeared. You see 1985 in this photograph?"

"Could be," Ward said.

"Look again. At the TV."

Ward squinted at the photo and he steadied Newton's hand which had begun to shake. He saw it then. On the television behind Ryan."

"We sure it's what it is?"

"Can only be one thing. That's the inauguration of Bill Clinton. 1993, no? Ryan was already gone a few years."

Ward took a closer look. "McNeely."

McNeely was already there. With a magnifying glass. Ward looked at the photo again. He nodded at Newton.

"That's not Ryan," Newton said. "The old guy had this photo in his room."

"Hidden behind the Bermuda picture," Ward added.

"But that's not Ryan. Now why would he keep this? Who is this?"

"The writing on the back. John 1 20. It's not a Bible reference. It's the date the photo was taken. The date of Clinton's inauguration. Gotta be. Always in January, right?"

"So he's called John. John Doe."

"My guess is this is your guy. The guy you chased."

"The guy who bears a striking resemblance to Ryan Novak."

Ward scratched the back of his neck. "Ryan's mother had another child. A stillbirth."

"You don't—do you think…" Newton's words trailed off into a forest of questions.

"We need to go back to Alice White," Ward said.

64

By the time Newton, Ward, Mallory and Poynter rolled out of the station parking lot it had started to snow. Small flakes of snow that dusted the roadside and sidewalks. Mallory managed to pull out a skid as he joined the street. As they left a car pulled past them into the parking lot.

"Internal Affairs," Newton said. "Nobody's told them. A long way to come for a wasted journey. We'll let Gammond explain."

"Snow," Ward said.

"Been coming a while now," Newton said.

They pulled into the cemetery entrance and drove up a short ramp, then swung left onto the eastern pavement. They could see a gathering of people up ahead and others making their way from the parked cars. There were dozens of parked cars, recently arrived from the Westmoreland Gospel Church where they had whooped their hallelujahs and Bill O'Donnell had been commended to God, his redeemer and judge.

Ward and Newton stopped a short distance away and Mallory and Poynter drew up behind them in their unmarked car. Nobody turned to look at them. Just walked with heads down, some bearing handkerchiefs, sobbing. A raven's distant call, and then another closer, shot through the somber moans.

And the people streamed up towards the grave and their numbers swelled. Many were black.

"From his church," Newton said but didn't need to.

They sat in the car as the flakes of snow settled on the windshield and then melted, fifty at a time, and then another fifty. There was a covering on the ground and Ward leaned forward and looked up at the sky.

"Okay, let's go," Newton said, and he opened the door and squeezed himself from behind the wheel, holding his breath as his back threatened to spasm.

They crossed to where the people snaked towards the graveside, moving slowly as if all were pallbearers carrying a giant's burden. Newton and Ward joined them and Newton turned to check on Mallory and Poynter. He saw the fidgeting shape of Mallory with binoculars.

They walked up the hill and as it leveled off the gathering masses of people had come to a halt and the people shook hands and they touched arms and some hugged. There was Principal Taylor. Other teachers and members of the school staff.

A hand touched Newton's arm and it was Alice White and her eyes were wet but her mouth smiled. Newton smiled uncertainly back at her and they walked together to the graveside, her arm intersecting his, and Ward followed behind, his eyes working through the people. There was a mist of calm cast over them all and the blanket of low snow clouds seemed to muffle the sobs and the murmured conversations as it came down thick and sticky.

The casket was there, suspended on straps fastened to a metal frame which bordered Bill O'Donnell's final resting place. Snow had already covered the top. The people circled it like crows in a meadow of marble and granite, and the sobs grew and silenced the murmurs. Reverend Adrien Baptiste weaved in and out of the gathering and offered comforting words in a deep rumble which seemed to spiral through his congregation.

As Alice and Newton reached the graveside, people made way for them and Alice said "thank you" and Newton let her arm drop but she grabbed his hand and pulled him gently forward. They stood at the head of the closed casket and Newton stared at it with teddy bear eyes and a tear ran down his cheek and he almost coughed out a sob but choked it back. Alice noticed and she gently turned him to face her so she looked directly into his eyes.

"He's found his peace," she said. "Now can you?"

And the sob came out. And then Newton gulped in air and swallowed the rest of it, his eyes streaming.

Ward had deliberately held back. From where Newton and Alice stood line of sight with Mallory and Poynter was lost, and Ward knew that Newton was lost now too. And he understood.

The Reverend took his place beside the casket and the sobbing grew in intensity and then he started to speak. Ward tried to remain still but he struggled to see as many faces as he would like and he rocked on his heels, side to side, with the rhythm of Reverend Baptiste's words and tried to crane a look at faces opposite, at faces beside him. None of the faces rang alarm bells. And as Reverend Baptiste's words settled on him like the snowflakes falling from the heavens, Ward turned to look over at Mallory and Poynter.

For a moment he didn't see the man. He saw Poynter tug Mallory's arm first. And then he saw him. Mallory was waving at Ward with both arms and indicating the man who strode towards him and Ward knew it was him. He wore a thick padded coat and a wool hat and an extra hood. He could take him before he got to the other grievers. Mallory and Poynter were out of the car, ready to make a move on Ward's order. Mallory shifted from one foot to the other like he was wearing tight boots. Ward turned towards Newton, who had his back to him, but Alice White was looking at Ward and looking beyond Ward and her eyes closed for a second or two and she nodded her head slowly. When Ward turned back to the man he was almost upon them but still far enough away for Ward to slip out and take him but he didn't. He settled into the service again and then he heard the footsteps running up the hill.

Mallory was sprinting towards the man and the man turned and saw him. He turned to Alice and then back to Mallory and he looked to turn and run but Mallory was there then and Mallory dived for the man's feet as the man made the decision to run too late and Mallory was on top of him as the man swung his arms, his scrambling feet struggling to grip on the snow-covered ground.

The commotion had the congregation craning to see what was happening and shocked voices gasped and murmured. Reverend Baptiste stopped speaking and he rose up on his toes and he bellowed, "What is this?"

Mallory was on top of the man, who wriggled

desperately to be free, but Mallory had his giant hands around the man's forearms now, pinning him to the ground. As the man struggled he tossed his head from side to side and the hat and hood shook free and Mallory looked straight into his face and he said, "It's you."

Ward dragged Mallory off the man and Mallory fell back and sat on the ground.

"What are you doing?" Ward said. "What the hell—"

Mallory looked up at Ward and said, "I'm making an arrest."

"We won't have this. Not here and not now," the Reverend boomed.

Ward said to Mallory, "Get away," and he tried to take the hand of the other man to help him to his feet but the man waved Ward away and he just lay there with his hands in fists at his temple, his eyes shut tight and his clothes spattered with dirty snow. Ward thought he looked like a little boy who had been beaten on by a bully.

It was Alice who went to him and calmed him down with soothing words. The man slowly and shakily raised himself up onto one knee and then both feet and Alice led him away, up to the top of the hill and the graveside where Newton still stood.

Mallory got to his feet then and he turned and stomped back down the hill, the snow underfoot once trying to fell him. Ward watched him all the way back to his car and Mallory jumped straight in and slammed the door closed and then Ward heard the deep voice of Reverend Baptiste start up again.

* * *

As Reverend Baptiste reached the end of the committal prayer a wail went up from somebody out of Ward's sight and everybody said "amen." Ward saw that Newton's hand was covered in dirt and Alice White took hold of it. The casket began its descent and Reverend Baptiste led the congregation in the Lord's Prayer and Ward joined them. The man's arm was across Alice White's juddering shoulders and Ward didn't take his eyes off him.

Then the Reverend started singing "Just a Closer Walk With Thee," and around thirty voices joined him and it became darker around them all or so it seemed.

"He's one of my children," Alice White said to Ward. Newton looked on and didn't say anything. "He'll come with you."

Ward had his hand on his handcuffs.

"He'll come. No need for handcuffs, detective."

Ward relaxed and he guided the man away. The man wiped his face on the back of his hand. And then again with the other hand. Ward waited until they were far enough away from the others before he softly uttered the Miranda warning. The man nodded to indicate he'd understood Ward. The man then looked over his shoulder and Alice White held up her hand. Ward walked him down the hill to the car. Mallory and Poynter drove away before they got there. Newton joined them a minute later and the journey to the station was silent.

65

Bill O'Donnell is painting some ironwork. He stops as Newton's car pulls into the school parking lot. Newton speaks from a distance and he notices O'Donnell's free hand clench into a fist.

"We found a truck, looks like yours."

O'Donnell waits until Newton has reached him before answering, and he speaks in a low voice, looking around him as he does.

"I'd have preferred it if we could've kept this away from the school."

"Don't you want to know about your truck? I would've thought that would be your main concern."

"My main concern is the whereabouts of Ryan." *He unclenches his fist.*

"Of course. Of course. But it's good news about your truck at least."

"You're trying to get a rise out of me, detective."

Newton smiles. "I'm just the bearer of good news."

O'Donnell returns to his painting and he turns his back on Newton.

"Just doing some tests on it. And then you can have it back."

O'Donnell stops painting again. He turns to Newton and his tired eyes become smoldering firecrackers. "I'll be out looking for Ryan after work. I'll let you know if I find anything," he says. He dips his brush in the pot of paint and pulls it out clumsily, splashing paint around Newton's shoes. Newton steps back quickly and glares at Bill O'Donnell. Bill O'Donnell sloshes paint onto the ironwork.

66

"We need the death certificate for the Novaks' stillborn child," Newton said to McNeely. "And run the prints you've just taken against the ones from the windowsill. As soon as you can."

McNeely watched Ward lead the man to one of the interview rooms.

"That our killer?" she asked Newton.

Newton shrugged and he still had the dirt on his hand. He went into Gammond's office. Moments later he left Gammond's office and Gammond followed, his face red and stern.

Ward was sitting opposite the man who looked like Ryan and Newton entered the room and sat next to Ward. Ward turned on the tape recorder and read the man his rights again. The man nodded again to show he'd understood and his eyes bulged as if he was fighting back tears.

"You should have an attorney present, son," Newton said.

The man looked up at Newton and then looked up

at the camera and shook his head jerkily.

"You have a name?" Ward asked.

The man looked beyond Ward. Didn't say anything.

"How should we address you, son? John?" Newton said.

Nothing came back. Newton looked at Ward, who just eyed the prisoner.

"Can we get you anything? You thirsty? Hungry?" No response to Ward's question.

"Okay, we're going to ask you some questions. We proceed on the assumption that you understand what's happening here as you nodded to indicate as such." Newton said it for the tape and the camera and the man nodded.

"Are you currently taking drugs?"

No response. Just the long stare, bloodshot eyes. Newton let the question breathe.

"Do you have access to drugs? Legal drugs? Medical drugs?"

No response.

"Can you account for your whereabouts on Sunday, January twenty-fourth?"

Just the stare.

"Were you in or near the Sunny Glade Nursing Home? You remember?"

A couple of quick blinks.

"Do you know William O'Donnell, known also as Bill O'Donnell?"

No response.

"We found some fingerprints on the windowsill of Mr. O'Donnell's room up at Sunny Glade. I think they're yours, aren't they?"

The man looked confused and trembled as if he was

about to cry. He looked down at the ink on his fingers.

"Okay. We need to make the questions easier." He invited Ward into the one-way conversation.

Ward said, "Did you murder William O'Donnell?"

The man's eyes focused on Ward. Ward waited for the question to settle.

"I'll ask you that again in case you didn't get it the first time. Did you murder William O'Donnell?"

The man's distant stare returned and tears started to form and he bit his bottom lip. Ward looked at Newton and Newton stood up and indicated for Ward to follow him out of the room.

"Please would you excuse us," Newton said.

Outside the room Gammond was watching the interview on a small screen. McNeely was there. And Poynter.

"Talkative little shithead, ain't he?" Gammond said.

Newton turned his back on him and said to Ward, "You think he could have killed O'Donnell?"

Ward shook his head. "No. But it would be nice to know what he's been doing up there."

"You think he's a bit simple?" And he pulled Ward away as Ward shrugged. Out of Gammond's hearing range. "Alice said he's her boy."

"We need to go talk to her anyway," Ward said. "We bring her back in? See if she can get him to cooperate?"

"Worth a try."

Newton said, "Looks like Ryan grown up, don't he?"

"He his dead brother? That would make him O'Donnell's grandson. I guess that's a reason for the visits."

"Why through the window?"

"Because he doesn't exist. He's a secret. And secrets don't walk through the front door."

"We need Alice to make sense of this. McNeely. You got that death certificate yet?"

"On it, sir," she said. "The prints. Positive match." And she skipped away.

Newton took the copy of the photo of the little boy from the evidence board as he and Ward grabbed their coats, Ward grabbed his hat, and they left.

67

The snow had stopped falling and already the thin covering had frozen to a crunch. Blue sky cracked through thinning cloud and javelins of sunlight stabbed the earth.

They were at Alice White's house inside of ten minutes despite the slow drive. Alice was at the open door and she disappeared inside as they walked up and they followed her in. They both stamped their feet. Ward left his hat on.

"Wonderful service. So glad you could make it," Alice said. "You two detectives like a drink?"

They both shook their heads.

"No, Mrs. White. Thank you," Ward said.

"Oh, we getting formal now, Detective Ward? It's Alice. Still Alice. I know you got to be formal in certain circumstances but won't have you call me nothing but Alice."

"We got your boy, Alice, but he isn't talking," Ward said. "He is your boy, isn't he?"

"I told you he's one of my children." She led them into the parlor.

"He have a name?" Newton said.

"Sir, he does."

"Would you like to tell me what it is?"

"He's called John. John, in the name of the Apostle. Says so on the back of that photograph you took."

"His surname?"

"Why, Detective Newton, he took my own. White. John White. But I guess you got him as John Doe or else you wouldn't have asked me that. He don't talk much and he's probably a little scared. He's not altogether bright schoolwise but he knows the rights and the wrongs." She seemed to lose her breath a moment and then she continued. "You know there's a theory about the painting of the Last Supper by Leonardo da Vinci says Mary Magdalene is actually in the painting. Now if that's true, it means John has disappeared. Where's John?"

Newton saw that Ward was examining the photographs placed all around the room, some on walls, the others on any surface that offered enough space. They overlapped in some places.

Newton said, "We have John."

Alice White chuckled and then said, "He's a good boy. He didn't hurt William. You all know that."

"Who is he?" Newton said.

"I just told you, he's called John White."

"Alice. We need you to be truthful with us here."

Ward looked around at the photographs.

"I ain't told a lie, detective. The Lord strike me down if I have. I'm cooperating."

"He one of these?" Ward said, indicating the photographs.

"No, sir. He ain't."

"Like John missing from the painting," Ward said.

Alice White smiled. "I suppose that's right."

"Do you have any photos of him? Photos you might have taken down recently?"

"I do," Alice said. "Would you like me to get them? They're just here in this cupboard."

Ward said, "Yes, please."

Alice bent down with effort as she opened the cupboard. She fished around inside.

Ward saw the framed needlework that read "Jesus is my savior. Christ is my redeemer". That's why he'd written it down in his notebook. Figured he must've done it absent-mindedly. He then noticed the photograph album he had flicked through the last time he had been there. The one with the dead babies. He opened it. He started to turn pages slowly.

Alice straightened up with Newton's help and she had in her hands a small grayed shoebox full of photographs, some in frames, some loose. The topmost ones were recent. She took one out.

"This is John," she said, handing the photo to Newton.

Ward was still flicking through the album, slowly.

"Do you have any older ones than that?" Newton said as he studied the photograph in his hand.

"Yes, sir, I do."

She dug into the box and came up with a handful. She started to flick through them. As she did so, Newton saw John White's life played out in reverse. There he was at eighteen. And then at fifteen. And now twelve.

Ward was still paging through the album.

John White at nine. At eight. And gradually, Newton's mouth opened wider. Until she got to seven.

"You know they sentenced John the Apostle to death. They tried to kill him but he miraculously survived. He lived to a grand old age. He got a second chance."

Newton took the photo of the little boy from his pocket.

"You interested most in these ones," Alice said, and she laid a few photographs on the small table next to her.

Newton spread them out and picked one up. And there, looking up into the camera lens was the same little boy in the photo that Newton held in his hand, the photo that had once been in Bill O'Donnell's room in Sunny Glade. Same clothes. Same scene. Same house. Alice White's house. The house looked different now but it was definitely this house.

"This is his grandson. Isn't it?" Newton said just before Ward let out a gasp.

"What you got?" Newton said.

"He's found the other John," Alice said. "One who died."

Ward looked at her. Looked back at the album.

"It's a dolly," Alice said.

Alice White said, "I didn't do nothing wrong," after she had been read her Miranda rights by Ward. Again Ward felt strange after being in the house. Those words on the needlework occurred to him now. "Jesus is my savior. Christ is my redeemer." He pushed the words out of his mind as he tried to piece together what was happening. His head felt twisted inside.

* * *

"Don't need no attorney, detective. I'll tell you the truth and be represented by the Lord hisself."

"Okay, Alice. Tell me why a dead child comes to be alive again?" Ward said.

Newton had sat this one out. He was talking to Gammond and sorting out a warrant to dig up the Novak baby's supposed grave. The final resting place of a dolly.

"It was back in 1986. Just past a year since Ryan went missing. One day there was a knock on my door. I answered it and there was William holding something in his arms. Didn't need the little squeak that it let out to know what it was. Only one thing come in bundles like that. And held that way. I asked him who it was. He didn't tell me at first. Just told me he would like for me to look after him. Well, I had doubts. Not of William. I told you he was a good man. I would never doubt him. I doubted myself. I had looked after many children. Even babies. But never delivered to me in this way. I lost my nerve a little but William said I'd be all right. And so I took him in." She looked over Ward's shoulder into the corner of the room as if something was there. It made him look around but there was nothing.

"Go on," Ward said.

"William went away and brought back some supplies later. Baby supplies. I realized then that the baby didn't have a name. So I asked William and he said the baby had none. 'None!' I say. 'Every baby's got a name!' And William said it didn't and he wanted for me to go ahead and choose. First name came into my head was John. After the Apostle. But I say I ain't going to choose a name. That's something parents do. And William told me his mama died in childbirth and I said that's so sad. And then he told me his mama was Janice, his daughter, and then it all made sense."

Ward said, "Why did it make sense?"

Alice said, "Child needs a mama."

"But he still had a father," Ward said, and then he realized and he nodded. "Of course. Presumably he thought the baby was dead."

"Uh huh," said Alice.

"So how did a baby that was supposed to be dead… I'm not understanding this."

"I don't know the part about how the baby gets declared dead. But of course they didn't have a little body to bury. You've seen the photograph, detective."

"The dolly. You're the Baby Dresser, right?"

"That's right. I admit right here and now that I dressed a dolly to look like the dead baby."

"Why did you do that?"

"William asked me to."

"Okay. And how did that fool everyone?"

"Not many people to fool as it happens. There was no body to get rid of in the first place. I just had to present my own baby for the service. Only person who saw it was the father. He was so drunk I could've put a dead possum in the casket. After that, the casket was closed. Nobody else saw."

"Not even the undertaker?"

"We didn't use one apart from to supply a tiny casket."

"So how did the baby get to be pronounced dead? Presumably a doctor needs to pronounce?"

"Like I said. I don't know the details of that. Never wanted to. I just did my duty to William, the child and to God who I knew wanted me to do this for His glory."

Ward let out a few liters of air.

"Detective Ward, William had good reason to do what he did. It's not my business what the why was. You've seen John. He's a good boy."

"He's a suspect in a homicide," Ward said.

"Oh, moonshine. You know he didn't do nothing to hurt his grandfather."

"Did he know his father?"

"Knew of him, later. Eugene got hisself killed before John was old enough to understand. William explained when he was a little older."

"Okay, Alice," Ward said. "I might have some more questions later. I'll get someone to bring you some tea. And cookies." He smiled.

"That would be nice," Alice White said. "Could I see John?"

"No, I'm afraid that's not possible at the moment."

"You charge him with murder?"

"Not yet."

"And you not going to."

"We don't know yet."

"You not going to," Alice said firmly. "Let me ask you a question, Detective Ward."

"Go ahead."

"You carrying something dark in your heart. I see it. Are you ready to meet your God?"

Ward almost jumped at the question. He left Alice in the interview room and he nearly crashed into Newton as he strode through the door.

"Ward," Newton said. He had something in his hand. A copy of a document. "Take a look at this." He jabbed the piece of paper.

"The death certificate. So—" Ward's words chopped off when he saw it. "Doctor Brookline signed the death certificate." He rubbed his eyes. "You think O'Donnell conspired with Brookline to fake the baby's death? That's what it looks like."

"It's what it looks like," Newton said. "He died a drug addict. My guess is O'Donnell offered him money to sign the death certificate. And Brookline signed the certificate and took the money to feed his habit. But if they were both murdered then it wasn't for this. For faking the death of a baby? That don't add up. It's the only thing connects them far as I can see. Did Brookline also know what happened to Ryan? O'Donnell spoke his name. Something spooked O'Donnell. Something that got him and the doctor killed. I think we're getting closer."

"Warrant come through to dig up the Novak baby's grave?"

"Should be soon," Newton said.

"What we going to charge Alice with?"

Newton said, "We're not. She can go."

Ward said, "Okay. We going to charge the guy with anything?"

Newton took a deep breath. Shrugged. "We ain't got a great deal apart from the fingerprints. If only he would talk he'd tell us he climbed into the window to go visit his old grandfather. I guess he was just keeping a low profile. He was supposed to be dead after all. I got no reason to suspect he's done anything but be a dutiful grandson."

"So, we're back to having nothing," Ward said.

"Not nothing. We've got the Brookline angle. The dead baby angle. We'll work at those."

"Damn it," Ward said.

And then the interview room door opened and Alice White was standing there.

"Let me speak to John," she said.

Newton looked at the frail old lady standing there in the doorway and for a minute he thought it was his mother despite Alice's color.

"Okay," Newton said. And he led her to the other interview room where John White—John Novak—sat, staring at the wall. He closed the door on them.

"You sure?" Ward said.

Newton went to the TV but it wasn't switched on. He tried the on switch but it didn't make any difference. He banged the side of it with his fist. Checked the cables. Still wouldn't switch on. Then he dashed over to the interview room door and burst in. Alice White had John White's hand in hers. She looked around at Newton.

"He can take you to where Ryan is buried," she said.

"She said what?" Gammond said.

"He knows where Ryan is buried. Ward's going to take a team out there. O'Donnell used to take the boy to his brother's grave. It's out over in the National Forest."

Gammond seemed confused. Not sure where to put his hands. "That means O'Donnell's the killer. You see?"

"We'll get the body and take it from there."

"But he must've done it. He buried the boy. You were right."

"Was I? What about Lafayette? You had him definitely done it."

Gammond's words wouldn't come out and he got red in the face.

"You going with Ward?" Gammond said eventually. "It was your case."

"It's Ward's case now. I messed it up first time around."

"Okay," Gammond said. He paused and then said, "Tell him he has everything he needs. Men. Chopper. All it takes."

"He's on it."

"You get to wrap up this case once and for all. Now, it's important you keep me informed on developments. This is a sensitive story still. And don't let it out. We keep a lid on this. I need to get my head around this. Dang."

Newton stood in the parking lot. He looked up at the sky and it looked set to fall again and the day had darkened. He put his head in his hands and his fingers ran up through his hair. He felt a pain in his chest like a sharp object skittering around in there. And then he felt the cold hand grip his heart and he made to grab at his chest but his arm was weak. And then he fell.

Newton was dead. That's what they told him later. McNeely's quick thinking and proficiency with the defibrillator which they kept at the station had cranked his heart back up. He would thank her later by buying her flowers. She would receive them graciously and then throw them into the trash on her way home as she'd always hated flowers. Remind her of funeral homes.

68

"It's been six months."
"I don't give a damn," Newton says.
"That's a hell of a quote," Larsson says.
"Listen here—"
"Now, don't let's get falling out, detective. I'm just doing my job here. Throw me a bone. Some gristle if you want. I've got five hundred words I need to pluck out of somewhere. How do you want this to read? It's basically your choice."

Newton takes in an ocean-deep breath and he silently mouths the numbers one through ten.

"Anything. I'll take some routine bullshit but I need to attribute it to a source," Larsson says.

After another short pause Newton says, "Make something up. Just... make something up," and he bounces the phone back in its cradle.

Bill O'Donnell is sitting in a tiny room which is filled with tools, cleaning equipment and a plethora of smells – oil, bleach, paint. The paint smell makes him feel nauseous and he thinks of Ryan. The only remaining piece of store cupboard realty is taken up by a child-sized chair which *creaks under his weight. He just sits there. The door is all the way open and heavy footsteps pound towards the room as the school bell sounds. Newton appears, fresh snowfall melting on his shoulders and head.*

"Where is the body?" Newton says. It's the first time he's called the boy a body but not the first time he's thought it. In fact, he'd thought it from the start if he was honest with himself. But honesty and denial had butted against one another for too long.

Classroom doors can be heard opening and the muffled cheerful clamor of children zigzags the corridors above them.

"How would I know that?"

"How would you know that? You tell me. What did you do with Ryan's body? You take it out in the woods? You bury it out there?"

"You dug up my garden."

"We'll dig up the entire National Forest if we have to but you could make it a hell of a lot easier on yourself if you just tell me where it is."

"This is harassment, sir," Bill O'Donnell says, and he stands up suddenly and faces Newton. "Do you have no respect? Do you know what you've done to me?"

Newton takes a step forward and bends down into O'Donnell's face and their noses almost touch.

"You killed him. I know that. And you're going to tell me where the body is. Right here and now. Let's go, you son of a bitch. Game's over."

O'Donnell stands and finds himself toe to toe with Newton.

"You get satisfaction from harassing a grieving grandparent? That it? Shame on you, sir. Shame on you."

"You killed that boy," Newton says, but his previously gusting words are a breeze now.

"I didn't kill nobody," O'Donnell says. "Thing is, you can't handle the fact that you ain't done your job. You ain't found the boy. You ain't done nothing but come at me."

"And I'll keep coming till it kills me," Newton says.

O'Donnell's eyes linger on Newton's and then he sits down.

"I wish I could tell you more. I really do. Fact is, we both know Ryan is dead. Fact is, neither of us knows where he is. Fact is, you've gotten nowhere with this. You ain't even looking no more. Be honest. Fact is, you've tried your best to pin this on me. And for what? What you got against me? I'm also a victim in this. Can't you see that? Ryan was my grandson. My flesh and blood. You think I could've killed my own grandson? You got children of your own? You could kill them? You don't know me. You're clutching at straws. After all this time you're still clutching at straws. Well, I ain't having no part of it no more. I'm done answering questions. I'm done being harassed. I want to get on with my life best I can. It's not easy but I take it a day at a time. Sure, I have guilt. But it ain't the kind of guilt comes with taking another's life. It's the guilt says I might have been able to stop Ryan being taken in the first place. The kind that says I should've been there for him. I wasn't, though. And that guilt will live with me forever. I carry it around like an overcoat on a sunny day. So with respect, detective, I'm done with helping you. You go on and get on with your life. Look at you. Just look at you."

It's a while before Newton speaks. His eyes are heavy with fatigue. His jacket has stains on it. He smells sour.

"You killed him" is all he says, and he draws the words from his shoes but they die off in the traveling. They are to be the last three words he will ever say to Bill O'Donnell.

Newton doesn't hear the last words O'Donnell will ever

say to him as he is already down the end of the corridor when they are said. O'Donnell just says, "I know where Ryan is buried but I didn't kill him."

69

McNeely noticed that Ward's left leg was set to jiggling.

"You go," she said. "I'd like to stay. That okay?" The question was directed at a nurse, who was injecting something into a tube that ran into the back of Newton's hand. The nurse nodded.

"You his wife?" The nurse said.

"His wife is on the way here. I'm a colleague."

"Strictly speaking it should be next of kin only," the nurse said, and Mallory and Jen walked into the room.

"We're his family," Mallory said.

Jen had been crying. She said, "Oh my…"

"How is he? Is he going to be okay?" Mallory said, his voice a little shaky.

"He needs rest," the nurse said.

"But he's going to be okay, right?" Mallory said.

"He's poorly but he's going to be okay," the nurse said. "And it's getting a bit crowded in here."

"We're his family," Mallory said, and he glared at Ward and McNeely.

"We're going," Ward said, and he stood and saw the look of anger swelling in McNeely's face. He gestured with his head for McNeely to go with him.

Ward turned to Jen and said, "Tell him... when he wakes up tell him I've gone to bring Ryan back."

Jen nodded. Mallory just gawked at Ward with his mouth working an unformed sentence. Ward put his hat on and stood at the bottom of the bed where Newton slept. The man in the bed lay like a toppled statue.

"And tell him... just tell him to take it easy, okay?" He took McNeely's arm and led her away.

"I saved his life and goddamn Mallory—"

"It's okay. You go home and get some rest."

"That son of a bitch—" McNeely said, and she punched the air in front of her.

"I know it but it don't do no good to let him get to you."

McNeely just growled and she walked away from Ward and he stood there and watched her and he could hear her grumbling as she walked. He turned and headed towards his car.

The cold was intense. Tiny ice crystals fell from the sky, seemingly jewels shaved from stars, and they blew in his face and stuck to his beard. It was still light but only just. The helicopter would be here soon and they had to move quickly.

He knew the chopper wouldn't fly if this weather got worse. He knew that he had limited time to get to the burial site before it was completely covered under a significant snowfall. He knew they had to go now to stand any chance of getting the job done before springtime. The job of getting Ryan's body back. And he knew that Newton needed the little boy.

He called the station. Poynter picked up. Asked for

news on Newton. Ward told him he was stable. He would be okay. Then Ward checked with Poynter if they'd got all the equipment ready. They had. They would be navigated by John White, who was still sitting in the interview room at the station.

70

John White still hadn't said a word and now the helicopter's rotor blades whupped like thunder and everything on the ground below them began to shrink. Packham, the medical examiner, was there, sitting with Poynter. They were behind Ward, who sat beside John White. John White pointed to a region of the National Forest on a map and Ward leaned over to the pilot and indicated where John White had pointed. The pilot nodded and then the nose of the helicopter dipped and Ward's stomach did a roll as they gathered speed. The pilot had told them he would have to fly low due to the weather and that had set Ward's nerves on edge. He had never gotten used to flying, even though he had done it dozens of times during his military service.

Ward turned to John White and asked, "Did your grandfather tell you anything about how Ryan got out here?" John White shook his head.

The town was soon behind them and it became a cluster of twinkling lights and stretched out in front was a gathering tide of white upon green upon white. In the distance the white mountain peaks stood like ancient pyramids and the trees seemed as ghosts migrating in parallax motion. They followed the interstate for ten minutes and then the pilot caressed the helicopter on a gentle curve rightwards and then all they could see when they looked down was forest and snapshots of a long narrow lake. In places the trees seemed smaller and greener where the forest had been scorched in years previous.

The pilot glanced around at Ward and Ward opened up a second map and passed that to John White. John White studied the map for a minute and then he again indicated a point on it and Ward showed the pilot, who looked at his navigation system and made a small correction left and then he straightened. Less than five minutes later John White said his first words.

"It's here," he said, and his voice was gentle and almost inaudible under the helicopter's rotors. "Sure looks different up above it."

Ward gave the pilot the signal of an inverted thumb and the pilot cast his head around, looking at the landscape below. He banked right and they turned a wide circle in the air.

Ward asked, "That look okay down there?"

They circled again and then the helicopter leveled off and began to descend.

"The ground will sure be hard," John White said as they unloaded the equipment from the helicopter.

They unloaded pickaxes as well as spades. Picks for the top layer of earth and spades for the finer work further down.

"It gets any colder we're going to need ice axes," Poynter said.

Packham had his own case and he was the last out of the helicopter.

The pilot said to Ward, "I'll be back in two hours and if you're not here you freeze to death in the forest," and Ward knew that wasn't negotiable. Anyone crazy enough to fly one of those things deserved the final say. Anyone crazy enough to fly one of those things was crazy enough to make good on such a threat.

Once they had all their equipment lugged onto their backs Ward said, "Which way?" and John White studied the trees around him and then started walking east and he led them from the clearing where they had landed and off into dense pine forest and they began to climb upwards. The engines of the helicopter whined but the sound was muffled already by the trees and they didn't see it take off. Ward checked his watch.

Ward was stripped down to his shirt already and he cast his hat onto his discarded clothes and wiped the sweat from his forehead and then swung again. And again. John White was right, the ground was hard, but they had already gotten down a foot. Poynter was willing but not as strong as Ward so Ward took most of the work while the others danced on the spot trying to keep warm. The medical examiner's face had started to take on a bluish hue.

They had cleared a rectangular perimeter of rocks that John White said he had recently put there so that he could mark the exact spot in case the vegetation got ideas of hiding the grave.

Ward stood and stretched his back and steam almost hissed off his body and then he threw the pickax to the ground and picked up the spade and removed the soil that he had just chopped up. The strapping on his hand had worked loose so he unraveled it and tossed it to one side and he gingerly clenched his fist a few times.

Then John White removed his own coat and he picked up another spade and he climbed into the shallow pit and he started to ease the spade into the soil carefully.

"Like this," he said to Ward and Ward nodded and knew the body wouldn't be much deeper. He stepped aside and let John White carry on working with the spade.

Fifteen minutes later John White stopped. He went down on his knees and started to scrape away the soil with his hands, slowly revealing the small shape of the boy's body wrapped in a sheet.

Packham was both amazed and delighted.

"It's like a mummy," he said, and he smiled to himself but nobody else was smiling.

The wrappings on the body had been toughened by some substance or substances known only, for now at least, to Bill O'Donnell and the sheet traced the contours of the small bundle so that you could tell it was a body.

They didn't unwrap it. Ward thought of Newton and thought the parcel that he lifted now, with the help of Poynter and John White, was a get-well gift to him.

The remaining hint of light was moving elsewhere now and they needed flashlights on their journey back to where they could hear the whup of the helicopter's rotors. Ward hoped the pilot would give them time to get there.

The wrapped boy was on a stretcher now and they loaded him onto the helicopter. John White touched him. He'd never been this close to his brother. Ward placed his hand on John's shoulder and smiled.

Ward said, "Thank you."

"Do you think he can come back here?" John White asked.

"Well, I don't know that," Ward said. "I guess there are regulations on burying people in the forest."

"Okay," John White said. "Will you find out?"

Ward said, "I'll do my best."

71

Newton was awake and he startled the nurse when he spoke. Startled his wife Maggie too. He said, "Thirsty".

"You shouldn't be awake," the nurse said, even though it was afternoon.

Maggie stood up and touched Newton's hand and Newton managed a weak squeeze.

"I'm still here," he said, and Maggie began to cry. "It's okay,"

Maggie held a cup to his mouth so he could drink a little and dribble a little down his chin. She mopped the dribble up with a handkerchief.

"Thought I'd lost you," Maggie said.

Newton said quietly, "Not again. Never again."

The nurse was fussing around the equipment that had kept Newton alive for the past few hours.

"He should be resting," the nurse said to Maggie. And she picked up a vial of something and inserted a syringe into it.

Newton saw the vial and suddenly tried to sit up in bed. The nurse put the vial and syringe down and tried to settle Newton back down. It didn't take much strength.

"Really now, Mr. Newton, you need to rest. Don't be going trying to sit up again. I'm going to have to give you something to sleep."

"I need a phone," Newton croaked.

"No, you don't," the nurse said, and she picked up the syringe and vial again. "No, you need to rest. I won't tell you again."

"The vial. I need a phone. It's the vial."

"I'll call," Maggie said, and she pulled out her cellphone. "Who do you want me to call?"

"McNeely. Call McNeely." He took a couple of breaths and then said, "Tell her to contact Grainger at Sunny Glade." He reached for the water and Maggie put it to his lips again and he sipped. "Ask Grainger to check the batch numbers on his morphine."

"That it?" Maggie asked. She was already dialing the station.

Newton nodded. And the nurse injected something into the intravenous fluid bag.

McNeely was there even though it was a Saturday. She knew what Newton was thinking. She had made the call to Grainger. Told him to not, on no account, let anyone near the pharmacy. She was at Sunny Glade within ten minutes. Grainger was waiting and he led her to the cabinet that contained the vials of morphine. She examined them all. The batch numbers on three vials of morphine didn't match the rest. "They're not ours, no, ma'am" was how Grainger put it. McNeely checked the batch numbers on the suspect vials against the numbers on the vials retrieved from Doctor

Brookline's house. Positive match. She called Ward.

Ward was with Packham. The medical examiner had managed to open up the mummification covering on the body of the boy and had cut his clothes off and he stood back admiring the little body.

"Pretty amazing really," Packham said.

Ward nodded but what he saw was a shriveled-up little papier-mâché figure.

"Mightn't look much to you but this is good. Very good."

"When might we get some results?" Ward asked.

"Give me a couple of hours for preliminary results."

Ward's phone rang.

"Okay," Ward said to the medical examiner. "You'll call me when you have anything?"

"Sure will," Packham said.

It was McNeely on the phone. She told Ward about the vials as he made his way out into the corridor of the mortuary.

"So someone placed vials of morphine from Brookline's house in the pharmacy of Sunny Glade," Ward said. "Why would someone do that?"

McNeely said, "To replace morphine used to kill Bill O'Donnell?"

Ward said, "So that nobody would notice any was missing. Make it look like whoever did the old man in brought in the morphine from elsewhere so we wouldn't think it was an inside job. So, we assume the old man's killer is someone who had access to the pharmacy at Sunny Glade. Only nursing staff, the on-call doctor and Grainger himself have access. Grainger told me. He keeps the key. Unless someone else got a hold of the key. Someone who would know where the key was kept."

"I wish I could help you with that but I ain't a detective, detective."

"You've helped a lot," Ward said. "We need those vials in evidence. Might have prints on them, though I'm guessing not, but check anyway," and he was out of the building and in his car. He turned his music on and then flipped it off again.

72

Property magnate James Kenny's house couldn't be seen from the security gate. Kenny buzzed Ward through the gate and the magnetic lock broke with a clunk and the gate swung open quietly. The road up to the house snaked through ornamental trees and rhododendrons and Ward stopped the car when his cellphone rang.

"Jake," Ward said.

The FBI officer said, "I got you something. This don't trace back to me. Never."

Ward said, "Okay."

"You have access to a fax machine?"

"No. Hang on. Let me get back to you."

"Hurry. I'm in a copy shop."

Ward hung up and continued his drive up to the mansion. He sped up and braked heavily in front of the house and left a couple of deep tire tracks in the gravel.

The gardens that Kenny's house towered over were immaculately tended. Lawns ran into shrubs which ran into expensively landscaped plantation woodland spread over a few acres. Like something Olmsted and

Vaux might have designed. The snow had settled on everything and made it opaque.

Kenny's door opened and the man stood there, all expression erased.

"Mr. Kenny," Ward said.

"I'm sorry, I can't remember the name."

"Ward."

"Of course. Now, Mr. Ward, I thought we'd had the conversation," Kenny said.

"Can I come in?"

"I'm a little busy."

"This won't take long."

Kenny backed off and moved to the side to let Ward step into the reception hallway. Ward's eyes immediately gazed upwards and the hallway stretched up three floors, a large French-style chandelier drawing his focus.

"It's a Saturday," Kenny said. "Don't you have anything else to do on a weekend, Mr. Ward? I certainly do."

Ward smiled. "Unfortunately crime doesn't take the weekends off."

Kenny said, "So, what is it that I can help you with?"

And then a mouse's voice called out, "Who is it, dear?" Kenny's wife, Ward presumed.

"It's okay, I've got it," Kenny called, and the voice wasn't heard again.

"Do you have a fax machine?" Ward said.

Kenny inhaled and his chest bulged out. "Are we playing games here, Mr. Ward?"

Ward said, "I'm sorry, if it's an imposition." He fiddled with his hat like a serf might do.

Kenny led Ward into his study.

"What's the number?"

Kenny told Ward the number and Ward called Jake back and read out the number and then he hung up his phone.

"I'm mindful that I don't have to talk to you, Mr. Ward." Kenny kept puffing out annoyance.

"It's Detective Ward," Ward said, his eyes settling on Kenny and staying there, unblinking. "And no, you don't have to talk to me. Would you prefer we do this down at the station?"

"Just say what you came to say. I've told you all I know in connection with the old man. And I have got things to be doing, so, let's get done."

"Well, we seem to have a little issue with some vials of morphine that appeared in the pharmacy at Sunny Glade."

"Go on," Kenny said, and his expression seamlessly went from annoyed to mildly curious.

"You see, the morphine you got in your pharmacy, that came from elsewhere. Different batch numbers."

"Oh, and where did it come from?"

"Do you have any idea where it came from?"

"Well, that's not my department, so I wouldn't know. I own Sunny Glade. I don't run it."

"Okay," Ward said as the fax machine started to whirr. "You see, it strikes me, sir, that the morphine used to kill Mr. O'Donnell came from your pharmacy and was then replaced by some morphine from another source. So's nobody would notice any was missing."

Kenny nodded as Ward was talking.

"So? What is it you want to ask me, Mr. Ward?

Detective Ward."

"Well, I asked it and you said you didn't know nothing about it."

"Well, sorry I can't be any more help. Now, if we've done here, I really need to—"

"Actually, that's not why I came. It's why I came initially but something else came up." He looked at the fax machine and the whirring stopped. Ward picked up the two sheets of paper from the tray. He looked at Kenny and then he studied the paper.

"This is becoming tiresome, Detective Ward. Now, I've got things to do and I'd like you to leave."

"Are you sure you don't want to do this here?"

"Just get the hell out," Kenny said, and he went to snatch the fax from Ward's hand but Ward pulled away. "You know my son's a lawyer."

"I'm leaving," Ward said. "Thank you for the use of your fax machine."

"What do you have there?" Kenny said.

"Potential evidence."

"Evidence of what?"

"Of your connection to the death of Ryan Novak."

"You son of a bitch, let me have that," Kenny said, and he again made a grab at the fax but Ward was quicker.

"I'll be in touch," Ward said, and he turned to leave.

"Do you realize who you are dealing with here?" Kenny shouted. "Do you know how much leverage I carry in this town?"

"Sir, I suggest you use all the influence you got to get yourself a comfortable jail cell."

"You son of a bitch. You fucking son of a bitch," Kenny said, but Ward was almost at the door and he turned and faced Kenny.

"You got a potty mouth there, sir." And he left.

He swung by the motel. It was the weekend. He'd neglected Jesús and it was their time together. The little old dog trotted over to him as he entered the door and he fussed around Ward's legs and he tried to jump up but a day of doing nothing had seemingly stiffened his joints. Ward attached his leash and they left, Jesús struggling to keep up on arthritic limbs.

"I'd like to bring in James Kenny, sir," Ward said to Lieutenant Gammond, who had just walked into the station.

"Whoa. Whoa, son," Gammond said, and he led Ward into his office. He turned abruptly and pointed at Ward with a shaky gloved hand. "You're in danger of getting yourself into a whole heap of shit here. Man's got power around these here parts."

"You two go to the same church? You sing the same hymns," Ward said.

Gammond's face reddened.

"He call you?" Ward asked. He knew the answer. "We going to be pushed around by golf club influence? That how policing works around here?"

"Look here, you dang son of a bitch—"

"Same preference in curse words too," Ward said.

"You treading a fine line there, boy," Gammond said, and his face nearly exploded.

"Sir, I'm trying to be respectful as I can but I'm kinda getting frustrated at being blocked from doing my job."

"What you got on Kenny? Tell me."

"There's the vials of morphine. Vials from the scene of Doctor Brookline's death found their way into the pharmacy at Sunny Glade. Replacements for the ones that killed O'Donnell. Tells me the same person killed both of them. And Kenny was there at Sunny Glade the night O'Donnell was killed. He would know how to get access to the pharmacy."

Gammond paused a few seconds, staring at Ward, then said, "Dang it, that's not enough to get someone like James Kenny into this police station. You ain't thinking clearly is all."

"And I think he's connected to the death of Ryan Novak."

Gammond backed away and sat down and the color seeped from his face. "How... you... you have something?"

Ward said, "I have something."

Gammond said, "What?" And his voice was in another room.

"I'd rather not say at this point because I'm still gathering things together."

"Tell me," Gammond said.

"Sir, I can't betray my source."

"To me, yes, you can. Tell me."

"Lieutenant, sir, no, I can't. Way I do things is I always protect my sources."

Gammond said in a tiger's growl, "Son, you going to tell me or I'm pulling you off this case."

"Well, that makes things difficult, then. I'll go see the captain." Ward made to leave Gammond's office.

"Hold on," Gammond said. "Hold on. Evidence

from a source you can't name isn't admissible. You know that, right?"

"Yes, sir."

"You're not bringing in Kenny. Get me something else."

Ward's blue eyes fixed on Gammond. Then he walked out of the office.

Ward was at his desk going through the interviews and statements of people at the nursing home again. McNeely was making Jesús feel special over at her desk. When he got to the young girl Penny Gilfoyle's statement he read it and then paused. He knew Kenny had been there that night. The girl hadn't mentioned him and Ward hadn't known to ask. He hadn't been aware at the time he'd gone to see her that Kenny had been there on the night of O'Donnell's death. He'd go and see her again. No, he'd call.

He spoke to the girl's exasperated father first and then the girl came onto the phone. She sounded excited to hear from him but at the same time disappointed that he hadn't been in touch earlier. She spoke first.

"Detective Ward. It's Penny. So nice to—"

"Penny, this is urgent and you could help me clear something up. Something very important to my case." He could hear the click of her smile.

"I'll try my best."

Ward said, "On the night of Mr. O'Donnell's death did you speak to anyone before you left Sunny Glade? Any of the staff there?"

"I spoke to the lady on the front desk."

"Anybody else?"

She went quiet.

"Did you tell anybody else what Mr. O'Donnell had said to you?"

"I can't remember. I can't..." She went quiet again, and then, "Yes. This old guy... I think he owns the place... he was there."

"Okay," Ward said. He twirled a pencil in his fingers.

And then Penny said, "He spoke to me."

Ward sat up. "What did he say? This is important, Penny." He could almost hear her thinking. It took a while for her to speak again.

"He... he asked me what the old man had said."

Ward said, "Good, Penny, good. And what did you tell him?"

Penny said, "I told him what he said. About a confession."

Ward was on his feet. "Was there anything else?"

"I don't think so. I told him he'd shouted 'Doctor Brookline,' that's all."

Ward said, "Well, thank you, Penny. Thank you so much. That's really useful."

"Cool. Do you need me to come down the station to make a statement?"

Ward was staring across at the evidence board. "I'll be in touch, Penny."

His eyes darted across the board. Looked at the photo of John White. Looked at the various scrawled words and phrases. Tried to put them together to make something. He was sure that Kenny was somehow involved in the old man's death. Ryan's too, almost certainly. But he didn't know exactly why. Couldn't work out his connection to Ryan. O'Donnell must have died because he'd known about the boy's death. He'd taken him and buried him in the forest. He hadn't killed him so someone else had and O'Donnell knew who and had kept quiet about it. There had been a cover up. Someone else knew and had been paid off, Ward was sure of that. Kenny's bank withdrawals, from the FBI corruption investigation, which his friend Jake had faxed over to him, suggested that. But not O'Donnell, despite his regular payments to Alice White. That money was his own hard-earned cash. To pay for the upbringing of John White. And then there was the suggestion of police involvement from what O'Donnell had said to the journalist, Larsson. Ward didn't like where his thoughts were taking him and he pushed that aside for now. Knew it would be answered soon. All the pieces were coming together now.

He fidgeted in his seat and kept the questions coming and one above all begged for an answer. Why kill O'Donnell now? Why after all these years of keeping the secret of Ryan's death had Kenny decided to kill him or have him killed? What was it that had spooked him? What was it that had almost certainly made him get rid of Doctor Brookline too? Was it just the fact that O'Donnell had mentioned the doctor's name? What did the old man mean by the word 'confession'? Was that what had spooked Kenny? But why would the old man just come out and say it? Why would he all of a sudden get agitated and come out with that? What was his confession and why didn't Kenny want him to make it?

And then it hit Ward full on smack in the face. He went over to McNeely, who had been watching him but rubbing Jesús at the same time.

"I need the newspaper. I put it in evidence."
"I'll get it."

He reread the story Penny had been reading to Bill O'Donnell when he had had his outburst. Nothing there. He slammed the newspaper onto his desk and as it landed he saw on the opposite page Principal Leon Taylor of Meriwether Elementary School. The school where Kenny's construction company was building a new science wing. The school where Bill O'Donnell had been janitor. "Time Capsule Makes Way in the Name of Science," read the headline. That's the page that O'Donnell would have seen while Penny was reading the one on the opposite side. Ward read the news article. The time capsule had been buried in 1986. Probably by O'Donnell himself. To be dug up in fifty years' time and reveal the secrets of a few dozen children. And the secrets of an old janitor, Ward thought. O'Donnell had buried something of his own in the capsule. That's why the story had spooked him. If they opened the capsule whatever secrets he had left in it would be revealed. Secrets about what happened to Ryan is what Ward thought. The time capsule was to be moved and reburied away from the new development, according to the article. He checked the details. The capsule was due to be moved next Monday. It couldn't wait.

He went over to McNeely and took Jesús's leash from her desk and the little dog struggled free of her petting hands and skittered after Ward, who was already striding out of the station. When Jesús caught up with him he bent and attached the dog's leash and then let it fall. He grabbed one of the pickaxes and one of the spades that had been used in digging up Ryan's body. Before he was out Gammond called out from the doorway of his office.

"Where you going?"

Ward stopped and looked over at Gammond, who stood there waiting, with his head tilted in curiosity, for Ward's answer.

"To the school," Ward said without further pause. "To dig up O'Donnell's secret. Maybe Kenny's too."

73

It was almost dark. Midwinter dark. The moon lit up big gray clouds that looked like huge misshapen beasts migrating south. These shape-shifting behemoths chased across the sky as if pursued by something bigger. And then he saw what they were running from. A huge stampede, altogether more yellow and carrying snow, obliterated the moon. Almost instantly the snow started to fall. Large flakes this time. By the time he reached the school, the ground was already covered with the fresh snowfall and the wheels of his car began to find grip a difficult task as he pumped the gas pedal gently and pulled up the ramp and onto a short driveway which led into the parking lot.

"Stay there," Ward said to Jesús, but the dog jumped over from the passenger side onto the driver's seat and straight out of the car like an excited puppy. Flakes of snow landed on his face and he shook his head and sneezed and snuffled and the leash flapped and rattled about him.

"Okay, but I don't want no trouble from you."

Jesús danced on the freshly fallen snow and Ward

smiled as he opened the trunk and took out the spade and pickax.

Ward walked around the south side of the main school building towards where the entrance was, where the new development was going to take place, and there he found a small area of lawn, almost completely covered in white aside from one edge which had been afforded some shelter by the school building. The grass was bordered with winter flowers and in the middle, just visible, was a circular indentation, about a foot in diameter. Ward bent down and wiped the snow away with his hand to reveal a plaque. He read the inscription – Meriwether Elementary School Time Capsule: To Be Opened 2036. The plaque was embedded into the ground and Ward took the pickax and levered the plaque out and rolled it to one side and then let it drop with a thud. The ground underneath it was a rug of anemic grass shoots and tangles of webbed roots and Ward took hold of the spade and thrust it into the ground. It went in an inch and he dug out a layer of soil, liberating the albino grass with it. He rammed the spade in again, harder this time, and he managed to go deeper. The ground here was not as hard as the ground in the forest which had held Ryan. He repeated this a few more times and his fingers became stiff with the cold, despite the gloves. His right hand ached miserably.

When the spade struck metal with a hollow clunk he stepped back and took a deep breath and he rubbed his hands to try and get some warm blood back into them. Jesús was straight in, scratching away at the capsule like a maniac. Ward let him have his fun for a minute and then pulled at his leash, which was soaking wet from the snow.

"Good work there, boy," Ward said to Jesús, and the little dog wandered off and took a leak on the flowers. And then he trotted away and disappeared around the side of the school building, his nose sniffing as much ground as it could as he went.

Ward started to dig around the time capsule then. He'd have to go deep to give himself any chance of getting the thing out of the ground. The soil yielded more readily as he dug deeper and a short time later he could see what he thought must have been most of the capsule.

The capsule had a lip around the top edge and that gave him something to grip onto. He could see the lid wasn't welded on and he was grateful for that. His fingers hooked under the lip and he tugged at it but it didn't move. He took the spade and turned it upside down and inserted the handle into the hole he had dug and he used it to lever the capsule. He did this all around it and eventually he figured it was loose enough. He tossed the spade to the ground and again he crouched down and started to tug at the capsule. Immediately it broke its sticky bond with the earth and he heaved it out and set it on the grass. By now he was covered almost completely in snow and he thought if he stayed still long enough he would become a perfect snowman in the middle of the commemorative garden. He took off his hat and shook the snow off it, then set it back on his head.

He tried the lid, which was somehow screwed onto the capsule like a soda bottle top, and it didn't budge. So he took the pickax and gave it a few whacks and tried again. With all his strength applied, the lid started to turn and it let out a high-pitched groan as it did so. Two or three rotations and it was off.

He took out his flashlight and shone it into the cylinder. There were three large sheets of paper which had been rolled up. There were little handmade envelopes with pretty personalized decorations on them, no doubt containing children's letters to their future selves detailing their hopes and dreams and predictions for the future, most of which would have been fanciful and unrealized. There were other knickknacks from 1986, some which only kids could have deemed important enough to preserve for posterity; a Transformer toy, a Rainbow Brite Color Kid, a copy of *The Wind in the Willows*, which the younger kids had read that year in class. And on the top of all this was an envelope, not manmade this one. And on the front it said something in pallid blue-gray ink. Ward carefully picked it out and turned it over and the words on the front read "Please Deliver to The police," written in an untidy but grown-up hand. The flap of the envelope had been stuck down in 1986 but the glue had since perished and the envelope was open. Ward shook off his right glove and let it drop to the ground. He had fresh strapping on his hand and yellow and blue bruising spread out from under the bandage. He slid the piece of paper out from the envelope. It was then that he heard the rumble of a car slowly pulling up on the other side of the school building where the parking lot was. Then he heard the car door close. He didn't pause. He opened the letter and began to read. On the second read he heard the snow-cushioned footsteps behind him. He reached into his coat but the voice stopped him.

"Take your hand slowly from your jacket, Ward." The voice had a nervous tremble coating it. But Ward recognized it. He took his hand from his coat and he held out both hands at right angles to his body, the letter in his gloved left hand, the bandaged one empty.

"Now turn around slowly."

Ward did.

"What you got there, son?" Gammond said.

"Took you longer than I thought to get here. Bad traffic?"

"Dang it. I said what you got there?"

"It's a letter."

"I can see that," Gammond said, and his gun hand shook as he spoke.

"It tells everything," Ward said. "'Bout what you did. Kenny. It's all there."

Gammond took a deep breath. "Well, that's a dang crying shame."

Ward said, "Why?"

"Why?"

"We can take this down to the station if you like," Ward said.

Gammond chuckled in his chest but his face was frozen, his lips tightly shut.

"I ought to read you your rights," Ward said.

"That's not how this is going to go, son," Gammond said.

"Just tell me why. Why does a cop do something like that?" Ward said, and he looked down at the ground. The spade, the pickax, the metal cylinder containing broken dreams and half-assed predictions of some sci-fi futuristic vision of flying cars and rocket packs.

"Dang. I just wanted… I was just trying to help, you know. It was an accident. Didn't I tell you not to go reopening ol' wounds? Didn't I tell you that, son? I told you that." And Gammond's shoulders slumped and his gun hand lowered slightly.

"If it was an accident we can sort this out," Ward tried but Gammond chuckled again.

"That's not going to work," Gammond said. He was quiet a moment, eyeing Ward, who stood motionless with his arms stretched out at his sides.

"You want to talk about it?"

"Not really." Gammond's shoulders dropped a couple more inches. "Dang. Dang it." And then he looked at Ward but almost over his shoulder, avoiding eye contact. "I was on patrol. Driving up Rochester and I saw the car and knew something was off. I gets out the car and sees the little boy. Boy was dead already. I tried CPR but he was gone. I was going to radio it in but then things got away from me. I was going to… I'd called Kenny on the boy's cellphone. Told him we'd got a situation."

"You called Kenny?"

"Boy had asked me to call him. Straighten things out. Truth be told I can't remember why I did it. I knew Kenny and… well…"

"You knew Kenny from the golf club, right?"

"I'd recently joined. He was one of my proposers."

"You'd done him favors before."

"Oh, little things, you don't need to know. We ain't got the time. You see, the little boy had apparently run out into the street and Arthur hadn't been able to stop in time. Ran him down. The kid was crushed under the dang wheels."

"Arthur?" Ward said, and he began to move from one foot to the other to keep warm.

"Don't be moving around," Gammond said, and he waved the gun. "Arthur is James Kenny's son."

"I still don't understand why you didn't call it in," Ward said.

"Well, you see, Arthur had been at the liquor. Was well over the limit. He was in college. Had a promising career ahead of him. You see how it would've been bad for the kid. Had big plans to be some highfaluting lawyer in New York."

"And then O'Donnell came, right?"

"Just as we was wondering what we was going to do with the body."

"And O'Donnell just went along with it? Just like that?"

"It was James Kenny we were dealing with. Dang. I told you about his influence but you wouldn't listen. You know how he influences?"

"Money."

"Well, that's just some of it. He has a way of putting things. People fall into his words like one of those pit traps you see in the movies. He's like a snake oil salesman."

"He'd paid you off before O'Donnell got there."

Gammond didn't say anything but scratched at his cheek.

"And it was you who talked O'Donnell into getting rid of the body. It was you Kenny sold the snake oil to. And you sold it on to O'Donnell. Don't go putting this all on Kenny. It was you brokered the deal and you took your commission."

"Dang, it was best all around."

"Best for who? Best for you who got rich? Best for the boy? Best for O'Donnell?"

"Boy was dead. Ain't nothing going to bring him back. No point ruining a young man's life. I just made it clear to O'Donnell that if he didn't go along with it he'd find himself in a heap of trouble in other ways. He worked with children and… you know. Rumors could start."

"And you didn't want to lose your heap of cash that Kenny had offered you."

"Like I said. It was better for everybody." He looked to Ward like he had some regret. "Anyways, we're running out of time here. I got to clean up this mess you made."

"No, tell me what happened to the boy."

Gammond looked directly at Ward now and studied him through slitted eyes. "O'Donnell said he would bury the boy. He was in pieces. So he took the boy in his truck."

"The truck that O'Donnell said was stolen. You took that call. You set it all up."

"Easy thing to do. I told him to get rid of the truck. Forest fire did the rest."

"You know why O'Donnell was out looking for the boy?"

"I guessed the boy had run off."

"He was being abused by his father."

Gammond paused.

"Don't tell me you didn't know that."

"Well, that poor little bastard," Gammond said. "Well, that's too sad. Dang. But don't change anything enough to bring the boy back to life."

"Kenny bought your silence and you engineered it all."

"Our Lord works in mysterious ways."

"I got his bank statements here and it wouldn't take much to show that the withdrawals he made found their way into your pocket," Ward tapped his pocket.

Gammond shouted, "Hey hey. Hands. Hands. I'm going to have to have those. And the letter."

Ward's hand went back towards his pocket. Gammond waving his gun stopped it.

"I'll take them from your body," Gammond said.

"You destroyed Newton."

"Collateral damage," Gammond said.

"You have any remorse?" Ward asked.

"Ain't got time for sentimentality, truth be told. Being police, you should know how that is."

"Why'd you get Lafayette to confess?"

"Oh, he ain't never getting out. Another kill to his reputation. Well, you know."

"And get us off the case."

Gammond shrugged.

"So, who killed Bill O'Donnell? That you?"

"I ain't laying claim to that."

"It was Kenny. And the doctor too. Kenny got spooked when O'Donnell had his funny turn at the nursing home last week and assumed O'Donnell had told his tale to the old family doctor. O'Donnell mentioned the doctor's name and that got the doctor killed too. That about right?"

"That would be speculation. But…" He sighed. "I ain't gonna question detectives' logic."

"Well, I guess it's all over for you both. And Arthur."

"I know you're a young man but you ain't that naive." Gammond put his hand to his mouth and wiped his lips. "You want to turn around?"

"You're going to kill me here?"

"Dang it. You ain't given me no choice. And I ain't taking you off somewhere. Here's as good a place as anywhere."

Ward let out a sigh. "I guess I would be wasting my time trying to talk you out of it."

Gammond nodded. And then Ward's cellphone rang. Instinctively, his hand went towards his pocket. Before the hand could get there he saw the muzzle flash and heard the report of the gun. The force of the bullet knocked him off his feet and he fell backwards, his hat flying off and landing a few feet away. He felt the heat of the blood spilling out inside his clothes and he couldn't breathe right and the overwhelming sensation he had was surprise. He watched snowflakes falling towards him and he felt like he was the one falling. The next thing he heard was a dog barking. From his position he saw a flash of black fly past him as he fought his own blackness.

Jesús didn't go for the ankle as most small dogs would. He leapt at Gammond's thigh and his teeth sank into flesh and the sharp canines tangled in Gammond's pants and Jesús hung there for a couple of seconds before Gammond batted him off with his free hand. He aimed the gun at the dog and fired but Jesús was already around his other side and Gammond twirled around and fired again, soil and snow exploding from the ground.

Ward tried to sit up but found that he had no strength in his left side and the pain in his chest, gnawing at molten nerves, made him cry out and blood gurgled in his cry. With his right hand he levered himself onto his devastated left side and his blood started to stain the ground.

Jesús was still barking and he pranced and ran, pranced and ran, and Gammond, in his whirling around, stepped onto the end of the dog's leash. Jesús tried to run and was snatched back by the taut leash. The dog fell over but was up straight away and he made another attempt to run away but he was snatched back again and Gammond took another shot but missed again. The little dog leapt away from the sound of the gun and the debris it threw up and as he did he ran right around Gammond. Gammond made his own growling sound and spun around to get another shot at Jesús and his left leg became snarled in the leash. The dog made a sharp turn and ran towards Gammond and then circled him and the leash tightened around both legs and Gammond's momentum took him spinning around and spiraling down.

Ward was seeing the blurry battle but he felt desolate and was sure that the little dog, who had lost one owner to a fatal shooting, was about to lose another. And then he saw Gammond's stocky frame start to fall. The remaining strength that he had in his right side was channeled into his arm and he slowly, too slowly, wrenched it up to his body and his hand clutched onto his coat and then twitching fingers grabbed hold of the zipper. He thought he'd counted to a hundred before enough of the zipper's teeth had let go and his hand crawled into the jacket. It couldn't have been a hundred though as he heard the thud of

Gammond hitting the ground and the gun firing into the air at the same time as Ward's fingers found his own gun.

Gammond shouted, "Hellfire," but the words were wheezed out by the impact. He managed to hold on to the gun but Jesús immediately went to work on his arm, yanking from side to side as his teeth penetrated cloth and then skin. Gammond cried out the same words again and then "dang son of a bitch."

The bullet from Ward's gun entered beneath Gammond's chest and exited his shoulder with a shower of blood fanning out over the snow. Ward saw that he was still moving and prepared to shoot again but he realized that the movement was caused by the dog's gnashing at the lieutenant's arm and Ward slumped back down and prepared to bleed out.

Before his eyes closed he saw the little girl standing at Gammond's feet. She had her back to Ward but he knew it was her. Her long dark hair. The clothes. So familiar. Tattooed on his heart forever. She stood motionless for a few moments and then she crouched down, leaning over Gammond's head as if she was looking into his face for signs of life. The dog suddenly stopped tugging at Gammond's arm and he looked directly at the girl and he sat in the snow and whimpered gently.

Ward's eyes opened partially and the lights in the hospital corridor caused him pain in his head and he tried to shield his eyes but neither of his arms would move so he closed them again but before he did he thought he noticed the figure of Mallory running alongside the gurney he was traveling on. He tried to take a big gulp of air but it felt like someone was sitting on his chest and he could hear a bubbling sound as he inhaled.

He didn't know he'd fallen asleep at that moment and he had no recollection of dreaming when he woke. No dreams of sinking in a field. No memories of a little girl. Simply a wonderful blackout without pain or panic or thoughts of death and an orphaned dog.

74

"I know you can't speak," said a voice. "Just listen. Gammond is alive. He's in a bad way but he's alive."

In Ward's disoriented mind the words seemed to come from everywhere at once and seemed to have traveled a long way. He blinked a couple of times and then he could see someone sitting next to his bed.

"I have the letter." Newton huffed gently. "And I'm kinda confused as to why Gammond would go and do what he did."

Ward's facial muscles made a massive effort to work a smile. Didn't work. He winked instead. He wanted to say something but couldn't. Wasn't sure what he wanted to say anyway.

"Most importantly, I guess, is that McNeely has fallen in love with your dog and you're going to be engaged in a tug of war to get him back. I may have to step in and mediate. She says she's taken him in as evidence but I'm not buying that. It was Mallory saved your life by the way. He kept you alive. Applied pressure to the wound and kept you warm. I won't say how he did that. Now, if your eyes can move the other way, there's someone else to see you. I'll leave you now." Newton moved off slowly in his wheelchair.

Ward turned his head slowly. Cherry was already holding his hand but he hadn't noticed as the anesthetic had sent his nerve endings to sleep. Her face was still beat up but Ward only saw the tears and the most wonderful smile in the world.

"Thought we'd lost you. You've been asleep for three days." She let go of his hand and reached down towards her feet to pick something up. "Your boss gave me this," she said. It was Ward's notebook. Cherry held it cringingly by the corners as it had dried-up blood on it. "It saved your life. The bullet was diverted away from your heart," she said, and then she sobbed. "Your heart. But the weirdest thing. This is weird. You remember what you wrote in there? Don't try to speak. I think you must have freaked out or something. Like you found religion. The last thing you wrote says 'Jesus is my savior. Christ is my redeemer'. You remember writing that? Don't try to speak. You wrote it anyway. I thought you'd found God or something. And then I realized. You see what it means? It wasn't Jesus saved you. He saved you! He saved you! Your dog."

And then Ward's eyes closed and Cherry's voice skipped away. He heard her calling his dog's name and he thought that she was the weird one.

75

"Kenny's gone," Newton said.

Ward's throat hurt when he said, "He's our man for Bill O'Donnell and Doctor Brookline."

"And the boy? I ain't told you this but the medical examiner found something. The boy was murdered. Strangulation."

"He was run down?" Ward stated it but it came out as a question.

"Both. Maybe his killer strangled him and then ran him over to make it look like an accident. The boy had bruising on his face too. He'd been recently beaten. What did Gammond tell you? This letter. What's in this letter that made Gammond go and do this to you?"

Ward took a deep breath and his lungs filled. "Nothing," he said, and the rest of the wind wheezed from his body.

"I'm not getting something here."

"He shot me for what he thought was in the letter. I bluffed him."

Newton almost laughed. He eased himself down onto the chair next to Ward's bed, both his hands sliding down his walking cane as he sat.

"It's Kenny's son who killed the boy," Ward said. "Arthur. Kenny and Gammond covered it up. Gammond told me. Kenny paid him off. Said it was an accident. Gammond blackmailed O'Donnell to go along with it."

"And O'Donnell took the boy into the forest to bury him."

"But you're telling me the boy was strangled. We need to get Arthur Kenny."

"He must have strangled Ryan and then run over him like I said."

"It's a guess. When Gammond wakes up we keep the bluff going." He took another gulp of air. "Otherwise he's going to clam up. He might give us more. He thinks the letter contains everything."

"When all it contains is O'Donnell's confession about John White. How he faked his death. With the help of Brookline."

"He didn't want him suffering the abuse Ryan did. Larsson said Ryan's father physically abused him."

"And he wanted it known what he'd done. But not till long after he and Brookline were dead."

"And the story in the newspaper about the capsule being moved. He probably thought the capsule was going to be opened. He wanted to warn the doctor. I'm guessing Kenny went to visit after hearing about his outburst. I'm guessing Kenny made up his mind that O'Donnell was going to tell about the cover up of Ryan's death."

Newton said, "He misunderstood that O'Donnell's confession wasn't about Ryan at all but about Ryan's brother."

Ward said, "Kenny made a mistake killing him."

"And the old man only ever wanted to do the right thing…"

"Gets killed for the wrong reason."

76

Newton bent down and placed the flowers on top of all the others that were still there, now just bumps under the snow which covered Bill O'Donnell's grave.

He placed another bunch on Ryan's grave and when he stepped back with wet eyes, Alice White took one arm and John White took the other.

"You walking without your stick," Alice said.

Newton nodded.

"You got no need to feel bad, Mr. Newton," Alice said. "What's done is done and it's done at the hands of God."

"Is this okay?" Newton said to John White. "I know you wanted Ryan to be returned to where we found him, but—"

"This is right," John White said. "Next to our granddaddy. Sure it's right, sir."

"I'm sorry this wasn't… I guess we could've…"

"You done your job," Alice said. "Like I said, you was driven by God. It's Him makes the decisions. You a good man, Mr. Newton."

77

Cherry was at Ward's bedside when Newton walked in. Ward thought he looked younger. Probably because he was feeling ancient himself. Ward's beard had started to grow back with flecks of gray he hadn't noticed before. He cursed whoever it was shaved it off in the first place. Cherry had said she liked it better with the gray as it made him look more distinguished.

"I'm not staying," Newton said. "Just wanted to let you know Arthur Kenny was picked up at a gas station just outside of Austin, Texas. Your neck of the woods."

"Thereabouts," Ward said. "What's a New York lawyer doing down there?"

"New York lawyer? He ain't no lawyer. He's a salesman."

"Okay."

"We already got the Bureau involved going through other missing children cases. Just in case. He travels."

"Any sign of James Kenny?"

Newton shook his head. "Nothing. Theory is he's skipped the country."

"I want to call Larsson. It's his story. I made a deal."

"That's fine with me," Newton said. He turned to

Cherry then. "I see what you mean about the beard. Kinda gray. Looking more like his mutt every day. But they do say that."

"He's gonna shave it off if we carry on with this and I like it too much for that to happen," Cherry said, and she went to stroke Ward's beard and he play-slapped her hand away.

"Leave me alone, you two sons of bitches. I'm recovering here and you two are setting me back. Nurse!"

"Okay, okay, I'm leaving. You get your rest," Newton said, and he turned to leave the hospital room.

"Hey," Ward said. "I thought you were retired."

"Captain asked me to stay on until you were back at your desk."

"You definitely bowing out after this is over?"

Newton didn't say anything. Ward thought he looked happy sad. He gave Ward a lackluster salute and left.

78

Arthur Kenny's lawyer had kept telling Newton that his client would not answer Newton's questions. Arthur sat there in the interview room with his head bowed, his baldness showing at that angle. And then his head snapped up.

"This is ridiculous," he said, and his lawyer tried to stop him saying anything else by placing his hand on his arm but Arthur Kenny shook him off and carried on. "I didn't strangle that boy. I did run him down, though. I'll admit to that. But I didn't strangle him. I mean, I ran over him but he must have been sitting in the road or something. He went under the car. I didn't see him." And the lawyer became red in the face and he threw up his arms in surrender.

"I thought we agreed I would handle this," the lawyer said. "You don't need to say anything that might incriminate you."

"Aw, to hell with that. I didn't murder that boy. I'll admit to running him down and that's that. It was an accident. An accident. I'm not sitting here and be accused of murder. It's plain ridiculous is what it is."

Newton left him enough space to say more but

Arthur's head went down again and the lawyer's head shook from side to side.

"We have evidence says the boy was strangled and we can place you at the scene, now by your own admission," Newton said, and now the lawyer's head went down. "We also have witness evidence that you were there and you conspired to dispose of the body with the help of others. You think a jury is going to believe you? Go ahead and take your chance. You admit to it now and you'd be looking at a reduced sentence. You deny killing that boy and you're convicted, you're looking at a whole longer stay in jail. Might never get out. So, what do you want to do?"

"I'm not confessing to doing something I didn't do. I'd rather take my chance with a jury. I'm not a murderer. It was an accident."

"Okay," Newton said. "Interview terminated at..." He looked at the clock on the wall. "...eleven forty-seven." He turned off the tape and stood. The lawyer was rearranging papers in his briefcase and Newton addressed him. "You've got some work to do with your client. I'll leave you a spell to figure things out and I'll be back." Before he reached the door Arthur Kenny spoke again.

"You spoke to the little boy? I mean, he'll be grown up now, but—"

"Little boy?" Newton walked back to the table and his finger was over the button on the recorder again but he didn't press it.

"Little boy who was there. I saw him hiding behind the tree and then he was gone. He must've seen something... everything. He can testify for me."

"Well, this gets better and better," the lawyer said.

"Arthur, listen to me. I can still help you but not if you won't take my advice. You don't need to say any more."

"Oh, shut up," Arthur said. And then he turned to Newton. "I'm telling you there was a little boy there. He saw me run over that boy. He must have seen me not strangle him."

Newton wanted to say there was no little boy but he just left the room to the sound of the lawyer mumbling desperate appeals about his client being tired and hungry. He went straight to his desk and dug his hands into a box. He came out with the picture that old man Filmore had drawn. He saw the four stick figures and the smaller shape of Ryan. His eyes then studied the other side of the road. The trees. One tree with a pair of eyes drawn on it. He folded the picture and ran to the door, grabbing his jacket on the way out. His footing was unsure on the fresh snowfall but he didn't slow down. He jumped into his SUV and he released the parking brake and the vehicle was moving before the engine started.

79

"Where's Jen?"

"Hey, you didn't stamp the snow from your feet," Mallory said.

"Damn the snow."

"It's just that when Jen gets back from shopping she's going to be annoyed about the snow in the house and she's apt to be blaming me and I'm already in the doghouse for trailing it in earlier, and—"

"I said to hell with the snow." Newton pushed past Mallory and walked through the house. Mallory paused a moment and then followed. When he caught up Newton had stopped in the living room and he had his back to Mallory. There was a well-made fire and Newton stood close to it and looked at himself in the mirror that was above the fireplace and he glanced at Mallory's reflection. The room smelled of burning trees and Newton thought it smelled of summer and winter at the same time.

"Sit down," Newton said, and Mallory sat. "When you married Jen you became my son. My own son don't talk to me no more so... you're my son."

"Appreciate that."

"Shut up. You're a poor substitute for a real son but for Jen's benefit I've tolerated you. Truth is, you ain't worth half a thimble of shit. But for Jen's sake... well, I've said it. Thing is, parents have a responsibility to their children and sadly for me I inherited that responsibility for you when Jen lost her senses and married you. But I've got myself a dilemma." He continued to look at his own self in the mirror as he slowly removed the paper from his pocket. "I've wondered for twenty-five years how this would end. That's my dilemma here." He unfolded the paper, the drawing done by the crazy old man Filmore. He held it down by his side. "I guess I'm looking for help. Help understanding all this." Mallory didn't say a word. "I think I understand but maybe you can help me. And help me solve my dilemma. You see, I've got a suspect down at the station who has admitted to being at the scene of Ryan Novak's death. He's admitted running him over."

"That's good, no?"

"Didn't I tell you to shut up?" Newton turned around to face Mallory, whose face was pale apart from the faint remnant shine of a bruise on the left side of his face which Ward had left there. "But according to the ME, Ryan was strangled to death. Thing is, our suspect denies doing that. And, you know what, I know he didn't do it. But he was there and things don't look good for him. The first part of my dilemma is this: do I let a man who I know is innocent go down for a crime he didn't commit?"

Newton handed the drawing to Mallory. "You were there," Newton said.

Mallory looked at the drawing. He held it in both

hands and stared down at it and he took a deep breath and then took another before he said, "I don't know what you're talking about, Dad." He glanced back at the drawing and shrugged and tried to hand it back to Newton.

"Don't you call me Dad."

"Look, what you doing showing me a picture? What is this? Are you okay?"

"You were there. You would have seen it all. But you didn't say nothing. All these years. You didn't say nothing. You were the last person to see Ryan alive. It's what you always said. A passing motorist saw you together. Thought you were friends. But you didn't say nothing about this. Never once said you'd seen Ryan run over. Why is that? Why didn't you say nothing about that? Look at the picture. You're there if you look hard enough."

"You got the guy did it."

"Why didn't you say anything?"

"You got the guy, didn't you? He murdered Ryan. You got your guy. You can wrap this up."

"Didn't I already tell you he didn't kill Ryan?" Newton was breathing heavily now and his hand found the tight place in his chest. "You can't neck a chicken," Newton said, and his shoulders slumped. "Why are you so squeamish about wringing a chicken's neck, big man like you? My God, Mallory. I know what you did. Don't you dare deny it neither or I'll put a bullet between your eyes before you can blink."

80

"I know you. What you got there?" Percy Mallory says to Ryan. But Ryan ignores him and keeps walking at a pace. Percy scuttles up behind him and grabs at his arm and tugs him so he spins around.

"I said what have you got?" And then he sees the tears running down the smaller boy's face. "Hey, you crying."

Ryan turns away sharply but he doesn't walk away, just keeps his back to Percy while Percy circles him to get a look at those tears.

"Stand still, will ya? You crying."

Ryan keeps his back to Percy but the bigger boy grabs his hand, which is clutching something, and then Ryan turns sharply and shakes the hand free.

"What you got?" Percy says again, and he makes another grab at the hand and this time his grip is stronger than the smaller boy's and he takes the hand with both his own and he sticks his thumb in Ryan's grip and starts to peel off his fingers as Ryan tries futilely to resist. Ryan tries to pull away but he can't so he jerks his whole body right and then left as his small feet scramble on the road beneath him but his hand is fast caught and it's beginning to hurt under Percy's grip. And then Percy bends back one of Ryan's fingers

further than it should go back and Ryan's hand opens and a five-dollar bill falls out.

"*Money,*" *Percy gasps as Ryan turns and starts to walk away, shaking the pain out of his hand. Percy stoops to pick the money up.* "*Hey, I ain't taking your money.*" *He looks at the money with twinkling eyes.* "*Unless it's stole in the first place. Is it stole?*" *He's skipping after Ryan now and he gets in front of him and puts his hands on Ryan's shoulders and stops him dead and Ryan props his chin on his chest and he cries silently with little involuntary shakes every now and then.*

"*Who'd you steal this money from? It's five bucks. Hey, I'm talking to ya. You can't speak? Somebody stole your voice?*" *He hears a car approaching and he steers Ryan off the road with his arm around his shoulders.* "*Better get off the road or you'll get knocked.*"

As the car passes the driver looks at the two boys and smiles and Percy raises an arm in something of a wave.

"*I know him. I know you. Where you going?*" *Percy says, and then he sees the fresh bruising on Ryan's left cheek.* "*Hey, you been hit. Come here, let me look.*" *But Ryan shakes his head and turns away.* "*Lemme look, I said.*" *And Percy clutches the tops of Ryan's arms so he can't wriggle away and he smiles as he says,* "*Woo. You caught a good one there. I hope you got a few licks in yourself. My dad always says to hit back and hit back harder. You catch him with one of your own? Woo, that's a good one. Gonna turn black and blue. I can see it's swelled. Bet it smarts.*" *He lets go of Ryan and Ryan just stands there, his head down and his eyes about closed.* "*Bet you stole this five bucks off them that did you that. You want it back you have to fight me for it seeing as that's how you come to have gotten it. I'll let you take the first swing.*"

Ryan just hangs there like he's on a clothesline but his own clothes are a few days dirty. Percy pokes the little boy's arm and Ryan jerks it away and wipes the snot from his nose on his sleeve.

"C'mon, have a shot," Percy says, and he sticks his face in front of Ryan's and he taps his own chin, goading the smaller boy. "In the face if you want." But Ryan just shakes his head.

"You are fighting me for this money I said so take your swing or you forfeit and I swing. It's your choice. Hit me. Go on. Hit me." The little boy just stands there so then Percy starts to jab at Ryan's chest. "Hit me, boxer. Box me. Hit me." And he jabs and jabs but Ryan takes a step back every time a bit further into the road. Then Percy gobs on his hand and wipes the gob on his forehead and straightens out the bill and slaps it on there. "Here, you got a target." And he gently swipes the side of Ryan's face with his spit hand. Ryan wipes his face and anger flashes briefly in his tormented eyes. "Hit me," Percy says, and then he starts dancing around like Muhammad Ali. He darts in and out, slapping a bit harder each time he moves in and Ryan takes another step back and then another.

Then, as Percy comes in again, Ryan shoves him with both hands and Percy rocks back and his eyes widen and he smiles. He resumes his taunting and he dances and slaps, dances and slaps and this time Ryan lunges and pushes harder and Percy is caught off balance and he nearly falls over and the smile leaves his face and he stops dancing.

"I wasn't ready. But we'll count that as your punch. My turn."

Ryan doesn't move but looks at Percy as if he's transparent. Percy clenches his fist as tight as a clam and he swings at Ryan and he catches him on the side of his head.

Ryan rolls back and sits messily on the road, the jolt of the punch and the fall vibrating through his entire tiny frame. Percy peels the five-dollar bill from his head and says, "I win." He stuffs the bill in his jeans pocket and he shakes the tingling out of his hand.

Before Percy can say anything else Ryan is up on his feet and he charges unsteadily at Percy, swinging both arms like a windmill and Percy takes a step back and then lunges at Ryan and his hands find the boy's throat.

"We finished and I won," he says in a gasp. "Money's mine. Fair and square."

Ryan tries to scratch at Percy's face but Percy leans back so his face is out of reach and he squeezes harder.

"Hey, hey. Fight's over. I won. Fair and square," and he continues to squeeze and Ryan snatches at Percy's shirt and he gets a grip on it but the grip isn't strong. "Fair and square. Fair and square," Percy keeps saying and he keeps squeezing as his face gets red and ugly and Ryan's gets bluish and then something sort of pops under Percy's thumbs and immediately he lets go and Ryan folds up and hits the ground like an empty sack and he doesn't move again.

Percy looks down at the little boy laid out in front of him and he kicks at his foot. "Hey, don't play possum. I know you playing. And I won that five dollars fair and square and you ain't getting it back and that's the end of it. Hey, get up. Please get up." A wet patch spreads on the crotch of the little boy's pants.

Percy starts to bend down to pull Ryan up but he hears the engine of a car and he starts to jump around and wave his arms at the little boy. "Hey, you better move or you'll get knocked. There's a car coming." He beckons Ryan to get up but the boy doesn't move. "Hey, come on. Car. You better *get up now. Please. This ain't funny."* And the growl of the engine is getting closer and Percy backs away from Ryan and walks backwards off the road, motioning with his hands for Ryan to get up. *"Get up now. This ain't funny no more."* His bottom lip starts to stiffen and then to quiver and his eyes become tear-filled and bloodshot. *"Aw, come on. Please get up. I ain't playing. I ain't playing no more. Fair and square. Fair and square."* And then he turns and runs, crying as he goes.

He can't make me do nothing I don't want to do. I'm not interested in stupid Harvard stupid Law. I told him but he's such a—Goddamn it, I'll show him. *Arthur Kenny, driving and banging his hands on the steering wheel. Seething. Turning the rearview mirror to look at himself and growling at his reflection and the reflection growling back. Invincible Arthur. To be reckoned with. Not a pansy lawyer, this one. Not Arthur Kenny. He'll take a sports scholarship. Flexing his muscles. A lawyer doesn't have these.* These will take me to the Superbowl. Quarterback for the Giants. Goddamn it, father. No. Hell no.

Ejecting the cassette tape from his car stereo and tossing it onto the passenger seat and grabbing another and dropping it into the footwell of the car. Damn it. Damn you, Father, and your stupid Harvard Law. *Looking at the road ahead. All clear. He reaches down to retrieve the damn tape. Fingers seeking amongst the scrunched beer cans. He touches the tape. Grabs it. Sits up. Nothing in the road. But bumping over something and braking quickly.*

Then he climbs out of the car to see what it is and expects to see a damn stupid stray dog or something.

He sees the body of the little boy with just his top half visible, the bottom half beneath the car, illuminated in blue light from the neon undercar lighting. He knows he is dead but he doesn't see any blood and he doesn't allow his eyes to dwell on the body for more than a few moments. He casts a look around in a full circle to see if anybody is about and he sees a small shape over the other side of the street, hiding behind a tree, but then the shape is gone. He turns back to face the other side of the street and he sees the house, set back from the road and maybe obscured by the trees that flank it either side. He turns back to the other side again and he sees the little shape, a boy, fleeing behind trees and he thinks to call after him but then thinks again and doesn't call.

He climbs back into the car and his first instinct is to drive away so he fumbles with the gear shift but the car engine is not running. And then he sees, in his side-view mirror, the patrol car pulling into the street a hundred yards behind and he slumps in the seat and he puts a hand on his head. He doesn't feel invincible anymore. Just feels like he could puke. And then he remembers the beer cans and he tries to scrape them under the passenger seat out of view and then the patrol car is stopped behind him, lights flashing, and the cop climbs out.

"Oh my—dang. Is he? He's dead, isn't he? You hit him? Oh, dang. I'll call this in. You felt for a pulse?" Officer Gammond is in Arthur's face now and he smells the sour smell on his breath. "Say, you been drinking?"

Arthur just stands there without voice, his eyes blankly staring at the cop. Gammond gets down on his knees and pulls the boy from under the car and feels for a pulse. He begins to pump at the boy's chest. He works the chest and *feels for a pulse. Puts his face close to the boy's mouth to feel for life breath. Goes back to pumping the chest. After a minute or so he sits back and stares at the boy.*

"Dead. Dang."

Gammond stands and starts to walk back to his car at a half trot and Arthur calls to him.

"No. Don't do that. Don't. My father is James Kenny. Please."

Gammond stops dead and turns around to face the young Arthur Kenny.

"Oh, dang," he says.

"Can... can we call him? I've got a portable phone in the car. Let me call my daddy. Please."

"Oh, dang, let me think," Gammond says. "Let me think."

Bill O'Donnell has been driving around in his truck close to home looking for Ryan and he pulls into the street and sees the police car's flashing lights and he pulls up his truck behind it. He sees the three men as he climbs down. Then he thinks it's two men and what looks to him like a boy. And then he sees the tiny shape lying in the road.

81

Mallory stood up. His eyes were bloodshot. He took a step closer to Newton until they were an arm's length apart.

Newton took a deep breath to keep his voice even. "And that's the second part of my dilemma. Is it enough that I know who did kill Ryan? Or does Ryan deserve justice? The only way I answer that particular question depends on whether I think I can destroy my daughter's life or not."

Jen's car pulled into the drive and the engine revved and then cut out. Newton heard a car door open and close. And then he heard another one open and close as Jen retrieved her groceries from the backseat. A few moments later he heard the door open and the stamping of feet and he knew Mallory was hearing the same. The two men faced each other and neither spoke. Jen could be heard grumbling about snow in the house. Then the sound of chickens clucking in the back yard coop. Mallory placed his hands on Newton's shoulders and he squeezed hard enough for Newton to try to wriggle free of the grip. Newton's hand found his gun and the hand sat there.

Mallory said, "So, what you going to do, Dad?"

When Jen entered the room she looked ready to go nuts on Mallory for the snow in the hallway until she saw her father. By then Newton's hand had dropped from his gun and Mallory's arms were by his sides.

"What's wrong?" Jen said immediately. The men looked at each other. Mallory was the first to speak.

"Nothing. Nothing's wrong," Mallory said. His words were tinny and annoying in Newton's ears.

Jen looked at both men. "Dad? What are you doing here? Something happened? Is it Mom?"

Newton's brain automatically tried to think of an excuse why he was there but his mouth said nothing. He shook his head and stared at his daughter and he knew he wasn't hiding the turmoil that was in his mind. But no words would come out.

"Dad? Is everything okay?" Jen said.

Her father looked at her eyes. They were her mother's. The inquiring look that always got to the bottom of what was on Newton's mind. The sense that women have. That wives have. He studied her and saw more of Maggie. Her genes in the smile wrinkles and her beautiful hair. The long flawless limbs. The perfection of their creation. The way she tilted her head when she asked a question. A question that clattered in Newton's head. That look. He felt tears building in his eyes but fought them back. His heart skipped as a father's heart skips when his little girl falls and comes up with bloodied knees and skinned hands. Mallory wasn't saying anything but Newton could feel his eyes on him. And now Jen's eyes filled with tears and the tears ran down her face.

"Dad," Jen said.

Newton's stare left Jen for a moment and he felt he was betraying her by gifting his gaze to Mallory, who now stood there, mute. He looked to Newton like the little boy who had walked into the station twenty-five years ago to tell a lie about what had happened to Ryan. The lie that had defined so much of Newton's life since. The fallout of a crime he couldn't solve. The drinking. So much of his life filled with bitterness, regret, uncertainty. The failure of his relationship with his son and near failure of his relationship with his wife, Maggie. Beautiful Maggie, who stood there before him now in his daughter's body. And he knew utterly the debt he had to repay to himself, to his wife, and to Ryan most of all. Ryan deserved justice. And he thought Mallory saw it in his eyes and Mallory opened his mouth but Newton looked back at Jen and Mallory's words never came.

Newton walked to his daughter, who was crying freely, her shoulders shaking.

"Daddy. What... what's happened?"

He took her in his arms and he held her there. He stroked her hair and she trembled in his grasp and he couldn't say anything more than "I love you." And then he left her and he walked out of the house, hauling his decision with him as Bill O'Donnell had carried Ryan into the woods. He slumped into his SUV and he cried and snow fell and the eternal Montana winter felt like his never-ending curse.

ABOUT THE AUTHOR

W.H. Clark is a native of Yorkshire, the most beautiful county in England. An End to a Silence is his first novel, fulfilling his second ambition in life. His first ambition, to be a park ranger, remains unfulfilled.

To connect with the author please visit his Facebook page at https://www.facebook.com/whclarkauthor

Printed in Great Britain
by Amazon